Echoes
— OF THE —
LOST WORLD

THE HIDDEN WORLD

BOOK ONE

First Edition, 2025

Library of Congress Control Number: 2025920573

ISBN 979-8-9997787-1-0 (Paperback)
ISBN 979-8-9997787-0-3 (e-book)
ISBN 979-8-9997787-2-7 (Hardcover)

Printed in the United States of America
Published by Sethworld Media, LLC, Atlanta, Georgia

Dedication

For every kid who's ever felt
too weird, too loud, or too much.
This one's for you.

Prologue:
The Girl Who Wasn't Ready

Ea'mara ✦ 537 AD ✦ Stonehenge

Stonehenge is burning. Unnatural light flickers with smoke and the ground trembles underfoot. I run as hard as my legs will carry me. Mud drags on the hem of my blue dress and my silver hair, once tightly braided, lashes at my face. With each breath, my throat is scraped raw.

I shouldn't be here... but I am. And that's the problem.

"Keep up, child!" Sir Pellinore shouts over his shoulder, his aura flaring as he drives his blade through a snarling beast on my left. His shield is cracked, his eyes ringed in exhaustion. "Whatever you do, don't stop moving!"

I nod, though something gnaws at my ribs. He still sees me as a child... and by Atlantean standards, I am. Just barely a novice mage. But I've lived through more lifetimes than he could ever fathom. I've studied more, seen more. None of it feels like enough now.

Smoke curls around us, thick with ash and magic. Barghests howl between the stones, and gnomes skitter past with evidence of gore, screaming taunts too garbled to make out. The air thrums with untamed power, raw and restless.

Then I see her.

Vaedra. The Atlantean mage from Dene-mearc.

She's sprawled near the edge of the circle, robes slick with blood. Her staff is half-buried in the churned earth. Just days ago she was teaching me how to coax warmth from crystals, laughter in her voice as my clumsy hands fumbled with light. Her teaching had been patient. Kind.

Now her eyes are blank, mouth still hanging open from a word she never finished.

I stop, chest heaving.

I don't want to believe it.

Sir Pellinore yanks me back into motion. "Grieve later! You want her death to mean something? Then move!"

I stumble trying to keep up. He's right, and I hate that he's right. Grief is a luxury we can't afford. But Vaedra's face burns behind my eyes as he pulls me to the center of the stone circle.

The magic is stronger here. It slices through me like a cold wind. My skin prickles under its weight.

At the center, Merlin and Arthur are fighting in a practiced rhythm... one casting, one swinging. Merlin's staff spins silver threads of power. Arthur's blade hums with intent. Neither look tired. Only focused.

"Ea'mara!" Merlin's voice slices through the chaos. "Now!"

Sir Pellinore drops his hold on me. Arthur is in front of me before I know it, leaping out of the way of a creature lunging from the left. With one swing of his blade, it crumples, his aura pulsing a regal purple. I stagger forward to the altar stone where Merlin kneels.

A round bronze disc rests atop it, etched with symbols that hover above the surface; alive, but unreadable. In the center, a jewel pulses: soft pinks, deep blues, flickering like thought.

I hover my hands above it, shaking so badly I can hardly keep them still. "I... I don't know what I'm doing," I whisper.

Merlin's voice is tight. "Put your hands on the mirror. Trust me."

My knees tremble, but Merlin's voice anchors me. I press my palms to the cold metal. It jolts, like it recognizes me. Energy floods through my limbs, fierce and unfamiliar. Merlin's power coils around mine, steadying me like rope on a fraying line.

The chill that rises after is one that gives me nightmares.

Titania is pressing at the Veil.

And Oberon's forces are attacking from this side.

Somewhere in the distance, Arthur curses under his breath. "Where are the others?"

"Still at Camelot," Pellinore answers his king. "Some damned trickster beast is keeping them busy. Blasted timing."

Merlin's hand lands on my shoulder. "The power's already in you. Stop fighting it."

I want to believe him. But the seal beneath us was built by Merlin, Titania, and those older and wiser than I will ever be. And now he's asking me to help hold it together? Why me? Why now?

Stonehenge groans and moans under Oberon's assault. Lightning crackles above the stones, twisting the shadows into something with teeth.

I try to steady my breathing, but Vaedra's face flashes again... and the guilt with it.

Merlin wouldn't have called me if we weren't desperate. That truth lands hard in my chest.

"I'm Atlantean," I mutter, half to myself, "but I've studied, not this..."

"You feel the magic. That's more than most." His tone softens just enough to make it worse. "And there's no one else left."

My hands tremble. Still, I dig deeper.

I will not let her death be for nothing.

I force the fear to the edges of my mind, pulling instead on memory... of her laughter, of Merlin's teachings, of every lesson I thought I'd have more time to learn. There aren't many of us Atlanteans left. Merlin and Vaedra are the only ones I have ever met.

My power responds, wild and jagged, surging through the disc. Merlin weaves around it, guiding, muting, protecting.

But I feel her fighting back.

Titania.

Her presence slides along the seal like a blade testing a crack. Cold. Patient. And for one terrible breath, I swear she laughs... soft and cruel, as if she's waiting for me to fail.

"Merlin," I whisper. "You said I wasn't ready..."

"You're not," he growls. "But we have no choice."

The disc vibrates under my hands as my control slips, magic lashing out.. not at the enemy, but at the world itself. The seal buckles.

Merlin grips my wrist. "Don't you dare let go!"

"I'm losing it!"

I clench my teeth and drive everything into the disc. Not with precision. Just pain, memory, raw blinding will.

Vaedra's face.

The screams.

The war I never asked to be part of.

The disc flares, white and sharp as sunrise.

A shockwave blasts outward... flattening monsters. The circle stills.

I collapse. The ground spins. My hands burn.

Merlin catches me, holds me steady. For the first time, his voice drops to something human. "It's done."

As the stones quiet, a faint hum lingers in the air, a reminder that the damage has been only mended, not healed.

I don't feel victorious. I feel empty. "How long will it hold?"

He doesn't answer. He wraps the disc in cloth, slipping it into his satchel like it's just another artifact.

I look across the battlefield. Bodies everywhere. The air is thinner now. Quieter. Never safe.

"Is it over?" I ask. Merlin stares at the horizon, as if seeing beyond it. When he finally speaks, it's barely a whisper:

> "When the old light fades, seven shall rise. Born of storm and silence, shadow and fire.
> They'll come, not as saviors... but as mirrors."

"Mirrors of what?" But he's already walking away, his form growing fainter with each step.

"Merlin!" I call after him.

He vanishes into the fog, leaving only silence.

Chapter 1:
She Knows I'm Here

Nia ✦ Afternoon (March 26) ✦ Botswana

I'm falling before I can even process what is happening. My hands hit the ground and it takes a moment to register that I've slammed my palms into dirt.

"Joo..." I gasp, the word stuck in my throat. "What... what is this?"

The world spins, and when I open my eyes I see nothing but stone.

Big stones. Leaning, jagged and glowing before they blink out of existence, flickering in and out of being. The dirt under my bare feet shimmers like it can't quite decide whether to be solid or liquid.

My stomach drops. I back up a step and the earth disappears. My heel hangs in midair, the dirt around it sucked out of existence. I throw my arms out to prevent myself from toppling over, but my hands no longer touch the dirt of Botswana's dry heat. It is soft and spongy, sucking at my fingers.

Fog coils around me, thick and heavy. The world feels wrong in its silence. I can't hear birds, or a breeze. There is a low vibration, like something humming in the air, like a giant grinding its teeth.

Silver to my left. A flash of a girl kneeling in the dirt, blood on her hands and her eyes blown wide with horror. I blink and she is gone.

A crash to my right. Two people in armor, swords raised, rending the mist as if it were smoke. Sparks fly. Shouts burn through the air, but there is no sound. One of them falls, and the mist swallows him before I can discern who he is.

Images stab through the vapor in quick, choking bursts. A broad-shouldered boy with something great casting a shadow across him. A bright, flickering girl whose hands shape the light itself. A boy with eyes so silver they are like a knife. A golden gaze that slices through the mist and disappears. A warm-faced boy lit by shifting green as the air around him folds and spills into corridors I cannot follow. Faces that disappear before I can focus on any one of them.

The sky rips. Blue and white tear the world in two like a wound. Gold spills through the split as if something on the other side is clawing to get here.

Then she is here.

She doesn't walk. She glides. A shape that sometimes coheres, sometimes fades to ash. Her cloak rends the mist; one moment solid cloth, the next shredded smoke. Her face flickers, shadowed by the mist and then crystal clear... marked by the light.

I stumble backward. My heart is drumming in my chest. My heel smacks a rock and I nearly fall. The wet dirt beneath my palms is sticky. It feels real. It feels wrong.

She kneels. One hand presses into a standing stone and the rock devours her fingers like clay. Images ripple across it, silver and blue and gold and then snap away until nothing remains.

Slowly she turns her head to face me.

The fog around her billows, a wave about to swallow stones, struggling, even the rend in the sky. Her eyes pierce through it all. Golden and bottomless. They do not flicker.

I can't breathe.

She saw me!

Mist curls at my feet like reaching fingers. Instinct outruns thought and I scramble backward. My feet are tangled, hands clawing at the slick earth.

"Wait!" I rasp. My voice cracks. "Who...?"

"Beware...."

The word is not spoken. It is a burn inside my skull, as loud as a drum and as soft as a whisper at the same time.

The mist lunges at me, hungry. I keep scraping away but the ground beneath me slips and the mist swallows me. I fall into nothing.

✦ ✦ ✦ ✦ ✦ ✦ ✦

Heat hits me and the world comes rushing back.

The baobab's roots shove into my back. Dirt is packed under my fingernails. I'm on my knees, my breath coming in gasps as my heart beats a fist in my throat.

She saw me. She was there!

I've had visions. Flashes of the past. Visions of what might be to come. But this: never have I felt the pull of the other side like this, like they reached back.

The letter is still folded in my pocket. Berlin. Professor Mara. The internship... and I am only 16. I am to board a plane in three days and leave this earth that smells of smoke and stew and warm skin.

Everyone is telling me I should go. Mom cried happy tears when the acceptance came. Dad smiled as if he's already placed a doctorate on my shelf. The elders have given their blessing. "Go," they say. "The ancestors will walk with you."

Then why does it still feel like betrayal to leave?

I press my forehead to my palms and try to breathe with the earth beneath me. Try to still the aftershocks the vision sent through me. It does not fade. The aftertaste of gold and cold and warning lingers like metal on my tongue.

The clack of a wooden spoon and smell of cooking smoke pull me back. Mogolo is at the fire.

The dirt path to the homestead is silent as I approach. The sun spreads orange across thatched-roof huts and the herb patch at the fence. Children yell from behind a hut. Smoke curls toward the sky. Everything is the same and nothing is the same.

Grandmother is seated at the fire, stirring. Her face is a tapestry of careful, patient lines. She does not look up when I kneel at her feet.

"You saw her," she says.

I drop down on the worn mat in front of her. Did she have the same vision? Did she see the same stones?

"She saw you, too," Mogolo says without pausing.

I pull the letter from my pocket, unfolding and folding it again with fingers that refuse to still. "My flight is in a few days," I say. "Professor Mara. Berlin."

She does not blink. "I know, ngwanaka."

"I want to go," I whisper. "But it feels like a betrayal. Walking away. Like leaving something unfinished. Like betrayal."

"You are not betraying us," she says gently. "You are a weaver of many threads, child. Our past. Our stories. Our future. You are not meant to weave only one tapestry."

I swallow. "What if I lose the old one while I chase the new?"

Mogolo reaches into her wrap and pulls out a small leather pouch. It is warm where she holds it, like it is a living thing.

"For protection," she says. "For focus. For remembering."

I press it to my chest. "You are not afraid?"

"Oh, I am," she admits, with a wry twitch at the corner of her mouth. "But not of you leaving. I am afraid of the world learning how amazing you are."

I look up. The sky is a deep purple now. One star pins itself to the baobab.

"I think something is coming," I say.

She nods. "It always does."

Chapter 2:
The Gathering Begins

Professor Mara ✦ Morning (April 20) ✦ Humboldt University

"There's a list of texts waiting for you at the front desk," I say, pushing the paper across the desk to her. "Comparative symbology. I want to know what ancient cultures share. Which images repeat across oceans and time."

Nia takes the paper, all curiosity and bright eyes. And far more resilient than she understands. I saw that in her the first time she walked into the room. I saw it before she said a word. That's why I picked her. But sometimes I wonder if she sees it. If she feels it too... that space between who she thinks she is and who she might be.

"Is there something in particular you want me to look for?" she asks, shoving the paper into her bag.

"Not yet," I say. "Just observe. Look for what shows up again and again. Patterns. Patterns say more than origin stories."

She smiles, already halfway out the door in her head, and I watch her walk away. Wondering, not for the first time. If she knew. If she ever knew what I see in her, would she still be here?

She's halfway down the hall when the door swings farther open and she nearly runs into a student chasing after a dog and dragging a bright blue leash. "Sorry! He just wandered in again. No one knows who he belongs to."

Nia automatically bends down and scratches behind the hound's ears. "You're a good boy, aren't you?" she asks, and the dog wags his tail in response.

"Thanks Nia," I murmur softly to the receding door, but I'm not looking at her anymore.

✦ ✦ ✦ ✦ ✦ ✦ ✦

Six files. Five of them neatly stacked in a corner, nameless, cross-tagged and cross-referenced in my own handwriting. The sixth one set apart from the rest with Nia's name on it. They all look like regular academic files. They are anything but.

They're all coming, not by chance.

I've arranged cultural exchanges and diplomatic conferences. Pressured a department for a student exchange. Talked a family into taking me on their vacation to Germany. Creative grants, selective approval, recommendations whispered into the right ears. Subtle. Purposeful. And it worked.

Nia was the first I found, and she came easily. It helped that her interests aligned. The others, not so much. I convinced an entire community to join a cultural showcase, pressured a liaison to send young representatives. One boy still thinks he's traveling by his own volition. Maybe he is, in part.

I've been looking for resonance... for years. Children who make a room feel awkward just by walking into it. Who hold power without understanding how, or even why. Some had a presence that I could feel after they left. An echo. Sometimes I found one. Rarely two. Never six, not until now.

I reach for the folder. As my fingers touch the cover, a cold flash goes through my chest. Not fear. Recognition.

The seal is failing. It's been cracking for weeks now. Like watching a frozen river fissure one line at a time. The pressure kept mounting and today it just burst. That's how I know. She's not just testing it anymore... she's pushing. Hard. Stonehenge is the only anchor point I have. Old magic, older than me. But it's failing, the ley lines shifting. Not broken yet, just unstable.

Titania. She's been clawing at the seal for weeks, but now... she's here. Not in metaphor. Physically. She's crossed into this realm and I felt it... the second it happened. Her power is cold, sharp, invasive. Familiar in ways I wish it weren't.

And if she's here, Oberon won't be far behind. Or worse.

I can't stop them. Not on my own. I never could. I nearly died the last time they came for the seal. I don't know the rituals to reverse what's happening now. Merlin had started to teach me, but he left before I was ready. Or maybe he left because he knew I'd never be.

He vanished after Arthur died. No warnings. No goodbyes. I spent decades looking for him. After a while, I gave up hope of finding anything at all.

The others are long gone too. All of them. Every single Atlantean. Killed, lost, died out, faded: I've heard the stories. We live for thousands of years, but not forever. I am the last.

There's no temple. No marker. No preserved archive. Atlantis isn't a myth... it was a civilization that's been wiped from history, and I'm all that's left. That reality isn't noble. It's heavy. Mostly, it's quiet.

But I'm still here.

And now, they're coming.

I pick up the files again. These six are barely beginning to wake. Most of their abilities are still dormant, or inconsistent. Misunderstood by the people around them, and more so by themselves. Some will fight it. Some will charge ahead without understanding the cost. None of them are ready.

But they'll have to be.

I open Nia's file again. Notes in my own handwriting: subtle reactions, energy sensitivity. She's likely unaware that she's seeing echoes, but it's there... in her behavior, in the way she hesitates before touching anything old. Her instincts are better than she knows.

And she trusts me, at least for now. She doesn't talk about her dreams. Not yet. She sees more than she's willing to admit, even to herself.

Merlin's last words to me come back. Not in some dramatic vision, just a phrase I can't quite shake. He said it just before he disappeared and I've never been able to fully decode it.

"When the old light fades, seven shall rise. Born of storm and silence, shadow and fire. They'll come, not as saviors... but as mirrors."

I don't know what it means. But I know where to start. With these six. And the seventh? I'm still searching. Hints. Whispers. Auras that don't quite match. I've felt a few that burned bright, then vanished. One of them was close. Too close. But nothing confirmed. Not yet.

The seal has been cracking for weeks. Now it's coming apart. The pieces are in motion.

We're out of time. And I'm out of excuses.

They must start learning who they are... before someone else decides for them.

Chapter 3:
The Pizza Helps

Balam ✦ Afternoon (April 23) ✦ Atlanta

Atlanta's airport is a hurricane of people. Shouts swirl in every direction, suitcases thumping past, echoes of announcements. It's alive... and I am at home in its movement. A businessman with a headset swishes his briefcase through the air without looking, but I swerve aside before he clips my ribs. A mother with three kids who all look ready to keel over wrestles them along, but I slip past without missing a beat. It's almost second nature now, and I guess I've always been good at moving with the flow of a crowd.

Something buzzes through my chest. This is it... this is really happening. I've never left Chile in my life... all 17 years of it, and in a few hours I'll be in Berlin, wandering the streets where my parents go on and on about history. They think it'll be a good way for me to connect with my culture. I hope they're right. I'm hoping it's more than that.

"¡Balam! ¡No te me alejes!" Ms. Ortega's voice rings out through the crowd, sharp and relentless.

I look over to see her glaring at me, arms crossed, shoulders tense. She's got that whole chaperone shtick down pat.

"I'm not straying," I tell her in English, and flash her my friendliest smile. "Just... taking in the sights."

She raises an eyebrow. "No quiero tener que explicarle a tus padres que perdiste el vuelo por andar tonteando."

I chuckle. 'Promise I won't get lost. I've got a compass right here.' I tap my temple. She almost smiles but still looks dubious. "Quédate cerca. Embarcamos en unas horas."

"Gotcha. No straying."

She stalks off, her posture never relaxing. I can't imagine spending your whole life that wound up.

✦ ✦ ✦ ✦ ✦ ✦ ✦

Near our gate, the rest of my exchange group is sprawled over plastic chairs, their eyes bright from phone screens. On the other side of the terminal, a group of teens in mouse ears bounce back and forth, clearly headed for a theme park or something. They're going to have a blast.

My stomach rumbles low in my chest and I realize I'm hungry. I follow the alluring scent of grease to a pizza counter, where a guy is flinging dough high in the air with far more flourish than I'd expect. I order a slice, lean against the counter, and stare distractedly at the passing crowds... cowboy hats, hijabs, business suits, muddy hiking boots. The world at its most local, and the stories, what I'd give to get inside each of their heads if there were time.

I take a bite... dense and cheesy and perfect. If the US is good at anything, it's pizza. Three bites later and I've demolished it.

I'm reaching for another couple slices when a figure cuts across the food court too fast... a dude in a baseball cap dragging a suitcase with one busted wheel. He doesn't see me and we're on a perfect collision course. I tense, ready to take the hit.

But then my body just moves... to the side, then back, then forward again... too fast, too weird. I kind of... glide around him. Awkward, sure, but it's not falling. My tray doesn't even tip.

The guy flinches around, staring at me. "Whoa," he says, voice hoarse. "How'd you do that?"

I blink. His face warps for a second... ears long and sharp, nose hooks, skin tints green, eyes a burning red... then gone. Just a tired guy in a baseball cap, staring like I've sprouted a third head. My chest hammers, but I force out a laugh anyway.

Jet lag. Has to be jet lag. No way I really saw that.

He shakes his head and wheels away, suitcase thumping behind him. I stand a moment longer, head swimming, like my body knows some trick my brain hasn't caught up to. Like I saw something I wasn't supposed to.

On the edge of the terminal, I catch a glimpse of blue hair... too bright, too unnatural... walking past. Small girl. Watching me. Smiling.

She didn't blink.

Guess I'm more jet-lagged than I thought.

✦ ✦ ✦ ✦ ✦ ✦ ✦

I see her.

By the window, a girl... maybe my age, but hard to tell at a glance... sits with one leg pulled in, twisting a coffee cup in her hands. She doesn't look sad, exactly, but all balled up. Like she's bracing for impact or something.

Normally, I'd walk on by. But something nags at me, an itch in the back of my mind: Talk to her. It's the same intuition that tells me how to flow through a crowd, the same instinct that helps me sidestep obstacles in the road. I can't explain it, but I know it's there. I trust it. And also, maybe, I'm just sick of eating alone.

I buy two slices and head over across the floor, trying to look nonchalant, not creepy.

"Hey," I say, pulling up at her table and smiling. "Mind if I sit?"

She turns to look at me, eyes sharp. "I'm not really in the mood for company."

I nod. "Fair. But..." I slide a plate in front of her. "I brought a peace offering."

Her eyes flick to the pizza. "You don't even know me."

"True." I shrug casually. "But you look like someone who could use not eating alone."

She pauses; as my hand brushes against hers, heat, some kind of charge, makes my heart stutter. Regaining my composure, I settle into the chair across from her, careful not to get too close, but not leave too much space either.

"I'm Balam," I say. "Like the Jaguar God... or the guy who won't stop talking, depending on who you ask."

She raises an eyebrow. "Aiyana."

"Nice name."

She nods once, eyes flicking back and forth between me and the pizza like neither of us is quite safe.

I point at the backpack by her feet. "Travel light. Fresh off the plane or getting out?"

"Connecting flight."

"Yeah? Where?"

She pauses a beat, like the answer still surprises her. "Berlin."

I shift in my seat. "No way. Me too."

She stares, a little dubious, like she's not sure if this is some sort of set up. "Cultural exchange," I clarify. "They picked me to represent my Inca heritage, although I think it's mainly because I never shut up."

She almost smiles. "I know that feeling."

"Yeah?"

She nods. "My grandfather pushed me to do it. Said it was time."

"Didn't give you a choice, did he?"

"Not really."

We sit in silence for a moment but it doesn't feel awkward. I breathe, slowly, savoring the steady sense of her there. For some reason, it's a relief when she doesn't tell me to leave.

"You don't strike me as someone who cozies up to random strangers," I say after a moment.

"I'm not." She takes another slow bite, chewing and swallowing deliberately. "But the pizza helps."

I grin. "See, told you... food diplomacy."

She checks out the edge of the slice like it's way more interesting than me, then sits up... "Thanks," she says, quietly, and she means it.

"Anytime." And I mean it. I got friends. Got plenty of friends. But most of them bounce when I stop trying to be the center of the joke. With Aiyana, I want something else.

She doesn't say much, but from the way she's sitting, all closed in, I can tell she's used to building walls around people. I feel it, like picking up a rhythm that no one else caught. And this time, I don't just want to slip past. I want in.

So I sit. Quiet and comfortable, giving her space to tell me to leave if she wants. For now, sharing pizza with a stranger feels like the start of something real.

Chapter 4:
Fry Girl

The Dubai airport is huge and polished to such an unreal degree, it almost feels like a hologram... glass and chrome and matte black, marble floors that glisten like they just got buffed an hour ago. Unreal, but I love it.

I haven't felt homesick yet. Everything just feels like an unopened gift, right now. The air tastes like espresso and perfume, and voices of people from every direction are bouncing off in at least a dozen languages. Loud, but in a good way... there's energy in the air.

"Stick with me, Tama." Uncle Manu's sitting next to me, relaxing but with that edge to his voice that's always there when he's spread too thin.

He's been hovering around since we left Auckland. It's not his fault, I guess. Six Māori teens on a round-the-world trip would keep anyone on edge. It's just that around me, he's even more protective than normal, probably because of last week... when I tripped downtown near the waterfront and sent a fire hydrant flying off its mounts. I didn't mean to. It just... happened. I'm bigger and stronger than people think I am. I am only 17, but I am bigger than most adults.

It really was an accident.

Just before I hit the ground, I'd seen a shape in a window. Large. Distorted. Scaled, possibly. It was the briefest flash of movement... and for a second, I thought it had eyes. Staring at me.

I jerked, heart pounding, and the toe of my boot hooked the base of the hydrant. The next thing I knew, I was sprawled out on the ground and water blasting out like a geyser.

Everyone just assumed I wasn't watching where I was going.

I didn't correct them. I haven't even let myself think about what I saw. I told myself it was a trick of the light. But sometimes I'm not so sure.

"Yeah, yeah. Right here, right here." I grin at him. "You can't get rid of me that easy."

He snorts. "Don't you worry, mate. Just... don't go off causing trouble, yeah? We don't need another incident'."

I scratch the back of my neck. "Me? Trouble? Never."

He mutters something that sounds like a quick prayer and turns away.

He gets it... he's afraid I'll break something or knock someone over. People are so used to underestimating me, they also assume I'm a big guy with zero impulse control. Lately, I've been trying not to give them any more reason to think that.

We fall in with the crowd. Business travelers are tapping at phones, families are juggling strollers; backpackers barrel past, one earbud in each ear. At home, people will usually make space when they see me coming. Here, no one's out of their own lane, and no one's going to slam on the brakes.

My stomach growls so loudly that Uncle Manu glances over.

"Food?" I ask, both hands on my belly like I'm starving.

He raises an eyebrow. "Didn't you eat on the plane?"

"Yeah. Yesterday."

He huffs out a sigh. "Fine. Quick, then."

I'm halfway to the food court before he can change his mind. The smell of grilled meat and deep-fried... everything tugs me in. There's a burger place with a practically nonexistent line. Sweet.

As I start to move for it, I catch a glimpse of someone across the seating area:

Bright blue hair, slicked back. Suit so sharp it could have been pulled straight out of a fashion magazine. Standing at a tiny table by himself, reading a real paper. Legs crossed, one hand holding his position, the very picture of self-control. Not even a glance when people walk past.

Strange.

I narrow my eyes a little. The paper doesn't move. Not even a page turns. But the back page, facing me, is a black-and-white ad. Or a photo.

And it looks exactly like him.

Same suit. Same hair. Same angle.

I suck in a breath. This photo isn't just familiar... it's now. Like someone printed a picture of this exact moment.

Right now.

For a second, the eyes in the photo shift... and they're looking right at me.

I blink... and BAM.

Boom. Crash. Squeak. Soda sprays across the floor. Fries go everywhere. One lands on my shoe.

I look down. A girl is crouched at my feet; she's tiny, with pink and blue pigtails, a frilly pink skirt, a bunny-shaped purse. She's gathering up fries like her life depends on it, her hands a flurry, like grabbing faster will un-spill them. She's muttering to herself, too busy glaring at the fries to notice me.

I laugh. I can't help it. It just comes out, loud and honest. She freezes mid-grab, eyes flying up. One hand clutches a fistful of fries. With the other, she's waving one fry at me like a tiny spear. "Hey! You made me drop my food!"

Chapter 5:
Trust and Pizza

Aiyana ✦ Afternoon (April 23) ✦ Atlanta

The airport food court is madness... scraping trays, layered voices, harsh fluorescent lighting reflected in every mirrored surface. I'm across from Balam at a small table near the window. The sun is hot against the side of my face. I sit up straight, forcing my hands to be still.

He's finishing his pizza like it's the best thing he's ever had. I've eaten more than I wanted to, and it's infuriating how good it tastes. Because I'm not sure I trust him... or anyone else.

Balam reminds me of the guys I tried to avoid back home: easy smiles, big gestures, full of bravado. But he also seems... real. Most have an agenda when they flirt, and I usually can tell. He doesn't give me that feeling. But I'm still wound tight, waiting for the moment he proves me wrong.

My grandfather used to tell me I was too closed off, that not everyone wanted to hurt me. He'd say I was stronger than I realized, and that I would get better. Hearing him used to help me... especially when the memories of what had happened got too close. But he's gone now. And the calm he gave me is gone with him.

Balam looks up, smiling like the world is a pretty good place to be in. It makes me uneasy. I wipe grease from my fingers, trying not to remember the last time I let my guard down... how badly that had ended. Balam seems nice. So did the last person who hurt me. I survived it, with my grandfather's help, but I'm not sure how to trust since then.

He's talking about some stunt he did as a kid, grinning like he's reliving it. My grandfather's voice echoes in my head, gentle and firm. Not everyone wants to hurt you, little guardian. But the memory that answers is not my grandfather's. It's a flash of feeling... the slick, cold grip on my wrist, the weight on my chest, the way my own voice felt stolen from my throat. My stomach twists into a knot of ice. I pull my hands into my lap, pressing my nails into my palms. Just a boy. Just pizza. It's not the same. But my body doesn't know the difference. It only remembers the chill.

I know a lot of loud, reckless guys. Most of them are attention seekers, but Balam isn't flashing his eyes around the room looking for approval. He's just telling me a story, like I'm an old friend. A tiny part of me almost smiles.

He catches it. His eyes light up. "See? There it is... your smile." I scowl before I can stop myself.

"You're ridiculous," I say, and it's supposed to be neutral, but it comes out soft.

He shrugs. "Better boring than forgettable."

I look over the terminal. His group is scattered about, lounging in seats, joking and snacking. Mine are huddled close but mostly silent. I tried to blend in with them...

didn't pan out. My chest tightens at the thought of home, of my grandfather. He would have known what to say.

Balam notices me drifting. "You good?"

I force a nod. "Just tired."

"Long trip," he says, and I know he means more than just the plane ride. He's eating the last of his slice. "And we haven't even made it on the plane to Berlin yet. I swear, airplane cabins smell like old socks and regret."

A short laugh bursts from my mouth before I can catch it. It's odd. Lighter than I'm used to.

We both fall silent. He doesn't stare, doesn't demand or expect anything. He's just there, open and relaxed. That makes me nervous in a different way... because kindness can trip you up if you're not careful. I know that well enough.

And then I feel it. A spark in the crowd, a jolt of energy I can't name. It shoots behind my ribs... cold and electric, like a draft coming through a closed window.

All I can see is a little girl. Flouncy dress, bright blue pigtails, ice cream smeared across her cheeks. She's spinning in slow circles between tables like she's in a ballroom and everyone else is standing still. Cute. Weird hair. She catches my eye, and for a moment she smiles, too wide, too steady, like she knows me.

The energy spikes, messy and loud, like too many voices trying to whisper at once. Not real voices, more like the echo of something ancient and wild trying to sound human. My skin crawls. The girl spins again... and something twists at the edge of my mind. A ripple.

Underneath it all, I can feel it. Not her, not exactly. What's inside her. Something impossible.

The air around her shimmers.

Not visibly. Not enough for anyone else to notice. But the presence behind her... coiled inside her... is gargantuan. I've never sensed anything that big, that focused. Not even close.

I wrench my senses back, like jerking my fingers from a flame.

Too late.

A flash...

A weight on my chest, breath knocked out. Cold hands. The helplessness. *Touched...*

No... not now... not here!

I shove the memory down so fast it leaves me shaking.

The voices, the energy, the wrongness... it's chaos and laughter with razor edges, sweet and poisoned. Not evil. But not kind, either. Not human.

It burrows deeper, and I flinch. My whole body jerks like it's been touched.

I can't stop it!

When I look again, the girl is gone. A chair screeches across the tile. Grease still sticks to my fingers. His voice is still there, constant, pulling me back to the present.

I've sensed spirits before. Gentle ones. Sad ones. Ancestors. Echoes.

Never anything like this.

Never anything that pushed back.

And for the first time in years, I'm scared of what I can feel.

Chapter 6:
Humiliations & Connections

Airi ✦ Afternoon (April 23) ✦ Dubai

BAM.

I go face-first into a wall. Not a wall. A person. A GIANT person. My tray tips, soda sloshes, fries fly all over the reflective floor. Heat blooms across my cheeks as I stagger, arms flailing. My comfort food... gone, all over the place.

The soda cup zaps my hand, buzz of blue static that pops with more intensity than it should. Lid bursts off, straw catapults like a rocket, soda spattering across my sneakers.

I yelp and drop it. Now I'm on the ground, sticky and embarrassed, surrounded by runaway fries. People are staring... DUH... they're staring... GREAT.

I lunge for the fries like the very act of picking them up will dispel the entire incident. My brain is a storm. Stupid, clumsy, why me.

Movement flits by. A shadow. The GIANT I'd hit bends down, wide shoulders eclipsing the harsh fluorescent lights. He's scooping up fries, easy like this is no big deal. Tattoos coil across his arms. He's murmuring something. Soft, maybe a joke? I'm too rattled to understand it.

So instead my mouth starts talking.

"It's your fault. You're a giant... *I'll sue you.*" I keep talking, burying the mortification. Standard operating procedure for Airi. (Seriously, what's wrong with me?)

He raises an eyebrow. "Pretty sure you bumped into me."

Heat floods my face. I open my mouth and it catches. "I... I... I'M SO SORRY!" I blurt, way too loud.

I drop to my knees, grabbing at runaway fries. He crouches beside me, calm. "Relax. It's just food."

"You were in the way!"

"You weren't looking."

"You're huge! Who just stands there, like that?"

"People in line?"

I groan and cover my face. "I can't handle this right now."

"Then let me do this."

My eyes flick up, suspicious. "You don't have to..."

"I know."

We scoop. Well, he scoops. I'm a tornado of soda and fries.

I stop, watching him. "Why are you doing this?"

He shrugs. "You looked like you needed it."

I stare like that's a language I don't speak. "But I spilled soda on your shoes."

He glances down at the cola. Shrugs again. "They'll be fine."

"You're weird."

"Takes one to know one."

I flinch, then settle. "You should've moved," I mutter.

"Didn't have time."

Arms crossed, glare on. "Still."

"You were light-speed."

"You're a human building."

He snorts. "Fair enough."

"I'm not usually this clumsy."

"Sure you're not, Fry Girl."

I practically vibrate with anger. "Don't call me that!"

"What, Fry Girl?"

"It's not my name!"

"Could be," he teases. "It's a pretty good origin story."

I groan. "It tells everyone I'm a klutz."

"Total klutz. But in a fun way."

I glare, then sigh. "I will sue you."

"With fries?"

Another glare. "I'm almost sixteen."

Shoulders still squared, but something eases. "I'm not a kid."

"I didn't say you were. You're a lot of attitude in a small package."

"You're really not going to let this go, are you?"

"Nope. Unless you give me something else to call you."

He doesn't flinch. Just grins, pinky out. "Deal?"

I hesitate, but hook my own finger with his. "Airi. From Japan."

He smiles down at me and his eyes warm. "Tama. From New Zealand."

But before I can decide what to do with that warmth in my chest, I see Dad and Mom walking toward the security check without me. My stomach slumps. Same formation as always: them in their own world, me... an afterthought.

"Raincheck," I blurt (*ugh, who am I even saying that to? Am I ever going to see him again?*), yanking back and running after them... I settle behind them in my familiar role as "kid who tags along." They never look back. I'm good at keeping up. They're talking seat assignments or gate numbers or some such... usual stuff. They didn't even ask me where I was. Last summer I *lost* them on the way to Kyoto. They didn't notice for three stops.

And me? Well, my heart's still racing. Analyzing. Replaying the brief collision. Fry Girl. I should hate the nickname. A part of me does. Another part is skittish but unsure, wondering if it's okay to feel... visible.

I take a shaky breath and try to focus on our next flight, but I can't quite shake the memory of how Tama grinned, the way he instinctively cared enough to help without a second thought. It's unsettling. I don't know what it means. I just know it matters. Maybe that's enough for now.

Chapter 7:
Smile for the Bloodline

Tristan ✦ (Midday) April 24 ✦ Berlin

I press the palms of my hands to the marble countertop, looking in the mirror. My reflection stares back, a stranger in a suit I didn't choose. The perfect son. The Pellinore heir. A 17 destined to a life of service and influence... I look for a flicker of myself in those dead eyes and find nothing. For a heartbeat, the urge to just... break something is overwhelming. To shatter the mirror, to see the perfect image crack along with my composure.

I rake a hand through my hair, shoving up the painstakingly precise lines of my parting, then I exhale. My shoulders unclench a fraction. If Mum walks in right now, she'll shriek. I almost want her to. Just so I can see her façade crack.

No one comes. Just the quiet whir of the fluorescent lights and the muffled clinking of silverware through the walls.

I give myself one heartbeat of rebellion... slumped over the sink, hair disheveled, true release. Then I push myself up by my shoulders and get back to work. Fix the shirt, cuff the sleeves, smooth the hair... but not too much. Leave it tousled, just a tiny bit of friction in a world full of smooth surfaces.

One more breath... in this sterile, impersonal chill. I leave the bathroom.

✦ ✦ ✦ ✦ ✦ ✦ ✦

The Pellinores have a history like few others. Our family tree traces back through the centuries, all the way back to King Arthur and his knights. One ancestor, way back when, claimed descent from the old knight Pellinore, and my family's made a business of it ever since... traditions, expectations, even the coat of arms in our foyer.

"Destiny and Duty." The family motto, which we've been hearing since birth.

The last few months have found us back in Berlin, this time for another round of diplomatic performances. Meetings, luncheons, photo ops. The running joke is that I've grown up on a steady diet of canapés and handshakes... raised on nothing but smiling for cameras.

Don't say the wrong thing, don't display weakness, keep the Pellinore name gleaming. It's a never-ending grind. I step into the ballroom, low conversation buzzing just under the din of chinking glassware and soft laughter. Everything just so... no wrinkles, no stains, no sudden joy. Just artifice.

I take my place at my designated table. Nobody even glances at me. Mum sees me, of course. Eyes flick over my hair... still a little messy. Lips purse. I smooth my hair back down. Mum relaxes a fraction and I can see it. Then her attention flicks to the French ambassador.

On stage, some professor, Ellen Mara, is making a speech from behind the lectern. Her voice is low, but it still carries, somehow slicing through the hum of the attendees.

"...the recurring motif of the serpent," she's saying. "From the Egyptian uraei to the Mesoamerican feathered serpents, this symbol manifests in thousands of cultures... guardian of wisdom, guardian of chaos, mediator of worlds."

A screen behind her shows an image of a sinuous serpent, haloed in white light. It's a bit cheesy, but she has a rhythm to her voice that's gripping in its own way. I remember Dad once calling her "One to watch." Meaning we might want to curry favor with her... or her connections, at some point.

The projector whirs, and the screen switches to another slide. More images of mythical serpents, otherworldly and golden. Professor Mara's hair is catching in the overhead lights... silver braided with a thin gold braid, like flames woven through ice. Her eyes scan the room, level and sure. Not creepy, but unplaceable. As if she knows things the rest of us only sense.

A slight chill runs under my skin, and I straighten in my chair.

In the crook of the stage, half-obscured by the curtain, is a girl operating the laptop. She's probably about my age... slight frame, dark skin luminous under the overhead stage lights, long braids pinned up behind her. Her jaw clenched, she's waiting for the professor's next cue.

She doesn't wriggle in her seat or dart furtive glances around the way the other interns I've seen at these shindigs do. She's watching Mara like she's analyzing the woman's every move. Not hero-worship, but close. Almost... examination.

Fingers touch the trackpad and slide it to the next slide. For a second, it feels like the symbols projected on the screen pulse with more power than they should. My heart skips a beat, a not-unpleasant jump in my chest.

And then...

For a heartbeat, the intern glows gold, bright and alive. Behind her, Mara shines silver... steady, sharp, colder. I blink, and it's gone.

I rub my eyes, and then I glance around. No one else reacts.

"Tristan."

My father's voice is quiet but perfectly pitched. It takes no more than my name, and I straighten as if on a string pulled by an unseen hand. Posture tight, hands now resting out of sight, no emotion, no sigh, no twitch of muscle that could be read as weakness.

"Sorry," I mutter.

He doesn't look at me. He's instead tapping one knuckle against the tablecloth, a silent rhythm... controlled, contained, and disappointed. That's all he needs to say: Don't lose focus. Smile for the cameras. Be the perfect Pellinore. Just don't ask me if I believe any of it is real.

I press the palms of my hands to my thighs, my hands itching to fidget, to move. I swallow hard, trying not to breathe too deeply or he'll think I sighed. This is the Pellinore way: every motion scrutinized, every image manicured. The same forced grace that got me up and into the bathroom a few minutes ago.

But a part of me wants to stand, wants to walk out. No scene, no shouting... just walk out. Leave the diplomats to do their politicking without me.

Of course, I don't. I sit. Silent. Still. Everything the Pellinore name demands.

At the back of the room, standing away from the diplomatic gathering... sitting alone, in a relaxed posture yet oddly frozen, as if he was only pretending to be calm.

A tweed coat and round glasses which, by themselves, would be unremarkable were it not for his hair... as bright as a neon sign, as though it's dyed to stand out from the sobriety of the ballroom.

The lights didn't flicker, but the world did. I blink and we lock eyes. The same eye-popping shade of wrong blue. He grins, a knife-edge grin, like he knows a joke at my expense. Or maybe on everyone.

A shiver ripples up my shoulders.

I blink, and he's gone. Not moved to another seat, not slipped out the door... just gone. The chair where he'd been sitting is now empty. No one else in the room reacts, like he'd never been there at all.

But I know he was there.

And then I hear it, a voice not mine, urgent and sharp: 'Keep going, child. Whatever you do, don't stop.'

Chapter 8:
The Queen in the Circle

Titania ✦ Morning (April 25) ✦ Stonehenge

The wind whips between the gray clouds overhead, sharp and cold. Stonehenge is silent. Shadows from the stones stretch across the dew-damp grass. It's heavy with tension, as if the air itself is waiting, holding its breath before a pronouncement.

I walk forward, the heel of my shoe clicking across the uneven flagstones. The charade has gone on too long: permits, paperwork, a committee of committees. A queen of Faerie, hemmed in by mortal regulations for daring to do her queen's bidding. Oberon sent me here. No, asked, or rather commanded me to.

Posture straight, hair pulled back, coat buttoned to hide my stance. To these mortals I am Doctor Eleanor Ashcroft, a respected historian with all the proper qualifications. They only see what I show them. It's almost laughable. How easily they accept the ruse, never looking past the surface. Mortal minds are not made to see my face... Titania, Queen of Avalon.

The security guards at the entrance shuffle past one another, three of them, shifting from foot to foot and glaring between me and each other as if they were a unit and not sure what to do. A man in a rumpled brown suit beside them wrings his hands as if they were all he was holding himself up by.

I smile politely. "Thank you for meeting me." He shifts, looking uncomfortable. "O-of course, Dr. Ashcroft. It is just... it's not common, closing the site like this. And for so many days." I tilt my head fractionally, even-voiced. "As I told you, my research is time-sensitive. We wouldn't want any damage to this historic landmark."

His shoulders slump. "Of course. No one would. It is just... three days is... an unusual request."

"Precisely what's needed." I say gently, but with finality. "And I cannot be disturbed for that time."

The window is narrow; I controlled the site for that reason.

He hesitates, then nods, shrinking under my confidence. "I shall... make sure of it."

"Excellent." I lower my voice in dismissal. "You have been most helpful."

"Right. Well... we shall leave you to it, then."

I give a single nod in reply. Regal. Final. They shuffle off, casting nervous looks over their shoulders. I watch them until they disappear behind the outer circle.

They wave their rules like iron clubs, proud and foolish. I will bend their will to me with a single thought. Lay them at my feet.

Then I let the smile fall.

✦ ✦ ✦ ✦ ✦ ✦ ✦

As I step through the stone circle, I feel the ancient magic thrumming beneath my feet... old, buried, but still beating. It surges through the soles of my shoes, a vibration that prickles up my calves and settles behind my sternum. The scent of wet earth deepens, twining with something older... like the air before a storm. I sigh slowly, the weight of years pressing against my skin. The magic remembers me. And I, in turn, remember the price, a fix that held but never healed. The wind gusts around me, whipping around the sarsens and the bluestones. The stones sing louder in memory and expectation.

I have stood in this circle before, in centuries past, braiding the seal with Merlin and the other Atlanteans. We had fought, straining to maintain the balance, to weave a wall of stone and sacrifice and vow. Oberon and I have fought to unravel it... and failed. For years I have worked from Avalon, and only of late has the circle begun to stir again.

I kneel in the grass, palms on knees, eyes closed. The touch of the girl's eyes earlier burns in my mind: raw, untrained, yet gold... bright, insolent. She should not have been able to touch me. And yet she did. The contact stung... hard, unwanted, far too direct. Not a threat, not yet. Curiosity and irritation coil inside me together. I do not like being seen when I do not wish to be seen.

The filament of connection pulses, taut and unbidden... a reminder of the day I was seen when I did not let it happen. She knew. Enough to know. I am unsettled by it more than I care to say.

But that can wait. For now, this needs my full attention.

A ripple of disquiet slides through me. Oberon has been ravenous, like a black root winding in his heart and caged by the seal as I am. Even for a faerie king, his hunger seems warped. Perhaps the shaking loose of the magic will loosen what's festered in him... though even as I think it, I know it to be a lie. If I tell myself this, then I do not have to give voice to what I suspect.

His hunger is not a byproduct of what he does, but the first steps of something else. I catch my breath... not from fear, but from something far more dangerous: doubt. Something darker... perhaps?

I take in a deep breath, centering myself. The incantation bubbles in my throat... ancient words that had echoed through this circle when we wove the seal. They flow from my mouth in a chant, and the wind answers, curling around my coat. The pins in my hair pull at their ends, strands loosening as the energy begins to pool around me. The first syllables drift on the breeze.

Then, as I force it, the air thickens. First draw, then let it settle; there will be more. The symbols carved into the stones begin to shimmer, drawn to me by my magic. Shadows slide across the grass, reaching for me like fingers. The seal groans under the stress. The price. Lines of energy flare just below the surface of the ground, fanning out from the central stones. My chanting rises. A bitter cold bites at my skin, but I do not falter. Impatience, strain... nothing more, I tell myself.

Magic is coming back... chaotic and raw, because the fabric is loosening. I can taste it in the air, feel it prying at the seams between worlds. Stonehenge shakes under the pressure, but holds. For now.

Soon enough Oberon will have his wish: the walls between Faerie and the mortal world will be broken again. The question is what else will seep through once we open the floodgates. On my terms, not his.

For now, I put my will into the unraveling of the seal, even as a part of me questions what fresh horrors may come from that. I will not indulge that fear. Not yet. It smolders below the layers of duty and will, but sharpens my focus all the same.

I must move forward, not because I know what will happen, but because to stop would mean admitting fear of what waits on the other side of that broken gate.

I can almost hear Merlin's muted grumbling... he and the other Atlanteans built this to protect the world. But that was then, and this is now. I will see this through.

My voice swells with power, echoing around the circle. The stones hum in answer. Energy crackles in the air, like the static before a storm.

This time, nothing will stop me.

Chapter 9:
What We Have Lost

Professor Mara ✦ Morning (April 26) ✦ Humboldt University

The room is half full, as usual. A few heads are down, a few laptops glow with everything but my syllabus. And yet... most of them are listening. They always do when I reach this part.

"The Battle of Camlann," I say, hands behind my back, steady. "Arthur is mortally wounded. Mordred falls. The golden age of Camelot ends in blood and betrayal."

I let the silence hang before continuing. "The stories diverge, of course. Some say the Lady of the Lake takes him. Others, three queens in black hoods. But the destination is always the same: Avalon."

I scan the rows, letting my eyes linger just long enough to feel the attention shift toward me. That familiar hush always comes at this moment: respectful, expectant. It only reminds me of what I have lost.

"A place of healing," I say. "Of rest. But more than that, a symbol of postponement. Not death... not quite. A delay. A promise. That he will return when the land needs him most."

Advancing the slide. The manuscript fills the screen behind me... Arthur adrift on glassy waters, painted with a reverence that makes myth look like memory.

"The legend becomes a lullaby here. A comfort. A way of handing off responsibility to a future that may never come. We love the idea of someone coming back to fix things. It absolves us of having to do it ourselves."

I glance toward the front row and frown. "Could someone pass out the handouts? I forgot... I gave my intern the day off."

One of the students stands and begins handing out the copies. I give a small nod, let my smile flicker across my face before fading again.

"What most versions do not focus on," I continue, "is what comes after. After Avalon. After the silence. What happens to Camelot without its king? To the advisors, the scribes, the... students?"

I look up, not at the ceiling, not at anyone. Just upward, as if memory lives somewhere out of reach.

"Merlin disappears too. Later. Quietly. Like smoke from a dying fire. No last stand. No farewell. Just... gone."

I step toward the podium. I don't lean on it. I just let it anchor me.

"He leaves behind a half-burned library, notes in languages only a few can read. And those who rely on him suddenly find themselves expected to lead. Overnight."

A dry laugh escapes, sharper than I mean it to be.

"Some of them are barely older than you. Imagine that. You arrive to study under the greatest mind of the age... and instead, he is gone."

I remember standing in that ruined chamber, smoke still clinging to the pages, ash smeared across my hands, pages stinking of smoke as I tried to decipher instructions that made no sense without him. They never would. I became the keeper of shards.

Someone coughs near the back. Another clicks a pen in the quiet. I look back at the image of Arthur on the screen.

"But the myth says Arthur will return. Merlin? He never promises anything."

Click. Blank slide.

"All right," I say, clearing my throat. "That's where we'll end today. Read the excerpts from Geoffrey of Monmouth and the alternate accounts in the packet. And yes, there will be a quiz."

They begin to gather their things... chairs scrape, backpacks zip. I watch them go. And only once the room is nearly empty do I let myself breathe. Let my senses stretch.

It's faint, but undeniable. Old magic... the wrong kind. Titania is still working to dismantle the seal. I feel the threads unraveling, breaking under pressure. The sensation coils in my spine, familiar and sickening. The same pattern I felt centuries ago, just before it all unraveled. It won't hold much longer. Hours, maybe less. And this time, there is no Merlin to buy us more.

Other pulses. Oberon... faint. Calculating. But the most concerning of them, the most dangerous, is too close.

A pulse I do not understand. Chaos, like a child tugging at threads.

I brush the podium with my fingertips. "The danger with stepping in too early," I whisper, "is that you rob people of becoming who they need to be. Or worse... you break something you're meant to protect."

But I can't wait anymore.

The protections around my office will need reinforcement. The initiations must begin... not just awareness, but the slow, dangerous work of teaching power to those who don't yet understand what it can cost.

It's time to start gathering them.

"We always expect the next generation to be ready," I say softly, to no one. "Even when we weren't. Too proud to admit it. Too late to learn what was required... I know what it means to be handed a burden too vast, too soon. I have carried that for lifetimes... and still, I ask it of them now."

Magic has always lingered... it chooses its vessels. Once, they were called gods. Now there are six.

Chapter 10:
Sparks and Circuits

I practically bounce into the Deutsches Technikmuseum (both tricky and fun to say), my brain working overdrive like an overclocked CPU. I haven't stopped pacing since Dad and Mom dropped me off here and gave me the brush-off. "...We'll pick you up later, sweetie; we have a meeting."... So I've been dying to look around. Mom and Dad aren't big on dusty old engines or futuristic robots, and here they dropped me off like I was a spare backpack. Typical.

They didn't even look back when they left. Not that I expect them to. I mean, that's like our thing: Drop-off, no check-ins, pick-up when you have time. I'm used to it, more or less. But still. It would've been nice. Just once. To feel like more than an afterthought.

But I don't care. I'm here. I'm here!

A million old locomotives, glimmering screens and creepily life-like robot demos. It's like walking into a living tech encyclopedia. I can feel my brain whirring. My feet are moving before I even think about where I want to go. Everything is shiny, loud, alive... and I want to touch all of it. At once. Maybe twice.

I stop at a line of classic computers... the monitors are the size of microwaves and the keyboards are clicky and rough. "Whoa... retro," I whisper, pressing my nose against the glass. My reflection is melded into the machines, pink and blue pigtails jutting out beside big gray boxes. "My phone probably has more CPU than all of you combined."

I press my nose against the glass, my reflection melding with the machines. For a second, I'm not in Berlin. I'm ten, standing proudly next to my robotics project at the prefectural science fair. It had taken me three months to build. A little wheeled bot that could solve a Rubik's Cube. I kept looking for my parents in the crowd, my first-place ribbon clutched in my hand. I finally spotted them near the back. Dad was taking a call, pacing. Mom was scrolling through her phone, a bored look on her face. They waved when I held up the ribbon, but they never came closer. I stood there for an hour, waiting.

I like machines. They don't cringe if you get too excited or say the wrong thing. They don't pretend to listen if they're on their phone. They listen and don't judge. They don't forget to ask if you're ok. Or forget you at school. Or forget to care.

And then I see it. The AI exhibit. Sleek, white alcove with rows of pulsing lights. Robots filed in silent precision, glowing screens casting streams of code like digital waterfalls. I take a shaky breath. This is it. This is why I practically dragged my feet here.

I step closer, my palms against the glass barrier and eyes wide. "I wanna build something like this." I mumble to myself. "I wanna bring code to life."

"Pretty cool, huh?"

I spin around. My stomach drops. A boy... blue hair peeking out from under a hoodie, grin too wide to be casual. Older than me, or maybe my age? He nods at the robots. "Pretty, yeah, but limited. Not really free. No real spark."

I furrow my brows. "Limited? Are you serious?" I wave at a nearby bot whose articulated fingers curl with fleshy precision. "They're almost alive."

He laughs, the sound skipping like a corrupted audio file. "They only do what they're programmed to, nothing more. Just imagine if they could break their own code. Break loose."

A cold feeling worms up my neck. "W-who are you?"

He tilts his head, grin sharpening. "Just a guy who likes to play, Cotton Candy."

My cheeks flare. "Hey! I'm not... " I catch a glimpse of my pink-blue pigtails in a nearby reflection. "Oh. Okay, fine, a little cotton candy. But still... "

He winks. The laugh again. That cringe-inducing laugh. "Careful Cotton Candy. Hop around like that and you'll run into another giant."

My stomach flips. "How do you... "

He's already shoving off the railing, walking away with suspicious nonchalance.

The closest display flickers as he passes, the LED indicators cycling from green to bright blue for half a second. Then a hard screen glitch.

For a moment, the screen is showing a video of... me?

But the me on the screen is smiling. Wide, too wide. The teeth...pointed, sharp.

I don't move. Can't breathe.

The smiling version of me didn't blink. Didn't breathe. Like it was waiting for me to notice.

Then the screen flickers back to normal.

I whip around to look for the boy. Heart pounding, he's already gone. The crowd flows around him like they don't even see him

I stare after him, rattled. He had to have hacked that display. What else would a reasonable person think? Right?

But something in my gut is tingling.

Wrong.

I herd myself back to the VR demo, working to squelch the nerves with awe. A life-sized dragon belches fire on screen, flapping its wings at a random visitor wielding a VR sword. People cheer. I bounce on my toes, but the line is insane. "I'll come back," I mumble and turn away.

I wander into the animatronics. My brain still running on the blue-haired boy... What did he mean, break free?

when I nearly trip over a roped-off display. My hands shake a little. I hate how easily I get rattled.

A mechanical cat blinks at me from inside the glass cage. I reach to pet it, my fingers skimming synthetic fur. The mechanical meow hums at my touch. The cat blinked, its gears whirring soft and even. Predictable. Safe. Machines don't smile wrong.

I should be in heaven... this is the kind of tech I go to museums for... but my mind can't stop replaying that exchange: the glitchy laugh, the flicker in the robotics.

I whip around, half expecting to see him. Bam... I crash into someone. AGAIN. Airport brain replays in my head. "Oh no, not again," I mutter under my breath.

I look up and forget to breathe. She's tall, with braids that flow down to her shoulders, and her skin is so warm under the overhead lights. She looks calm, centered, everything I am not. And for some reason, I want to be near her. Like if I get too far away, I'll miss something. My cheeks heat, not just from embarrassment.

Her eyes meet mine, and for a moment, I can't think of anything to say. My heart tightens in an entirely new way... like the flutter of a hundred butterflies fills my chest.

"You ok?" she asks, voice quiet, kind.

I nod too fast. "Yeah! Totally fine! Super fine! I just... got excited about... uh..." I wave at some random panel behind her. "That!"

She laughs... low, soothing... and it does something to my insides that I can't name.

"You're funny," she says, holding out her hand. "I'm Nia."

It takes me a moment to register... I'm supposed to shake it. "A-Airi," I stammer, cheeks on fire. "From Tokyo, if that wasn't obvious." I cringe. Why did I say that? Why am I still talking?

She just smiles. "It's cute. Your hair, I mean. I like it."

People don't usually say things like that to me. Mostly they tell me to quiet down or ask if I'm lost. But she said it so matter-of-factly, like it wasn't weird to notice me. Or like... maybe it was okay to notice her back? My brain scrambles to process it... admiration? A crush? Just wanting someone to like you? I don't know. I've read about this stuff. It's not the same as living it.

"Th-thanks," I mumble. "Your braids are really pretty."

She nods, and we stand in silence for a second. My skin buzzes with so much awkwardness. But also... interest? Is that the right word?

I want to say something clever. Something poised. But everything I can think of sounds artificial or stupid. I open my mouth and shut it. My hands start doing that again. I shove them into my hoodie pocket. Then yank them back out. Do something normal, I scream in my head. But what even is normal?

"So, hey. Are you here for the museum?" I say, too loud, too fast. Duh, Airi... she is at the museum. Ugh.

"Yeah," Nia says, something darkening her face. "Got the day off, so I am here, on my own, exploring."

"Oh, same! I mean, alone. My parents dropped me off. They had... other things to do." I bite my lip. My hands are flapping again. Stop flapping. I press them to my sides.

We stand in silence again, and I could say a hundred things. I want to ask if she wants to go and explore together. The words are there but choke on them.

Instead, I glance sideways, hoping she'll say something. Anything.

But she's just smiling, soft and calm, like she's waiting.

And then... she offers.

"Want some company?"

My heart skips. Her eyes are locked on mine.

"Wait... like, me and you?"

She nods. Most people roll their eyes. Or walk away. She just smiles, like my noise doesn't scare her off. Like maybe it's okay to stay.

I grin before I can stop myself. "I mean, if you insist."

We start walking together. I point at a half-melted robot and go off on a tangent of design issues and AI rights and probably too much else. But she doesn't seem to mind.

I glance at her again, and that warm flutter in my chest returns. But not panic. Something... nicer.

I don't know what this is yet. But I want to find out.

"C'mon," I say, tugging her forward, before I explode from too many *unsupervised* thoughts.

Chapter 11:
Bones & Bros

My sneakers squeak on the polished floor. Every step reverberates like I'm stomping for show. This place is massive... at least twice the size of any museum I've been in before. Back home, history is etched into wood or stone. Over here, dinosaur bones the size of trucks dangle from the ceiling like it's some weird ornament. Surreal.

I stop in front of a giant egg. The thing is easily the size of my head, cracked open on one side. The plaque reads Titanosaur Egg – Late Cretaceous Period. I don't know what all of that means but it sounds fancy.

I lean up to the glass. "Guess it's either scrambled or sunny-side up," I whisper, mostly to myself. I glance around to make sure no one heard that. Sometimes all it takes is for one person to see a big guy cracking wise to decide he's an idiot.

Uncle Manu's voice echoes in my head. Don't forget your respect, Tama. The past isn't just old things... it's our history, it's our ancestors... living with us. I usually roll my eyes and grit my teeth when he starts getting all philosopher on me. But he's also right more than he's wrong. Uncle chuckles to himself: "You gotta watch that strength, boy. People will read things wrong."

I lower my head slightly in a bow, more out of instinct than any actual intent. It feels right. When I straighten back up, the weird pressure in my chest lifts a little.

Skeletons of ancient beasts arch overhead in the bright lights, their shadows creeping across the floor. They look like sentries, keeping watch on the living. I pass a T-Rex skull with teeth as big as my hand.

"Sorry, mate," I whisper. "Didn't mean to wake ya." It stares back at me, its hollow eye sockets staring like black holes. Goosebumps rise along my spine. Something about all of these fossils feels... wrong in a way... like the passage of time hasn't quite taken them down.

"Okay, spooky stuff," I mutter to myself. "They're just bones, not gonna start wandering around."

A sauropod skeleton arches across the hall on an exposed neck so long, the head nearly brushes the ceiling. "Guess how many forests it took for lunch?" I ask, mostly to hear the echo of my own voice. It's oddly low. Sort of like a kid's voice.

A nearby voice snickers. "Would've been one hell of a lawnmower."

I look over. A guy a few years older than me lounges on a railing... perfectly turned out, hair just so. He exudes a breezy confidence, like he's made public appearances since birth. Or something like that.

I grin and rub my hands on my thighs. "Bet he could clear a rugby pitch in one go."

The guy snorts. "Then he'd be saving a bundle on landscaping."

I extend a hand. "Tama. New Zealand."

He shakes it, firm and deliberate, not taking the liberty. "Tristan. Cornwall, England."

I tilt my head. "You've got some wild sea stories over there, I'll bet."

Something flickers behind his eyes, gone in a flash. He grins at me. "You could say that."

I choose not to pry. Everyone's got their baggage. Instead, I point my chin at the immense skeleton. "Crazy, huh? We've got some legends back home about things like that. Sometimes they protect people, sometimes they tear their houses apart. Depends on how they're treated, I guess."

His eyes light up. "Yeah? Like what?"

"Taniwha. Protectors of rivers, lakes, ocean caves. Some call them ancestors, some call them monsters. My uncle says they keep everything in balance, so you respect or else they'll make you feel your place." I snap my fingers to punctuate.

Tristan nods slowly. "That's wild. Never heard of Taniwha. Guess every country's got its own legends."

"Yeah," I say, something small snagging in my chest. Back home, no one sees me as much as a big guy. And those stories are important to me too. "Guess so."

We stare back at the skeleton.

"If this guy were real, he'd be having a million TikTok followers for sure," I say. "Crushing cars, getting shared every day."

Tristan laughs. "Sponsored by the lawn mowing companies, no question."

I chuckle, clapping him on the shoulder. "I like you, man. You're alright."

He smiles back. "You're not half-bad yourself."

✦ ✦ ✦ ✦ ✦ ✦ ✦

We explore further into the museum, more bones and mythology references dotting the hallways. It's surprisingly easy to talk to Tristan. Feels like I've known him for years, not five minutes. At the same time, another part of me is bracing for him to make assumptions. Like everyone else does... you're just a big dude, all muscle, and brain matter was obviously optional at birth. So far, Tristan hasn't done that.

We stop at a placard featuring a fossilized skull. Dire Wolf, the tag reads. The teeth are curved in a cruel arc. I huff a whistle. "Mean-looking dog. Wouldn't surprise me if he didn't like fetch."

Tristan smirks. "He might've fetched people. Some think dire wolves inspired werewolf legends... big, deadly, hunted in packs."

I feel a cold knot in my gut, imagining glowing eyes in a moonlit forest. "That's... creepy. I could see those guys working the night shift."

He nods. "Makes you wonder how many so-called myths are built on something real."

We move through a mythology-inspired gallery of fossils: eagles alongside griffins, ancient marine reptiles next to old sea serpent stories. A dragon skeleton sprawls above us, wings outstretched.

And then we stop, and I don't breathe.

A Taniwha carving stands in a glass case: sinuous body, carved wooden scales, fierce eyes. The placard says it's Māori legend. Tristan's mouth goes slack as he reads it, eyes flickering back to me.

"This is what you were talking about, right?"

I nod slowly. "Yeah. They can guard a river or swallow a canoe whole. Not evil, just strong."

My uncle's voice echoes in my head. Show respect.

But I don't hear the words anymore. I'm transfixed on the carving.

I've seen eyes like these before. Last week in Auckland, just before I tripped and opened that hydrant. I told myself it was just a reflection in a shop window.

It wasn't.

Now the same eyes are staring at me again.

My chest tightens. The air feels dense. I step closer, fingers grazing the glass.

A jolt strikes me... cold, electric, sharp. The carving's eyes flash. Not the light. Not some trick of the glass.

It's looking at me.

My vision swims. For a second, I'm back on that street. Water bursting, my own body slamming on the pavement.

I flail into the railing. Metal creaks beneath my hands. I can feel it bend, hot and soft like plastic.

I release quickly, heart thumping like a drumline in my chest. Staring at the bent metal, a cold dread washing over me. That wasn't right. I'm strong, sure, but this was different. Effortless. Wrong. Uncle Manu's voice rings in my head, a low warning he's given me a hundred times. "You gotta watch that strength, boy. People will read things wrong." They'll see a monster. A brute. A big guy with zero impulse control who breaks things because he can't help it. And what if they're right?

Tristan takes my other arm, grip firm but gentle. "You okay?"

"Y-yeah... it just... startled me."

I pat the distorted rail, as if that'll help. "Guess that's some cheap museum-grade plastic."

Tristan arches an eyebrow, but he nods. "Sure... it must be cheap."

We keep walking, but I don't feel steady on my feet.

Like something in that case had seen me.

Or worse... recognized me.

We walk on in silence. But I feel it... something out there watching. Not bones or ancient legend. Something alive. Something waiting.

Chapter 12:
Ball of Energy

From the outside, the Deutsches Technikmuseum is like a steampunk fever dream: an ancient brick building with a full-sized airplane bolted to the roof. Inside, it's all chrome walkways and humming engines and blinking lights. Tourists call it a must-see. I came here because I hoped it'd be loud enough to block out the noise in my head.

It isn't. If anything, the noise carves out my pulse.

My dreams last night still stick to me like cobwebs... wisps of a woman wrapped in shadows, a sky tearing open, a voice that almost made sense. Almost.

I walk past oxidized steam engines and ancient-model radios labeled "prehistoric tech." At home, some of this stuff is still used... necessity, not nostalgia. The dissonance clenches something in my chest.

Tourists surround me. Kids shriek with delight at the robotic arms and vintage toys. Their energy sticks to my skin like static, too much and not enough. I try to find stillness. I don't.

Then I see it... a flash of electric blue out of the corner of my eye.

My body tenses. I pivot, pulse racing... but there's nothing there. Just a gaggle of teenagers crowded around a flight simulator, shouting in three different languages. Normal.

But that color...

That blue...

It's the same shade as the man I saw at the lecture. The one with the thin grin and eyes that didn't blink. The one watching the blonde boy like he was prey... or a puzzle.

I press two fingers to my temple and breathe. Center yourself. My grandmother's voice, deep as bedrock. I try to listen to it. But the heaviness in the air won't go.

Then it comes.

Something behind my eyes.

A flash. The world lurches. I see black, see stabs of artificial light. And something huge. A gargantuan figure looming over me, eyes glowing, tusks sprouting from a snarled maw. Its skin is cracked and parched like old stone and in its hand...a club the size of a tree trunk.

It raises the weapon above its head.

And brings it down...

I gasp, jerking backwards.

My shoulder smacks the wall behind me. I'm back at the museum. Bright lights. Tourists. Tech noise.

I'm breathing too fast.

What was that?

I haven't had a vision come at me like that since I was a kid. This one was uninvited.

I swallow and scan the crowd. No blue hair. No monster. Nothing but people and machines and the buzz of electricity.

✦ ✦ ✦ ✦ ✦ ✦ ✦

I push into a new wing... new exhibits, brighter lights, sharper noise. Holograms spin overhead while robotic dogs pace in glass cages. It's sensory overload. I press my back against a wall and exhale slowly.

And then I hear it.

A laugh, clear and delighted like someone cracked a window open inside my chest. I turn.

She's bounding from display to display like a spark given legs: small, colorful, impossible to ignore. Pink-and-blue pigtails bounce as she points out everything to no one in particular, eyes wide, mouth open. Her energy isn't just bright. It shimmers.

For a moment, I just watch her. All motion and color, like sunlight bouncing through a prism. Something about her makes me feel... anchored. And weightless. At the same time.

Before I know why, I step toward her. Then another step.

She spins too fast and bumps straight into me. A squeak escapes her mouth as she stumbles, flailing for balance.

"You okay?" I ask, catching her elbow.

"Super fine!" she blurts, waving vaguely toward a VR exhibit like that's what did it. "I totally meant to do that. Like... friction-based navigation?"

I blink. Then laugh, unexpectedly. She's chaos in a hoodie, and I can't stop watching her.

She flushes. "Sorry. I get excited in museums. Or airports. Or, um, general life settings."

"I noticed." I smile and offer my hand. "I'm Nia."

She eyes it for a second, then shakes it like she's not sure how long to hold on. "Airi. From Tokyo. Obviously." Her face twists like she regrets saying that.

"It's cute," I say, meaning the name, the hair, the awkward blur of it all.

Her blush deepens. She shrugs, trying to play it cool, but I see the hint of a frown she doesn't mean to show.

"My parents kinda ditched me here," she says, waving a hand. "They're off doing... business things. I just told them I'd meet them at the exit later."

The lightness in her voice sounds practiced. I know the tone. I've used it myself.

"You come to museums alone a lot?" I ask, gently.

She shrugs again. "Alone's kinda my default setting."

Something in my chest clenches. That wasn't just a joke. That was a quiet truth, wrapped in glitter.

"Want some company?" I ask before I can stop myself. I don't usually invite strangers into my orbit. But something about her, messy and bright and real, makes me want to try.

Her big eyes widen comically, blinking fast. "Wait... like, me and you?"

"If you don't mind."

She grins like she's trying to contain it. "I mean, if you insist."

We fall into step together. She points out a half-melted robot and mutters about design flaws, then launches into a tangent about AI ethics and how she once programmed a calculator to tell jokes. Half of it sails over my head, but I don't care.

Then something flickers in the corner of my eye again.

We pass a robotic dog display, and one of them... black-plated, sleek... pauses. Its LED eyes shift from green to blue. For half a breath, they glow with that same unnatural shimmer I saw this morning. It tilts its head... and stares at Airi.

I freeze. A cold shiver dances across the back of my neck. Not fear, exactly... more like dread.

But then it blinks, wags its tail, and turns away like a normal exhibit. The spell breaks. I glance around. No blue-haired man. No shadow in the crowd. Just noise and lights.

Still, I take a step closer to Airi. Just in case.

She doesn't notice. She's rambling now about how she wants to invent something that changes lives. Her voice softens, almost reverent. "Not for fame or anything. Just... something real. You know?"

I nod. "I think you already are."

She stops mid-step, like I hit a nerve. Then keeps walking. But slower now. Like she's not sure what to do with being seen.

And honestly? Neither am I.

I don't know what this is yet... friendship, fate, something else entirely. All I know is that, for the first time in a long time, the weight in my chest feels a little lighter.

Maybe we're both just lonely weirdos with sparks to hide. Or maybe this is the start of something bigger.

Either way, I don't want to walk away.

Chapter 13:
Ghosts Speak Too

Aiyana ✦ Afternoon (April 26) ✦ Neues Museum

The air is thick in the Neues Museum, like a humid fog settling on my skin. My fingers twitch at my sides as I walk through the exhibit hall, heart beating wildly. It's not just the silence of a museum, the hush of tourists and security cameras and voices muffled by objects made sacred by time... it's heavier than that. There's pressure here. Something unseen bearing down on the artifacts and on me.

Each relic... a carved mask with hollowed eyes, a statue smoothed by time, a spear half-swallowed by the earth and rusted solid... is humming with the energy of a remembered voice, vibrating with the echoes of lives lived, histories passed and half-lost. That's just the way it is for me. The past is so clear to me sometimes. Like it's not even past at all. But I can usually handle it. I can usually filter the noise. Right now, though, it's just too much. Too many voices.

Focus.

I close my eyes, breathing slow. Feel the earth under your feet, my grandmother would say. Let it center you. The thrum of voices and swirled energies quiet a little, retreating behind a screen of calm. I breathe out, and crack open my eyes. This always happens in places like this. In old places, full of memories. Objects remember, and they don't forget to make sure I remember them.

Glass cases line the hall, each glowing softly with the hum of a whispered grief, each object tagged with the smaller tags I know are meant to identify it as "historic" or "ancient" or some such. But I can tell they're more than that... more than historical relics. They're more than pieces of wood or stone or metal. They're something alive, a connection to peoples and cultures that live, or have lived, in some form. They're not supposed to be kept in airtight cubes, or displayed for tourists. They belong outside. In the world. A spark of anger flares in my mind, and a voice cuts it off before it can fully ignite.

"Creepy, huh?"

I spin around, nearly dropping my bags. Balam. The boy from the airport... the one that flirted with me over pizza. He's standing a few feet away, hands in his pockets, half-smiling with an eyebrow cocked between amused and interested. My heart stutters.

I swallow. "You didn't scare me," I say quickly, without meeting his eyes, trying not to hear the sudden flutter in my chest.

He raises an eyebrow. "Sure. You looked like you were about to bolt."

My face flushes. He's grinning now, obviously amused. For a moment I want to snap at him, but... I can't. Because the other part of me is relieved to see someone I recognize... to see someone other than the girl with a mop of wild hair who flirted with me in an airport. It's a small thing. But it matters.

I clear my throat, moving back to the mask in front of me. A carved wooden mask with cracked paint and paint flaking in spots, the eyes hollow and black. "These things aren't just old. There's more to them. Meaning. History. It's just a lot, sometimes."

"Deep thoughts?" he mocks lightly. He looks at the mask, and his expression turns thoughtful. "Yeah, man. It's a lot. Kinda freaks me out, actually."

He shifts from foot to foot, folding his arms like he's bracing against the cold. I can feel that he feels something, even if he can't quite name it. That surprises me.

"You feel it too?" I ask, watching him.

He nods, taking a step toward me. He's taller than I remember him being, and the heat of his presence makes me jittery in a good way and a confusing way. "Not to the same degree, I imagine," he says, "but the eyes... man. They're not supposed to be that real."

A chill ripples through me... part from the mask, part from how easy he gets it. I expect most people to look at me and shrug off the atmosphere. Ignore the lingering energy around ancient things.

I watch him, heart thumping in my chest. "Yeah... me too."

We stand in silence for a moment, the museum sounds turning into a dull hum in the background.

He laughs, shaking his head slightly to loosen the tension. "So do you think these were really worn? Like for ceremonial dances, or whatever? Or was it just decoration?"

I blink, not expecting him to have stayed on topic so long. "They were worn," I say. "Used in ceremonies, dances, a way to cross boundaries. To reach out to spirits, or to become... something else."

He whistles, low. "So you just put on a mask and then you're not just you?"

"Or you're still you," I correct him, "but... more. Like you're reaching into something else."

He tilts his head at me, truly interested. I realize I'm feeling that flutter in my chest again. And it's not just the mask's energy. He's listening. To me. Listening. Which is... not something that should surprise me, but here we are.

"It's kinda cool," he murmurs. "Do you think people really... change like that?"

I pause, shifting my gaze to him. His eyes are warm and open, I can tell. "I think there's a lot of things in this world people don't understand," I say. "Sometimes we connect to them. Leave echoes, or pick up echoes other people left. Maybe that makes us different."

He stares at me. "You're kinda intense, aren't you?"

I roll my eyes, but my face is flaming and I know it. "You're kinda annoying."

He grins, toothy and charming. "But you like it, though, right?" he teases, leaning into me just a little.

My breath catches. My heart flips. I shove him lightly, face burning. "Don't push it."

He chuckles, but it's softer than before. The air between us relaxes. Feels less hostile, less strange. More real. More... us.

We continue down the exhibit, floating from one display to the next. He's genuinely interested. Not pretending or acting like he just wants to be friends with a random girl. He points out stone carvings that look a lot like his grandmother's, tells me about growing up around digs and artifacts in Africa. I talk about dances, stories, how they keep me connected to my home when I'm so far away. He listens. Really listens.

It's unsettling. I can feel this uncomfortable bubble of relief growing in my chest... like maybe I can trust him a little. Just a little. Enough to let down my walls, just a crack.

He moves closer as we stop in front of a display of old weapons. Glancing down at us, I realize it doesn't even seem odd to be standing next to him. My heart is ticking up, faster and faster. Am I... attracted to him? The idea tangles in my head. I've never seriously considered opening up to anyone before. Not since... not since I've ever even had the time. But this is something. Something I can't ignore.

He suddenly twists to face me, catching me looking. My face heats and I look away, but he just smirks, not put off or gloating or anything. "You really like this stuff too?"

I shrug, trying to act nonchalant. "Yeah. Surprised?"

He laughs, and it's warm enough to draw my tension out. "Not anymore."

I smile softly. It's okay, right? Maybe it's okay.

Eventually, he rubs the back of his neck, suddenly sheepish. "Hey, um... I think we were kind of off on the wrong foot the other day. Or I was just being a jerk. But... I would like for us to be friends. If that's cool?"

My heart stutters. Friends. It's not too much. Is it? But it's enough to make my chest tingle. "Yeah," I whisper. "I'd like that. Friends."

He breathes out in relief, grinning in a way that makes my stomach flip like crazy. "Good. Friends it is."

I let out a shaky laugh, my mind whirring with relief and something else... something more than friends that I can't quite name. But friends. We're friends now. We're friends.

✦ ✦ ✦ ✦ ✦ ✦ ✦

A flicker of blue catches the corner of my eye.

A woman in a crisp, tailored suit is standing by a display of old jewelry. Her hair is the same shock of blue I thought I imagined in Atlanta... that I thought belonged to a strange little girl who grinned too big and stared too long. But this time, it's not just the color of her hair that seizes me.

It's the silence.

The air around her is wrong, like the music has been sucked out of the room. Her shoulders are too still, her hands too still, her face too serene... until you look in her eyes.

Her eyes.

They're watching me. Watching us.

Not in a curious way. Not in an angry way. Just... calculating. Like she's studying a bug in a jar, like she's observing and waiting and ready to tap on the sides to see if I squirm.

And then it shifts.

Not her. But the air behind her ripples. My stomach drops, my skin prickles. I feel it again. The thing in that little girl. But it's bigger now. Sharper. Clearer. Ancient and endless and...

Wrong.

It doesn't need to invade me like it did before. It doesn't need to. It just waits.

My stomach twists. "Balam," I whisper, leaning toward him. "The woman. She's wrong."

He moves with me, and I can feel him freeze beside me. "Yeah... I see her."

I want to step back. I want to run. I want to put distance between us. I want to scream. Every instinct in me is screaming at me to get away, to keep moving, to run. But I don't. I stand still. Stiff and frozen and... maybe if I don't move too quickly she won't notice I'm afraid.

My chest clamps. I rub at my arms, trying to shake the chill working into my bones.

Balam sighs, then glances up at me. "Are you okay?"

No. But I nod.

And then a gaggle of tourists floods between us, shattering the moment... and when they've passed, she's gone. No footsteps, no warning. She's just gone, like she was never there at all.

We look at each other, uneasy, wordless. Something passed over us, but it didn't stop.

We continue walking, the easy mood broken by the sense that something, or someone, is still watching us. Still observing. Still testing. Still waiting.

But when Balam's arm brushes against mine, a flicker of warmth overpowers the chill. We're friends. We're friends. I cling to that thought. It's something solid in a sea of other weirdness.

Chapter 14:
Charm & Consequence

We move away from the Taniwha carving, but something still feels heavy in the air. I keep my shoulders loose, my hands in my pockets, my expression neutral. But I can still feel my heart beating.

The way that carving flickered to life... the way Tama twisted and the metal railing bent like foil... it keeps flashing in my mind.

Tama is walking beside me in silence, head tilted down. He's tall and broad shouldered, easily the type of guy who would stand out in a crowd. But he appears scared, hunched in on himself, with his eyes darting nervously to the fossils around us. He has a hand clenched and unclenched at his side, as if he's not sure what to do with it.

The corridor we're walking down is dark. Spotlights on ancient mammal displays cast twisted shadows across our path... saber-toothed cats and dire wolves and giant sloths. The skeletons are posed in dynamic stances with jaws agape and claws extended, frozen in attack. The lighting is low, soft spotlights highlighting the bones and casting jagged webs of shadow across the walls and floor. My footsteps echo unnaturally in the quiet.

Tama keeps looking over his shoulder, as if he's afraid something will lunge out at us. I want to say something to reassure him, but what? Hey, sorry you accidentally snapped a railing... that's fine, right?

I want to say something, do something. I don't know what would help. And I hate that.

I take a deep breath, forcing my "Pellinore calm" to the surface... the right way to stand, the polite expression, the unnamable confidence I was born to have. I feel like it's cracking. Inside, I'm shaken.

A bark of laughter breaks the quiet: "Hey! You there!"

I start, spinning to one side. Tama is tense next to me, with his knuckles turning white. My heart is thumping in my chest.

A burly museum guard is marching toward us. He has his feet wide apart, fists planted on his hips, chin jutting. A thick beard bristles on his chin, his uniform strained over broad, solid shoulders and chest. He's not a man I'd like to mess with.

"You bent the railing," he says, voice booming like an avalanche in the distance. "What were you thinking?"

I glance at Tama, who is staring at the floor in shock. But then, just for an instant...

Not in the lights. In the air. Around the guard.

There is... something. Faint, like smoke at the edge of a fire. But real. Ghostly outlines glowing around his figure that shouldn't be there. Golden?

I blink, and it's gone as fast as it came.

My heart skips. What the hell was that?

Tama opens his mouth to speak but nothing comes out. He glances up at me, helplessly, with eyes so full of guilt and confusion they almost pain me to look at. He doesn't know what to say. I don't know what to say, but I take a step forward anyway... on instinct and something more.

I force a diplomatic smile, practiced and perfect from years of Pellinore dinners and fundraisers. "Sorry about that," I say, light and polite.

But there's something in my voice that isn't me. The moment my words leave my mouth, there's a hum in the air. Not loud... just enough for me to feel it, a plucked string against my ribs. The guard blinks. His expression softens. His shoulders relax an infinitesimal amount. His frown doesn't deepen. It... pauses.

"We didn't realize the railing was loose," I go on, voice carrying a weight it shouldn't. "My friend leaned on it and, well, it gave. We'll be more careful."

The words fall like stones. Too heavy. The guard's eyes wander... not confused or hypnotized, just... deviated. Like my voice... plucked that string in him that agreed. I have no idea how.

"That wasn't 'easy,'" he says, though his voice has lost its bite. It's more a grumble now. "You'd have to be built like a bulldozer to warp steel that thick."

He flicks his eyes to Tama and regards his wide shoulders and broad frame. "Weightlifter, are you?"

Tama forces a shaky chuckle. "Nah, bro... I just... got bigger than I look, I guess."

He swipes at a shrug, but it's stilted.

I laugh casually and pat Tama on the shoulder. "He's got the genes, you know? Some people are just lottery winners."

The guard takes a long look at us both. Then, unexpectedly, he shrugs.

"Just stay away from the exhibits, yeah?" he mutters. "These aren't playground toys."

He glances back toward the Taniwha carving.

"And I wouldn't try and stir up any spirits that don't want stirring."

Chills run down my spine.

"Spirits?" I echo, voice lower now.

The guard's smile goes faintly apologetic, like he hadn't meant to say that. He clears his throat and adds, "Also... museum's closing in ten. You boys need to make your way to the exit."

A long sigh. "Some of these relics have... presence. A lot of them do. But that Taniwha piece they just put in here... since they installed it, weird things. Be smart. Leave it the hell alone."

Before I can ask what he means, he turns and walks away, boots thudding across the polished floorboards.

I breathe out slowly, only now noticing how tense my shoulders had been. Tama still says nothing. He is really shaken... not just by what the man said, but that he was so easily swayed. I feel it too.

That was too easy.

And the flicker of gold... I didn't imagine that.

I look at Tama. His aura... yes, aura... is red now. Solid and sure. Firm as earth. I don't know how I know that. I just do. And me? I look in the reflection of the case next to us and there's nothing overt, but at the corner of my eye... in my mind's eye... there's silver. I rub my temples.

What the hell is happening to me?

I don't ask Tama if he saw that too. I don't think he did.

But I did.

And I'm starting to think... maybe there's something in me that's been waiting to wake up all along.

The two of us trudge onward. A quiet heavy between us. My father's voice rings in my head, Keep your cool, Tristan. Always. I try to do it. I do. But questions swim. What was that presence by the Taniwha? How is Tama that strong? This doesn't make any sense. This isn't supposed to make sense.

Spotlight from a high window floods the corridor, highlighting more fossils and prehistoric beasts. We approach an archway back to the main hall with families milling about a café and gift shop. Normality beyond that arch. Ordinary.

But just as we pass a line of hulking skeletons...

I see a man. In cargo shorts. Standing beside a placard on prehistoric sea reptiles. At first he's a perfectly normal tourist: a pasty, pinkish sunburn and uncombed hair and an ill-fitting polo. He even has the look of a normal tourist until I catch the color of his hair. A bright, unnatural blue that sticks to the sides of his balding head like liquid metal.

A flash of recognition flickers. Like I've seen this color before. Like the man from the gala... the one that looked so out of place. He must feel me staring because he looks up. His eyes glow the same vibrant blue and he cracks a knowing smile and curls his lips into a wolfish grin. Before I can see more, a gaggle of chattering students streams between us and I lose sight of him.

By the time they pass, he's gone.

My heart skips. Something about that smile... it slices through my veneer. I swallow hard and try to focus. Normal tourist? Probably. I mean, it's possible. But it feels too deliberate, too much like that man I saw in Berlin days ago... the man with the bright hair that shouldn't exist.

Tama tugs on my sleeve. "Tristan? You okay?”

I blink, looking around. Nothing. No stupid hair. No sneering expression. The light from the overhead spotlights are bouncing off dinosaur skulls and shiny signage and there's nothing out of place. "Yeah," I force out. "I'm good."

I'm not good. My palms are sweaty in my pockets. I can feel it. Something is watching us, or following us, or... something. I glance at Tama's white-knuckled fists on his side, remembering how Tama bent steel like foil and how afraid he must be of his own power.

We shuffle into the main hall, where tall windows are letting in afternoon light. Families chatter happily and there's a line at the café and postcards and stuffed dinosaurs and dinosaur pendants line the gift shop shelves. It all seems so normal... so jarringly normal, when inside I'm on edge. On edge and keyed up and too freaked out to properly enjoy myself.

I clear my throat and turn to Tama. "So that was... something," I say quietly, softly. Hoping to at least strike up a conversation and get us both off our feet.

He gives me a tiny nod, glancing everywhere but at me. "An understatement."

I want to say it'll be okay, that we'll figure it out, but I can't ignore the tingling at the back of my neck. I keep watching my reflection in the polished kiosk at the corner of the room. Expecting to see the man with the blue hair. Expecting him to jump out at me.

But he's gone. For now.

"I... let's just get out of here," I finally say, mustering a smile that doesn't quite reach my eyes. "We've seen our fill of bones for one day."

Tama sighs. "Yeah. Good idea."

We head for the exit with every other visitor in Berlin staring past us with eyes that think they're boring teenagers. But inside I'm rattled. If the guard was right and we've somehow crossed some forces that don't want to be disturbed... well, I have a feeling this is only the beginning.

And as much as I've been trained to perform under pressure, this is nothing like some photo op that Pellinore friends of the family can smooth over with money and influence. This is something else. Something bigger. Something older.

Something is watching us. I think it's waiting for me to break character.

Chapter 15:
Echoes of the Past

Friends. The word hangs in the air between us, both a promise and a wall. I force a grin that feels brittle at the edges. Of course, friends. What else would we be? But a stupid, selfish part of me I hate had been hoping for something more. I push the thought down. Friends is good. It's more than I had five minutes ago. It has to be enough.

I'm trying not to walk on eggshells, but I keep stealing glances at her.

She moves with purpose, but also ease. Like she belongs in this place. Not just the museum. But in the space between the past and the present... like the history is alive around her, and she's a part of it. Like she doesn't just look at the artifacts... she hears them. She almost reaches out and touches them, like she knows they'd speak if you listened.

She's still closed off. Guarded. Quiet. But... not so tense. She's not so withdrawn. There's more openness to her now. Curiosity.

And yeah... beautiful.

Not just her face. Not just that. But I'd be lying if I said that wasn't a big part of it. But it's her perspective, the way she sees things. Like the stories behind the glass enclosures are as real to her as anything outside them.

I've never met anyone like her.

Friends is great. I'll take that. I'll take that all day. But a little part of me... stupid, selfish, probably doomed little part of me... wants more.

I want to be the one who makes her laugh without thinking about it. I want to be the one who makes her drop her guard. I want her to look at me the way she does at this history: with respect and wonder.

My throat goes tight and cold. Chill. It's fine. I barely know her. She's not giving those signals anyway.

Just friends.

That's good. That's more than good. That has to be enough.

I clear my throat, trying to shake the thoughts away. "So... where to next, friend?"

She gives me a look, a twitch of a smile at the corner of her lips. "I thought you were leading."

That little almost-smile? Like someone punched me in the gut. I force a grin. "Guess I am."

I take a glance around the room and spot something familiar. "Carvings. There's a section with stone tablets... there's some Incan pieces there, I think."

Her eyes light up.

The whole room could've exploded into supernova, and she'd still be the brightest thing in it.

"Really?" she says, and already she's taking a step toward the exhibit.

My chest constricts. "Yeah. Come on."

I start walking ahead of her, before I do something stupid like reach for her hand. I can't stop the buzzing in my palms, or the static under my skin. She moves next to me, keeping pace with a warm, steady presence. Close, but not too close. Like a fire you can't get too near.

I try to focus on the history. On the exhibit. On anything but the way her hair glints in the light or how her fingers dance like she's always holding something invisible.

We stop in front of a large glass case. Inside, stone tablets lay on a soft cushion, under diffused light, etched across their faces.

Patterns. And... language?

My breath catches in my throat.

"I know this one," I say, leaning forward, my grin spreading fast. "No way."

Aiyana tilts her head, eyebrows furrowed in curiosity. "What?"

I point at a tablet near the center of the display. "That was discovered by my parents."

Her eyebrows shoot up. "What? Seriously?"

"Yeah. Coastal Chile. They found it buried under a layer of dirt and rock. It was... deep." I glance at her. "Seeing it here's... weird. Kinda like finding an old family photo in someone else's house."

She blinks, looking between me and the tablet. Her eyes go soft.

"That's... incredible."

I force myself not to fangirl too hard. But seeing that look in her... my heart misses a beat.

"My dad always said the symbols were alive," I add quietly, after a moment. "Always said they were carrying voices. Stories."

She leans in closer, shoulder nearly brushing against mine. "Do you know what it says?"

I swallow, nod. "Yeah. Some of it."

I trace a few lines through the glass. "This one tells the story of Inti... the sun god. His journey across the sky, watching over the world, giving it warmth and protection."

Aiyana's gaze deepens, and something's happening there. Something behind her eyes.

"You have stories about the sun?" she asks, slow, the edge of her voice.

I nod. "Oh, lots. We believe the sun is alive. It sees us. Protects us." I smirk. "Not just a giant fireball in the middle of space."

She laughs... quiet, but real. Like she means it.

"It's a guardian. A protector." She says, now.

The timbre of her voice has changed. It's lower now. Steadier. Like she's drawing on something she knows, by heart.

"My grandfather used to tell me stories about the Sun Dance. The Wiwáŋyaŋg Wačípi. It's a way to connect to our ancestors."

I glance at her. The way she says grandfather, there's weight in it.

It hits me: Aiyana doesn't talk about her family the way I do.

She doesn't talk about them.

At all.

Before I can ask her anything, she turns the question around on me.

"What about your parents? Still doing digs?"

I nod. "All the time. Peru, Bolivia. Sometimes back home. Dad's got a thing for Incan and Mayan sites. Mom's more all over. She's worked on everything." I grin. "She once spent an entire year doing research on a single type of pottery, just because she 'had a feeling.'"

Aiyana's lips quirk. "That actually sounds kinda amazing."

I laugh. "It is. But that also meant growing up with more artifacts than furniture. I knew how to clean ceramics before I knew how to ride a bike."

That gets a real laugh out of her, and man... it's so worth it.

I press in close, grinning, my voice quiet. "What about you? Anybody else in your family into this stuff?"

She hesitates.

Pauses.

Then, slowly: "Not really. My grandfather told me the stories. Taught me the traditions. Made sure I knew where I came from."

Past tense.

There's something in her voice, but the words she chooses don't say it all.

But before I can ask her anything, she smirks. "You talk about your parents like they're rockstars."

I shrug. "Hey, they did find this tablet." I point. "Kinda legendary."

She rolls her eyes. "You would say that."

I press a hand to my chest. "Guilty."

She shakes her head, but her eyes are still smiling.

And I'm gone.

Not just because she's pretty. Not just because I want her around. But because she listens. Because she gets it.

I clear my throat, trying not to stare. "Anyways, wanna go see the other carvings?"

"Yeah." she says. "Let's go."

We pick up our pace again, voices quieter now. Easier. Still riding the high of being around Aiyana... her warmth, her smile. It feels good. Real.

Then out of the corner of my eye, I see her again. The woman by the exit. Sharp suit, crisp lines, electric blue hair cropped short. Older, probably in her forties. But those eyes, ice cold.

She's not just watching us. She's hunting us.

When her eyes find mine, they don't flicker. They just stare.

Like she's sizing me up.

My stomach clenches. I tense. I want to protect Aiyana.

I look over. She's tense too, eyes narrowed, obviously creeped out.

Like Aiyana said earlier, something about her just feels... off. Dangerous.

I need to get us away from her... fast.

Without warning, a faint green trail appears in my mind. Like a dusting of glowing powder, spilled across the floor. The same green light illuminates that woman, and then the doorway to the next exhibit: the burial hall.

No time to think. I step forward and give Aiyana a gentle nudge. "This way."

She follows without question.

Still feeling those cold eyes at our backs, we've seen enough of the creepy, watching woman.

Time to see what else the museum has to offer... which means stepping into the burial exhibits. Cool!

Chapter 16:
The Tricksters

The crypt exhibit is trying way too hard. Moody lighting, overdramatic shadows, everything whispering respect the dead while smelling like lemon polish and decaying linen.

I lean on a column in my favorite power suit: heels sharp, blazer sharper, lipstick somewhere between scandal and venomous intent. Wall Street dominatrix chic. A little something to get on Oberon's nerves.

I sigh dramatically, dusting off my sleeve.

Time to gather the rest of me.

The air ripples. Shadows stutter. And, with a pop, the rest of me steps in.

Little-me bounces in first, tutu bouncing with her. "Ooooh! Skeletons! Can I touch one? Just one? Just a finger?"

Hoodie-me follows, grumbling. "Ugh. Smells like a crypt in here... oh wait."

Glasses-me surveys the space with a clinical sniff. "Delightfully curated. Overcompensating with the lighting. I give it three stars."

Professor-me straightens a cuff. "Ah... the eternal human fascination with mortality. Always charming."

Polo-shirt me ambles in, slurping soda from thin air. "This place could really use a nacho stand."

Six of me. One mind, six moods, infinite sarcasm. Who needs friends when you have personalities?

Right away, the chatter begins.

Little-me sprawls on a bench. "Balam and Aiyana making goo-goo eyes at clay pots. Kiss already or break something."

Hoodie-me mutters, "Airi's falling like a phone with no case. Crash incoming."

Glasses-me adjusts his frames. "Classic. All six wobbling toward disaster, and none of them notice the pattern."

I smile, nails glinting. "Adorable. Tragic. But adorable."

Professor-me chuckles softly. "Love, as ever, proves itself the most elusive of the elemental forces. Even to the gifted."

Polo-shirt me slurps the last of his soda. "And the boys? Robin Hood and Little John, lost in a museum like they're LARPing Jurassic Park without a plot." He hums a few bars of Oo-De-Lally, off-key and weirdly upbeat.

Little-me spins in place, arms wide. "Robin Hood and Little John runnin' through the forest... Oo-De-Lally, Oo-De-Lally, what the heck are they doing anyway?"

Glasses-me groans. "We're being held hostage by this slow narrative pacing. Who writes this stuff?"

I glance at you dear reader. Oh, don't look at me like that, reader. You wanted answers? Buy a different book. This one's about the tease. Wink. "Don't worry," I purr. "We're about to shake the jar."

Little-me squints at me. "You're going soft. You want them to win."

Glasses-me tilts his head. "Incorrect. I just don't want the story to end too soon. Academic curiosity."

Then the air shifts. The chill, the sudden hush, the flickering lights.

"Oh good," I say, a loud yawn following my words. "Here we go again."

"And now," I mutter, mostly to myself, "a very special episode of Overlords Who Need Better Timing."

Oberon arrives: a big coat, a bigger mood. The cold wind follows him like he invented winter. Very theatrical. Very him.

The dead don't stir, but they'd probably roll their eyes if they could. "Report," he says.

Six of me grin: six sparks of curated chaos, perfectly timed for maximum annoyance.

Teen-me throws a lazy salute. "All present, Your Royal Gloominess!"

Glasses-me adjusts his frames. "Mara's chasing shadows. The chosen are wobbling. The seal hums on cue."

Businesswoman-me doesn't bother with preamble. "They're dancing to your tune. Every thread's fraying right on time."

Little-me swings her legs off a nearby bench. "Can I break something yet? Please? Pleeeease?"

Professor-me, ever the steady voice, murmurs, "Patience. The cracks are forming."

Polo-shirt me drains the last of an imaginary soda. "Mara's hoarding heroes like they're limited-edition cereal prizes. Not a great long game."

I roll my shoulders and flash a grin that could slice marble.

"They're just wandering," I say. "The unraveling. The choices. That delicious moment where they look down and realize there's no floor."

Oberon's power flares.

Dramatic. Expected. A little stale, if we're being honest.

"Puck!"

His voice could cut glass. "They must not advance. Ea'mara's reach grows. End them. Now!"

Silence.

Then...

We laugh. End them? Oh, I could. Quicker than you think. But then you'd lose the performance. And I do love a performance.

Six mouths, one melody. Mischief layered with menace.

"Kill them?" little-me giggles, childlike and sinister at once. "So last century."

"Too quick," hoodie-me mutters, already half-submerged in shadow.

"Where's the fun?" Glasses-me asks. "I want to see the exact moment they realize they're doomed."

"I love this part," I say, voice low and amused. "The tension. The meltdown."

Oberon's power tightens, corners of the crypt darkening. "This is no game."

In unison, all of me turn. Six sets of eyes glow with the same promise. "Oh, my King," hoodie-me whispers as he dissolves into blackness, "everything's a game."

I smirk, the rest of me reflecting the same sharp grin.

Little-me drops her tiara, but it vanishes before it hits the ground. professor-me gives a courteous bow. Polo-shirt me just shrugs, adjusting his waistband.

And I? I vanish last, a grin lingering in the air like an afterimage. "Let's see if they can keep up."

Finally loose. Finally free.

Chapter 17:
Whispers of the Dead

The museum empties, closing around us as we cross the threshold into the next gallery... the Crypt, Balam is calling it. Shadowed light, low and gray, illuminates skulls and desiccated remains. Skeletons behind glass, grinning skulls contorted in mute screams, fingers curled as if trying to grasp at something lost so long ago. Mummies swathed in brittle cloth, hollow eyes staring into nothingness. Urns and grave goods laid out carefully... food, drink, tools, carefully curated to fit the predilections of modern scholarship. Offerings intended to ensure the dead found the path to the afterlife. Utterly alone.

I exhale, my breath a waft of stale air, viscous and oppressive. The smell of dust and mold and musty old paper is heavy, but underneath is something else. Dryer, older. It sticks in the back of my throat. The quiet is wrong here. Too still, too charged.

Balam steps closer to one of the displays, a murmur to himself. "It's amazing, isn't it?" He whispers, voice hushed and reverent. "Who would not want to see this? The fascination is understandable... these were people. These were once real, living people, warriors, and kings and priests and artists and... all of them preserved, given some kind of immortality... frozen, like ghosts in a museum. Poetic, in a way."

He leans close, studying the carvings on one of the sarcophagi. His voice changes then, soft and uncertain. "Aiyana? I think..."

I have been quiet, almost wordless, since we entered.

He turns to find me smirking, expectant. But instead, my hands ball into fists against my chest and I hunch over on myself.

"It's wrong," I breathe. "All of this. All of this shouldn't be here."

His brow creases. "You mean... the remains?"

I nod, my voice hollow and far away. "They're... restless. Trapped. They shouldn't be here."

His jaw tightens. The air thickens. Static coils between us.

"They were meant to be allowed to rest in hallowed ground," I whisper, my voice cracking. "Allowed to rest, surrounded by their families, by the land that had given them life. Instead they're here, behind glass. Disembodied. Nameless. No purpose."

A tremor rolls through me. "They're lost."

He glances around us, eyes wide suddenly, as if he hadn't realized just how far we were when we entered. The walls seem to close in, tight and unrelenting. The lighting is too low. Every shadow is too deep.

He opens his mouth, as if to ask me what I mean... I whisper, "I can feel them"

That's when the scratching begins.

On the other side of the room, a janitor is polishing the glass on one of the skeleton displays. His movements are frantic, the cloth flapping furiously against the pane, shoulders jerking at every stroke. He's a little man, short and stocky, arms thick and corded with muscle. His beard is the striking part... huge and wild, like a lion's mane, half obscuring his face.

He pauses, tilts his head just enough to let us know he's clocked us, and his voice comes out gravelly and oddly formal. "Museum's closing. Time to make your way out," he says, then goes back to scrubbing, muttering gurgled words I can't quite make out.

Balam leans over toward me, voice low. "That guy's...intense."

I don't blink. "He's not normal."

The janitor pauses in his scrubbing.

Balam's pulse picks up. "Let's... keep moving."

I nod. Neither of us look back.

✦ ✦ ✦ ✦ ✦ ✦ ✦

We try to leave.

But the museum won't let us go.

Corridors snake around us. Exit signs blur and shimmer. Every turn we take leads back here. The air is off... wrong. Heavy and cold and deeply unnatural. It presses into my bones, sinks into my lungs, makes every breath shallow and burning.

I rub my arms, but it doesn't help.

"This way," Balam says, his voice steady but stressed with urgency. He had heard me when I spoke, earlier, when I told him we needed to leave. He had not asked questions, just grabbed my hand and pulled me along.

But we're still here. The corridors keep stretching out in front of us, looping back in on themselves.

Balam's fingers tighten on my wrist as he searches for an exit. But he's not finding one.

My heartbeat thumps in my ears.

"Balam," I murmur.

"I know," he says.

With every step, the air grows thicker, presses in more. The overhead lights flicker; not enough to pitch us into darkness, just enough to make the shadows seem to move in ways that shouldn't.

I glance behind me.

Nothing.

But I can feel it... some weight pressing against my back, something just out of sight, lingering. It touches all of my instincts to flee.

Balam hisses, pulling hard around another corner. We move faster.

And then it starts... not around us, but in my head. A hissing, snarling, cacophonous roar of voices... pain and fear and anger and confusion! Screams all at once!

Not words that I can understand. But screams of loss and crying out in rage, sobbing in despair. Speaking in ancient languages, some I can identify from half-forgotten myth and legend, some I have never heard. But all of them dead.

It crashes into me like waves, battering me, relentless. I ball my hands over my ears, but it won't stop. I can't make it stop!

The emotions batter through me: hopelessness and rage and cold dread. Like drowning in an ocean of emotions.

"Balam..." My voice is raw and broken, not more than a whisper.

He spins, eyes wild as he sees me shaking, straining to maintain myself. "Aiyana, what's wrong?"

I open my mouth to scream... The lights flicker, the air snaps tight... And the dead move.

Chapter 18:
Strength & Strategy

Tama ✦ Afternoon (April 26) ✦ Invalidenpark

We step out of the museum, and I finally feel like I can breathe again. The cool Berlin air floods my lungs, clearing out the stale tension still clinging to my skin. My hands remain clenched into fists, the memory of that warped railing looping in my head like a broken record.

I bent it. With my bare hands. Like it was plastic.

Sure, I'm strong. I surf, wrestle, lift weights... but that wasn't normal. It was something else. Something... not normal.

And Tristan... he just talked our way out of it, calm and smooth, like he had the script memorized. Who does that?

None of this makes any sense.

I want to tell myself it's a bad joke, that none of this is real. But every time I try, my skin prickles and my stomach twists tighter.

We walk in silence, putting distance between us and the museum. The streets revert to normal... cars humming, people chatting, wind rattling bare branches. I try to ground myself in the everyday routine, pretending nothing's changed.

Then we round a corner. And all hell breaks loose.

Screams. People running... some stumbling, some shoving. Panic flooding through the park like a wave. A vendor in a red apron staggers past, clutching his bleeding arm, eyes wild. Tables are overturned, food spilled everywhere... ketchup smeared on the pavement like blood, a rolling beer keg foaming over. Glass shatters. Somewhere to the left, a woman shrieks.

And then, like a nightmare punchline, an empty baby stroller rolls by, slow and surreal, bumping off a curb into a trash bin.

I freeze, instincts flaring. This isn't just a fight... It's chaos swallowing everything whole. My heart pounds so loud I can barely think.

Tristan stops beside me, rigid. "This isn't good," he mutters, voice clipped yet controlled. "This is..."

"Bad," I finish. "Really bad."

Then I feel it. The air changes... heavy, static, electric, like right before a storm. That same feeling I had in the museum.

Then I see them.

At first, my mind screams for logic: kids? A prank? Some gang fooling around? But my hands tremble, and my whole body tightens. This isn't fake. This is real. This is happening.

But they move wrong. Too fast, too twitchy, like they're fighting against their own flesh.

Their faces... jagged teeth, sharp noses, eyes glowing like hot coals. Their skin is the color of pale wood, and their hands end in claws. Scraps of clothing hang loose, tattered jackets, mismatched hats.

And on every head... ratty pointed hats. Crooked. Mocking.

"What the...?"

"Gnomes," Tristan says, grimacing. "Not the garden kind. Real ones."

I stare. "Come again?"

"Gnomes," he repeats, voice grim. "From the old myths. Tricksters. They feed on chaos."

I let out a bark of laughter that sounds crazier than I feel. "Right. Next they'll sell lawn chairs on the weekend?"

He doesn't smile.

One gnome yanks a woman's scarf so hard she crashes into a trash bin. Another upends a food cart... grill and all... sending flames licking across the park. Plates crash, bottles burst.

They laugh, high-pitched and mean, drilling straight into my skull.

"How do you even know what they are?" I ask, struggling to steady my breath, forcing my brain to keep up. I can taste their sour breath and feel their claws scraping my skin. My heart hammers, but my mind reels in disbelief.

Tristan doesn't blink. "Folklore. Myths. English lit. They show up in stories all over Europe."

"And you're just accepting this?"

He finally meets my eyes. "You bent a steel railing in half."

Point taken.

A gnome leaps onto a woman's back, clawing her hair, forcing her down. Another darts between her legs, tripping her hard. Her head cracks hard against the pavement, and the gnomes pounce... ripping through her purse, tossing her wallet, her phone, even her shoes, cackling all the while.

She groans, barely conscious. Bleeding. They just laugh.

Her blood stains the ground, and I feel frozen for a split second... helpless, desperate. Then fury floods me, hot and wild, burning through the confusion. Heat surges through my veins. My fists clench tight. My vision turns red. I'm furious, terrified, and confused all at once. How can this be real? Why are these things here?

Then one of them looks at me... stares really. This little bastard perched on the woman's chest, wiggling its fingers in a smug wave. It sticks out its tongue and blows a raspberry.

"Oh, hell no." I move.

Tristan calls my name, but I'm already gone.

I rip a metal trash can lid off the ground, swinging it like a discus.

WHAM.

It nails the gnome square in the face with a crunch. He flips back, crashing through overturned chairs. Debris scatters.

The woman scrambles up and flees.

Satisfaction flares in my chest.. a moment of victory, a win.

The vibe shifts.

Laughter dies. Every gnome freezes. They twist toward me, heads jerking unnaturally, as if pulled by invisible strings.

Their grins vanish.

Their lips curl back, revealing jagged, rotted teeth.

Their eyes darken to black voids.

Their nails stretch into hooked claws.

Shadows writhe beneath them, alive and hungry.

Then they charge.

The first slams into my chest like a brick, claws tearing my jacket, scraping skin. I yank him free and toss him aside...

Two more replace him.

Weight crashes down, claws raking my scalp. I slam into a pole, something snaps. The creature screeches and falls...

But they keep coming.

A sharp sting flares in my thigh.

I look down... one's biting me. Teeth sunk deep.

I snarl, heart hammering, and kick up, punting him away. He tumbles into a cart.

I brace myself for torn flesh, blood pouring down my leg. Instead, when I look... just bruises, teeth marks pressed into the skin, angry red but not broken. My scalp's bleeding, scratches sting along my arms, but nothing close to what it should be. Not after that.

Too little damage. Way too little.

Fear claws in beside the anger. Something's wrong. Seriously wrong.

It doesn't matter now. They don't stop. They swarm in, piling on me. Claws slash my arms, yank my hair, dig into my shoulder.

I fling one off, another takes its place. The lid swings, but for every gnome I knock out, more crowd in. They're too many, too fast, too savage.

Something grabs my wrist, claws digging in. More hands grip my other arm, my legs.

I'm dragged down. My balance tilts. My back hits the pavement... hard.

Air whooshes out of my lungs. Now they're on me.

Clawing, biting, tearing.

I thrash with every muscle, but the weight is too much.

I'm losing.

Chapter 19:
System Overload

This place is magic.

Not sleight-of-hand, not cheap trick magic. I'm talking wizard level, Doctor who, opening theme blaring in the background magic. One corner of the room is a drone demonstration, and a hologram in another is giving a lecture. An AI is composing music live next to a 3D printer that's casually spitting out a prosthetic hand like it's printing homework. There's even a bipedal robot that's tracking motion...perfectly. I waved at it and it waved back. I almost cried.

My brain is doing backflips. Drones buzzing overhead, holograms flickering, robot dogs wagging tails they don't actually have. I want to pet every bot, push every button, pull every lever and know exactly how all of this works. It's a candy store for tech nerds and I am a child who snuck in.

A soft chime pings overhead, followed by the intercom: "Achtung, das Museum schließt in zwanzig Minuten... Attention, the museum will be closing in twenty minutes." Another chime. Another tiny stab to the heart.

Nope. Not listening. Not today.

I crank my smile brighter like I can drown it out.

I don't want this experience with Nia to end.

I glance over at her... calm, focused, that quietly intense furrow to her brow. She's not bouncing all over the place (who is?) but she's listening. Actually listening, like what I say matters. If I pretend hard enough, maybe twenty minutes can last forever.

Why is my heart trying to do cartwheels? Don't stare, don't stare, don't stare! Okay, maybe just a quick peek... is my face always this pink? Probably. Man, she's so calm. How? How does she do that? I wish I could be like that. Instead, I bounce around between 'don't say something stupid' and 'say ALL the things.'

I'm about to melt. She's so pretty. She's glowing in this lighting... soft, radiant. Not literally glowing... but the lights in this place are reflecting off her braids and her eyes are shimmering like they're HDR-rendered or something.

My heart flip-flops and I spin toward the nearest VR display, hoping it'll distract me.

"Oh my god, look at these robot puppies!"

Tiny robot dogs wag their tails and blink their LED eyes. I squeal.

"I want one. No... all of them."

Nia laughs, and the whole world seems a bit warmer.

"What would you even do with all of them?" she asks.

"Take over the world, obviously." I grin wide.

She laughs even harder. Her face lights up and I float. Then... because my brain has clearly stopped working... I grab her wrist and start dragging her toward the VR dragon slaying portion of the museum.

Wait, wait, wait... this is bad. This is really bad. My head's a kaleidoscope of flashing lights and error messages and I want to scream but I can't. Oh god, my face is on fire, my heart's pounding like a marching band and my brain is yelling 'ABORT! ABORT!' but my hand is clinging on. This is happening. Too real. What is happening?

The second our skin touches my system glitches.

Oh no. Her hand. My hand. We're touching. Oh god, we're touching. My eyes go wide, my cheeks go mega-pink and my brain just...

ABORT, ABORT, SYSTEM OVERLOAD.

I let go, spinning back around to the screen, furiously trying not to look like I'm dying but really just trying not to scream.

"Uh... s-sorry! Got excited."

Nia smiles, quietly. "It's okay." Then, almost too soft to hear, "I like your excitement."

Did she just say that? Me? Someone actually likes... me? No, no, no, don't freak out, don't freak out, but wait... my chest feels like it's about to explode with happiness and panic. Why can't I stop smiling? Oh man, stop smiling, you look like a total dork!

I nearly short circuit. No one's ever said that to me before. Not my parents, not my teachers, nobody. I don't know how to process the feeling so I blurt out:

"So cool... I wish I could do that. Like, for real."

She tilts her head. "Do what?"

"Be a hero."

Her expression softens. "A hero?"

Be a hero? Me? Yeah right. But... another little corner of me, quiet, stubborn... wants to believe it. That I could be brave, or strong, or the kind of person who doesn't run away when things get real. But what if I can't? What if I'm just a scared kid who stumbles through things? No capes though. Definitely no capes.

"Yeah. Like the ones in anime... brave, strong, the kind of person who actually does something when things go wrong."

Nia's face softens even more. Then she says, "I think you already are, Airi."

My brain bluescreens.

"W-what?"

"You're kind, you're smart, you make people happy." She pauses. "You make me happy."

You make me happy. The words echo in the sudden silence of my mind. Not, *you're so smart, Airi.* Not, *you have so much potential.* Not the empty praise from teachers who didn't know what to do with me, or the distracted nods from my parents. She didn't say I was useful, or gifted, or interesting. She said I made her happy. Just by being me. My chest aches with a feeling so new and bright I don't know what to call it.

Dead. I'm dead. Bury me under the robot puppies.

✦ ✦ ✦ ✦ ✦ ✦ ✦

Why is it getting so cold? Not just cold...bone-deep chill that makes my breath catch in my throat. The lights flicker and dim like the museum is turning off on us. My stomach clenches. This can't be real, right? Right?

I glance over at Nia to see if she is seeing this too... she looks like she's made of gold light but she's frozen. Frozen! I start shaking her, panic clawing up my throat. No response. Why isn't she moving? Why is my heart about to jump out of my chest?

"Nia?"

Silence.

Her breathing is even, but she's stiff, frozen. Her eyes are unfocused and she doesn't react when I shake her shoulders or call her name. Panic tears through me.

She's glowing and frozen, and we're alone in a glitching museum. I press my forehead to hers, trying not to cry.

"Please come back..." I whisper.

Then the sound starts.

Deep, grinding growl, like stone shifting under terrible pressure. The floor beneath my feet starts to vibrate. I turn.

It steps out of the shadows... massive, horrifying. Riot armor is draped over its massive frame like rags... cracked, rusted, stretched over its arms that should not be wearing human body armor. A half-shattered helmet dangles from one of its biceps. Its face seems hewn from stone... cracked, jagged, almost human but not quite. It's eyes glow with an awful blue light.

It breathes in through a cracked gas mask and the stench... burning metal and wet earth and old decay... hits me like a wall. I gag. My eyes water. What is this thing?

Then it roars.

The sound tears across the museum. Glass shatters, walls rumble, and I fold in on myself. I go down on my knees, hands over my head, ears ringing. The lights flicker overhead.

It moves, far too fast for something that big. It smashes through a display case like paper... shards of glass fly, the steel frame bending under its weight. The floor cracks open beneath its mass.

And it's seen me.

I freeze, mind blank, unable to move or scream or do anything but wait for it to be over.

Sudden sharp gasp.

Nia!

She inhales like she was drowning. Her eyes refocus; she's back.

"RUN!" She screams, and I snap up and grab her wrist. We run.

We tear through halls and galleries, flickering lights above us. A garbled robotic voice chirps in a hundred languages, some random audio guide. Behind us... BOOM... the monster's club smashes into the floor, the ground buckling in on itself. The force sends me stumbling.

"Nia... move... MOVE!" I scream, shoving her forward. My lungs are on fire. My legs feel like rubber. The troll is behind us, the museum warping around us... glitching screens, flickering holograms.

We tear past robots and mechanical exhibits. My ankle rolls, and I go down, pain flaring up my leg. The troll raises its club. It's over.

Nia hauls me up, pulling me out of the way. As the the club smashes where I went down.

We run again, ducking behind a display... a dead end, no escape. The troll looms over us, eyes glowing with rage.

I close mine. I wish I was strong like the anime heroes who stand tall no matter what. No matter what is about to happen.

I wish I had that power.

Something inside me... warm, bright, fierce. My hands lift like I am on autopilot. A surge builds in my chest, crackle of lightning and fire and static all at once.

"Kōgeki suru!" I scream, the words ripping out of me before I can stop them. I don't even know why... I think it was the first dumb thing my brain latched onto.

Why did I yell that? Oh god, kill me now. Except not literally.

Energy explodes out of my palms, pink and blue streaks tearing through the air like a final attack move. It slams into the troll's chest, armor shattering. It flies backward, smashing into the wall, which collapses in on itself with a metal-and-glass crash.

Silence.

I stand there, shaking, breathing like I've run a marathon. The glow fades. The power drains out of me like someone pulled the plug.

The troll is down. Blasted through a wall.

Nia stares, wide-eyed, speechless. Awe, maybe terror in her eyes. I don't know how to respond either.

Chapter 20:
Command & Chaos

Tama goes down.

One second he's slicing and stomping gnomes like a juggernaut... spinning, tossing them to the ground. The next, they're swarming around him in a writhing tide of teeth and claws, overwhelming him by sheer number. My stomach drops at the sight, and I grab the first improvised weapon I can find... a metal tray from a toppled food stall.

The whole square is a disaster zone: tables flipped, festival banners shredded, food splattered on cobblestones. People scream, some running, some fighting back. Flames flicker from where a grill had toppled onto a tarp.

A woman stumbles in front of me, a gnome clinging to her coat. I rip it off with the tray, shoving the creature away. She sprints off. A few stalls down, a shopkeeper is perched on top of a fallen table, swinging a rolling pin, clearly outmatched by the snickering little fiends. Another gnome is clinging to his back. I grab a broken lantern and throw it... the glass shatters, sending the creature skidding off the man. He gasps, spins, and thwacks another one with his rolling pin.

I dash for Tama. He's nearly buried beneath a writhing pile of claws and snarls. His arm breaks free for a moment, then gets yanked down again.

No! My heart pounds.

I notice a bent tent pole on the ground nearby, grab it up. Then something snaps into my field of vision... My eyes adjust, and I start to notice a shimmer around each figure.

The gnomes all seem to be outlined in flickering, sickly blue auras, feeble but unstable.

Many of the festival workers and shopkeepers have a gold or silver fringe around them... some pale and dim, some oddly bright as though there's a contained spark. I even notice a couple with short, thick builds, dwarf-like in the way my old world myth books describe them.

No, that can't be true. Or can it? I blink, and for a second, I remember those glimpses I caught previously, but then they vanish as though they were never there. It's not a trick of the light. This is actually happening. Right. Now!

No time to figure it out... it's real. I scan the area: Gnomes are hunting the stragglers, trying to pick them off. Shopkeepers are banding together behind overturned carts. Some have brighter auras than others. Right now, all that matters is that we have to stop the tide.

I charge at Tama, swinging the pole. I connect, knocking three gnomes off him. Another leaps... I jab mid-lunge. I don't know how I'm doing this, but I can't stop. I have to keep going."

Tama bucks, and I bring the pole down on the last few crawling over him. They screech and skid away. He stumbles to his feet, shirt shredded and bloody, but still finds a grin.

"Took you long enough," he pants.

I glare, heart still thundering. "You dove in there by yourself... what did you think was going to happen?"

He shrugs, out of breath. "Somebody needed help."

I almost argue, but I get it. He sees trouble and can't help but jump in. Fits the Tama I know.

The gnomes regroup, snarling and baring fangs, their blue auras flaring at the edges of my strange new vision. They're smarter than they look. Can't let them swarm us again.

Tama meets my eyes, wincing. "Plan?"

I let instincts take over. "They're picking off stragglers. If we split their attention, they can't swarm anyone. See those shopkeepers?" I point to a group of them making a rough perimeter. "Go help them. I'll take care of the rest."

He follows my gaze... people swinging rolling pins, brooms, random metal tools at the monsters. Many of them have a faint magical glimmer. "Meet in the middle?"

"Yeah." I say, hoisting the pole back up. "Try not to get buried again."

Crooked grin. "No promises."

He charges back into the fray, using a barrel lid as a shield. I spin away in the opposite direction, leaping over a fallen grill. A father is crouched behind it, shielding his daughter. A gnome snarls inches away... I slam it with the pole, shoving it back.

A festival worker screams as a gnome latches onto her arm. I bash it off, telling her to run. Out of the corner of my eye, their blue auras spark and flicker as I hit, like I'm literally shattering that crackling energy. Creepy, but can't think about that right now.

Something clamps onto my ankle. I look down... a gnome, lips peeled back in a snarl. I wedge the pole between its claws and my leg, then kick it hard into a twisted metal cart. It falls, aura flickering out.

Across the square, the butcher... a short man with a surprisingly bright silver aura around him... is fighting off two gnomes with a cleaver. I sprint over to help, batting one away with the tent pole. The other shrieks and scurries off.

Nearby, beer mugs are flying through the air, shattering against gnomes. The beer vendor is perched on what's left of his stand, lobbing steins like grenades. Another gnome leaps at him... he catches it mid-flight with a half-empty keg, cursing loudly in German.

A few steps away, a woodcarver... again short and stout, and glowing with a faint gold... is taking on a gnome with the most ironic weapon possible: a carved wooden gnome that he normally sells as a souvenir. He whacks it across the real creature's head, staggering it. The real gnome bellows in outrage at being battered by its own likeness.

Finally, the beasts seem to notice that their "easy prey" is no longer there. All that remain are people fighting back. Their shrill laughter and taunts are swallowed up by a mass of snarls, sparks of blue dancing at the edge of my vision. My arms burn, lungs scream, but I grit my teeth.

"Don't let them circle around us!" I shout, some old battle instincts kicking in. "Hold the line!"

A few shopkeepers gather around me, a ragtag collection of people with random tools. Each of them has hints of gold or silver in their auras... some brighter than others. No time to figure it out. We all press the gnomes from one side, forcing them to charge at us head on. They slam into our line, testing left and right. We hold. Adrenaline buries fatigue. We do not yield.

Suddenly, we do. The gnomes recoil, a few squealing as they dart behind carts or scramble into dark corners. They vanish as quickly as they arrived. The square is left in a battered silence.

I drop the tent pole. My arms tremble, my legs threaten to buckle. I suck in air, sweat stinging my eyes.

Tama waddles over, equally bruised and bloodied, still wearing that irrepressible grin. "Well," he pants, "that was fun."

I release a breathless chuckle. "Sure. Loads."

Blue emergency lights flicker... sirens. Police are pouring in, shouting orders, scanning around in confusion. They spot us: two battered teens in the midst of a wrecked festival. One officer stiffens, reaching for his weapon. "Ihr zwei... Hände hoch!"

We freeze. I raise my hands up a bit, mind desperately grasping for a plausible cover story. "We can..."

A shout from a nearby vendor cuts me off. "It wasn't them!"

The butcher, still cleaver in hand, steps forward. "These two saved us!"

Others chime in, gesturing to the sprawled carnage, commending our efforts. Cops exchange baffled looks, the tension eases.

Tama and I exchange looks. Time to go.

While the crowd argues with the cops, we weave around the smashed stalls, slipping out into the side street. A few nod or wave as we pass. The butcher nods at me, the beer vendor claps Tama's shoulder. We melt into Berlin's darker streets... battered, bruised, and breathless, but unbound.

Tama rubs a sore spot on his arm, voice slightly tremulous. "So... not in cuffs. That's a win, right?"

My heart is still racing. "Definitely."

We start walking again, surreal memory of flickering blue auras and glinting gold in the corner of my vision. Don't know what it all means yet. But we lived. That's something.

Chapter 21:
Breaking Bones

We're trapped.

The dead are on all sides of us, lurching and jerking in an imitation of life. Bones scrape on bones. Their eyes are a sickly blue glow, glowing embers of cold fire in their hollow sockets.

There are too many.

There shouldn't be this many.

Aiyana is pressed up against my back. Her breath is ragged in my ear. I can feel the tremble of her skin, the pounding of her heart pressed against my chest. "They're everywhere," she hisses. "We're surrounded."

I grip the staff tighter. The carved wood digs into my palms.

My senses flare. I see the faintest shimmer of glowing dust, trailing after the things, tracing movement, illuminating threats, picking out the edges of shadows and even faint suggestions of exits that wind their way through the carnage.

I don't even remember picking it up... must have been when the glass shattered, must have been when the first corpses rolled free from their display cases. A reflex, I guess. A flash of green from the staff caught my eye.

But now that I have it, something thrums inside me, like it's not just wood and knots.

It feels alive in my hands.

Warm in a way that isn't temperature... a sensation that's more motion, more energy. The moment I closed my fingers around it, a hint of memory I don't even recall flooded through me.

The wood is carved with pumas, claws extended, ready to pounce. I trace one with my thumb. For a second, I think I see them move. The faint green light is still in my vision.

I gasp. Must be imagining it.

No time to think about that now.

The dead shuffle in through the door. Quiet moans, the soft clicking of jaws. Mummies with linen unraveling. Skeletons with snapped bones. All of them with something hungry inside them, or something angry. Doesn't matter which. They're coming.

"Let's just break through," I say, voice thick.

She shakes her head, darting her gaze. "They're dead, Balam. They don't feel pain. They won't stop."

I stare at her. Seeing her like that, afraid, makes my chest ache, but I'm more afraid for her than for myself. "Everything breaks," I whisper. "Even the dead." The staff thrums under my hand. It's alive with energy and possibility. "Especially the dead."

She glances at the bodies. Her expression tightens, fear etched in every line. Then she straightens her shoulders, nodding. "Then let's break them."

A mummy lurches forward, brittle fingers fanning out. Its jaw hangs open in a silent shriek.

I move.

The staff arcs in my hands. It feels so natural, like I've been wielding it for my whole life. It crashes against the creature's ribs, splintering them like they're nothing. The body folds in half before it even reaches the ground.

A second one bolts forward, advancing on us. I drop low and spin, staff singing. Bone crunches... skull shatters. I land in a crouch, a cloud of dust kicking up around my boots.

They can break!

Something inside me clicks into place at that thought, like a spark setting off a wildfire. I move faster, swinging with power and precision. I smash every one in the ankles, ribs, the spine. Bones collapse like dead twigs. Wrappings come loose. Corpses fall apart in heaps.

Beside me, Aiyana is wrestling with a piece of splintered wood, her movements hard and desperate. She is slamming each one away, sweeping them clear of us. Her eyes are wide, her jaw clenched, but she does not hesitate.

The way she glowed just a minute ago is still fresh in my mind. That scared me. But I shake that thought away. I have to keep her safe, no matter what.

"Left!" she yells.

I duck, the staff's blade connecting with a clean arc.

"Behind you!"

I spin, pivoting on one foot, bringing the staff down like a spear. Bones spray across the floor. But even as we bring down dozens, more are surging up out of the shadows. The entire exhibit is a swarm of undead. That can't be right. The museum didn't have this many displays.

The air shimmers. Shadows twist around one another like snakes. It's as if something is breathing life into the remains, pulling them out of corners that don't even exist.

They keep coming.

Even the ones that are shattered are crawling after us, using broken fingers to drag themselves forward. Bones scrape the floor. Jaws snap at our heels. Linen wraps snag on our ankles.

My lungs burn. We can't stay in here. "We're running out of time," I grit out, voice scraping. "Move!"

I tug on Aiyana's wrist, and we take off, staffs sweeping through anything that dares try to close in on us. My heart is in my throat. We're running as fast as we can, sprinting toward the emergency exit sign at the far end of the hall, blinking red in a bright red light... like some kind of salvation.

So close...

Aiyana gasps, tugging on my arm. "Balam..."

The shadows shift, and more corpses pour out from behind us. Another wave... blue eyes glowing, rotted fingers raised in defiance.

They're cutting off the hallway. Just like that.

"No," she breathes. "No, no, no... We were almost there."

They pile up into a wall of dead flesh and blood, broken armor and empty stares.

I lift the staff, jaw clenched. I am not going to let them trap us...

Then Aiyana glows.

At first, it's just a shimmering under her skin... but then the heat hits me. Not temperature, exactly... more like pressure. The air is bending around her, folding in on itself. My breath catches in my throat. Every hair on my arms is standing on end. The staff in my hand thrums once, like it's responding to her.

Her eyes are ablaze with gold. Her skin is lit from within, every line etched in white fire. She's shaking... trembling like her body can't contain the thing that's waking up inside her.

She opens her mouth. And when she screams...

"STOP!!!!!!!!!!!!"

The order echoes out, not just sound but raw energy.

It ripples through the exhibit, the force slamming into glass cases, knocking down undead. I can't move for a second... my whole body freezes. Every mummy, every skeleton is frozen mid-lunge, arms and hands outstretched, jaws agape. The sickly blue fire in their eyes flickers like a candle in a windstorm.

Aiyana is heaving for breath. The glow around her is flickering, like it might fade at any second. But she hasn't collapsed.

"They're not monsters," she gasps.

I stare at her, chest heaving. "What?"

She swallows, eyes still glowing. "They're trapped... they're scared." Then, barely louder than a whisper, "They're draugr."

Draugr. I've heard the word in stories and games... undead warriors, cursed and relentless. But this?

This is real.

I open my mouth to ask how she knows, but the blue fire in the corpses' eyes flares again.

The stillness breaks.

The draugr burst back to life.

"Time's up," I growl, grabbing her hand. "We go now. Just us."

We run, crashing through the line of dead bodies. My staff carves a swath through them. Bones scatter, clattering as we bulldoze our way to the door. We reach it... slam against it.

It bursts open. Alarms blare, red lights strobing. Cold air slams into my lungs. We're outside.

Alive and free... for about three seconds.

Then shouting. A whole group of guards burst around a corner, yelling in German. One is barking into a radio, eyes wild. Sirens wail in the distance. Flashlights slash through the fading twilight.

Aiyana staggers beside me, the light gone from her arms. Her whole body is trembling. We don't have time to explain or rest.

I grip her hand. "Run."

"Balam..."

"No time!"

She doesn't resist.

We run. Hearts pounding. Alarms shrieking behind us, dust and death still dusting our clothes as we disappear into the streets of Berlin.

Chapter 22:
Blind Spots

The air is thick with dust, soot, and debris, choking my lungs and scalding the back of my throat. My heart hammers in my chest, still reeling from the post-panic rush. My legs are lead, my breaths ragged gasps. I feel wired on adrenaline... every nerve in my body buzzing like live wires... frayed, overloaded. Shattered. By how close we just came to dying.

And Airi...

She's trembling, hands splayed out in front of her, fingers twitching, eyes huge in horror and disbelief. The cloud of pink and blue around her has mostly dissipated now, but it lingers, tendrils of color still fading like a firework remnant. I can't drag my eyes away from the point in space where that beam of light just shot out of her palms. She did that. She blasted that wall of raw impossible power. And now, she's as lost and petrified as I am.

But before I can even wrap my head around it...

The troll groans.

Groans. It's alive, somehow still gasping, clawing, moving underneath the tangle of overturned displays and collapsed shelves and twisted metal supports. I hear it... a wet, rattling breath, and then the sickening scrape of stone and metal grinding together. Like it's healing. Like all our frantic onslaught did was buy us a few more precious moments. The thought twists in my brain, sending frissons of dread up my spine. Is that even possible? Anything that big supposed to heal like that?

It lifts its head, glaring at us through the shifting clouds of dust and rubble. Eyes blaze that sickly vibrant blue, and I suck in a ragged breath, panic welling in my chest. I know this feeling... from the back alley before. Except now, it's like my lungs have actually seized. And the freeze-brain moment where I realize this thing is on its feet and coming for us.

It snarls, the sound ripping through the museum's battered PA system. I'm shivering internally, drowning in my own fight-or-flight response. All I can think:

"Damn. What did we just do?" I blacked out... for a few seconds? A minute? All I remember is feeling cold. I remember a tangle of illusion and disorientation. Airi screaming at me to get back. And then a troll? It's too much, like I missed a beat of time.

The monstrosity roars, the sound shattering glass around us. Walls crack farther, even more chunks of shattered display cases and glass sheets raining down, and I feel the ground tremble beneath my feet.

"Airi! We have to go!" I shout, half yelling, my voice a sharp croak of desperation I can't help. But she barely reacts. She's half blank, half catatonic with shock, spiraling in her own brain. The troll hoists the ruined club... like chunk of what might once have been a banister and turns, shambling in our direction...

I seize her wrist, tugging her to our feet. We take off.

We're running, careening through the flickering hallways, my heart thundering in my chest, lungs desperate for air. Lights stutter overhead; an intercom prattles half in German, half in garbled distortion. Our footsteps slap stone, the troll's pounding close behind. We cut a corner too fast... Airi stumbles, her knee skids across a jag of broken display bracket, and she sucks in a breath as a thin red line opens on her skin. "I'm fine," she lies, already yanking free. The troll roars again, the floor quaking, and we run harder.

Then I see him... the blue-haired guy from before, standing in the chaos, hands on his hips, shoulders slouched in casual amusement, eyes rolling in that sickly blue light. I see him, and something in the air twists, and I know: illusions. He's making the halls lopsided, looping back on themselves, creating fake walls and doors that disappear and shift. He's the reason I keep coming across hallways that lead to blank dead ends.

I feel him snicker, soft and self-satisfied, a sound thick with derision: "Run, little fireflies... run faster."

Cold dread twists in my gut. He's got the place warped around us, illusions piled on top of illusions, and I know: the troll is real, the grating, mindless thrash of stone and metal. But the building rearranging itself... that's him.

I grit my teeth and refocus, mentally kicking myself back into gear. I think of all the years training with my grandma and mom, the deep steady breathing, the silent chants, all the visualization techniques I was made to practice to hone my ability. I remember the way Grandma said, time and time again, that this gift was never just about seeing the future or spirits. But about piercing the Veil of illusion and deception. Bending perception and seeing through the tricks of the mind.

I would never have imagined using it like this, hightailing it out of a museum warped by some creepy troll magician boy.

I take a breath and try to center myself. Breathe, in. Breathe out. Breathe in. I can do this. I can do this. My hands shake on Airi's wrist, but I'm trying to focus. I center my breathing like Grandma taught me. Concentrate. Focus. See what's real.

My vision clarifies. Slowly. It takes a second for my eyes to adjust to the undercurrent of illusion, but it happens, and the cracked edges of the hallway's misalignments begin to shimmer, the false walls and twisting passages shimmering like a glitching hologram.

Focus, Nia. See the truth.

Slowly, through the haze, I see the way the real door should look. The exit. The way out.

"Follow me!" I half-yell, hauling her forward. She lurches after me, limping now... each step a hitching stumble. She squeezes my hand anyway, jaw set, and we veer past a plummeting light fixture. Shards of robotics twitch on the ground, metal limbs sparking. She hisses as the leg buckles once, blood threading down her shin and darkening her sock, then grits through it and keeps pace. My lungs are on fire. Everything aches... muscles screaming, breath stuttering, ears ringing... but we don't stop.

The troll smashes another wall after us... CRASH. Wood splinters, rubble flies. The sound is so loud it rings in my ears. I risk a glance back. Mistake. It's right there... glowing blue of its eyes, a thundering colossus eating the hallway in brutal strides.

I force my focus forward. The illusions snarl behind my eyes, but I peel them back... edges stutter, seams undone. There: the real path. The front atrium, all glass and night beyond.

The troll heaves something... a large computer, and hurls it past us with impossible force. It hits the curtain wall with a gunshot CRACK. A spiderweb skitters across the glass. A second throw... KSHHH... blows out several panels. Cold air rushes in. Alarms wake in overlapping languages, red strobes pulsing.

"Go!" I yank Airi toward the gap. We sprint, lungs burning. The floor is a glittering beach of safety glass; it tinkles under our shoes as we vault the metal frame. A shard kisses Airi's knee; she hisses but keeps moving. Night air slaps my face. We're outside... alive, and running before the next roar finds us.

Berlin's afternoon sunlight greets us in a wall of wind. The sky swirls purple and orange, the street below alive with passersby. People milling around on the sidewalks, cars on the streets, and the world goes on. We don't dare stop. The troll bellows somewhere in the distance, and we take off again, a dervish of fear weaving through a field of milling strangers and honking horns.

✦ ✦ ✦ ✦ ✦ ✦ ✦

It's an eternity, but eventually, our lungs beg us to stop, and we catch sight of a small coffee shop a block away, small glowing windows beckoning to us. We burst inside, hearts thundering, clothes still dusty and ragged.

The barista stares, mouth open, wide-eyed, but he says nothing. Airi manages to stutter out our orders; hot chocolate for her, some tea for me, our voices rasping in our throats. We fall onto one of the chairs, clamoring in a booth like our hearts might burst out of our chests, adrenaline still pumping through our veins. I take a sip of the hot liquid in my cup, burn my tongue on the caffeine buzz, but it helps. My hands are still trembling.

I look over at Airi, the faint ripples of pink and blue still dancing around her hands, magic crackling like aftershocks around her skin. I rub my arms raw with the effort of trying to shift the illusions, the visions, the sick, lumbering roar still ricocheting around my head. I can feel every bit of fear still jittering through my veins.

The silence is deafening. We both fall into an exhausted daze, the murmur of the coffee shop around us growing in contrast to the stark relief of finally being safe. Steaming milk, the scrape of cups on saucers, the quiet chatter of patrons, voices murmuring in the background, ticking over in a quiet haze.

It's the mundanity of it all that makes it seem surreal. The grotesque cruelty of having such an absolute normal backdrop for what just happened to us. I can still see the troll's face when it was near me, its eyes bloodshot, its roar that sickening bass boom in my head. I can still see the boy's expression, too, in the quiet reflection of the shop windows, smirking like he'd won some twisted game, his own face shifting and rippling in his own reflection, the air around him alive with the erratic flicker of his powers.

I pick up my mug again, take another sip, and the tea is so hot it almost burns. It feels grounding, in the way my grandmother always used to say that tea was supposed to make you feel. My heart still races. The adrenaline is finally ebbing away, but it's like I'm trying to suck in air, and nothing is there. I try to still my breath, let the tea calm my nerves, but every time I hear his laugh in my head, I know I never feel quite the same.

I wrap both hands around the cup, willing the burn to steady me. My fingers brush the little leather pouch tucked in my pocket, and for a moment the panic ebbs. Grandma's words echo... protection, remembering. I cling to that like a rope in the chaos.

I don't say anything, but neither does Airi. We sit in that coffee shop, the clock ticking on, and I can feel the whole thing, the trip, the narrow escape, the shattering afterimage of that roar. It's dizzying.

I make an effort and sip my tea again, watching it calm my nerves, if just a little. I take a deep breath, too, and then I finally see it. In Airi's eyes, or maybe just behind them. I can see the white of her eyes, the rawness of it.

She's so white, so pale, like she's still on the other side of that fear, still shaking from that blast she just unleashed. I shake my head, trying to calm my breathing. It's been a long day. But if I'm being honest? I'm still shellshocked, too. I know magic is real, but that? It's something else. Something new. Something... terrifying.

I can't bring myself to look away from her. I know how strong she is. How she was able to blast through that wall of energy, cut that beast to pieces with her magic. I was running for my life... and she was there, ready to back me up.

A smile cracks across my face. "Thank you..." I whisper, every word a rasp, like my throat might close up on me. "For saving me."

Airi opens her mouth, but I know she can't find any words. She reaches out, stretches her hand across the table to meet mine, and I take her hand without thinking, shaking off the static between my fingers. It crackles. Dust and scorch still cling to her skin, and her fingers are ice cold, but she squeezes back.

The world fades for a moment, and it's just the three of us. The shop, her, me. The customers around us, busy with their own lives and worlds. And the coffee. Good strong coffee.

I don't even know how to find her, if I can. I don't even know what to ask her, how to bridge the chasm we just leaped. We both got away, and yet...

But I can at least say thank you. And for now, that's enough.

Chapter 23:
The Ritual Continues

Magic is thick in the air.

It thrums beneath my fingers... old, bound, carved into the earth with purpose. The barrier shudders under my touch, ten thousand threads strung so tight they hum.

This seal was never meant to be broken. Even as I work to unravel it, I feel its brilliance: Merlin's voice weaving Atlantean and druidic syllables, binding a knowledge already lost to the world. Their civilization is dust, yet the seal endures... calm, intricate, relentless.

I breathe slowly, murmuring the words that loosen knots one by one. Each syllable pulls at a filament without breaking it. This is not a spell to command but a negotiation across ages. The seal does not trust me. The strain is not in power, but in patience... knowing that one false note will either unlace everything... or snap back with ruin.

And the whispers don't help.

They flutter at the edge of my mind, shadows of a language I tried to forget. Not fae. Not Atlantean. Older. Hungrier. Sometimes I think they come from Oberon. Other times, I fear they come for him. *Zamukhar.*

He speaks with conviction these days, but it rings hollow, rehearsed. Behind his words, I sense something moving... something not entirely his own.

The threads tighten. I know he is near before I see him.

"Oberon," I murmur, without looking. The air knots like a noose around me.

He steps into the circle, silence cleaving around him. The ground seems to bow beneath his feet. His robes are darker than mine, silver etchings faint, like runes forgetting their meaning. His hair shines pale as frozen water; his eyes burn too bright in the dusk.

"You're not making fast work of this," he observes.

"The seal is not a door to be kicked open," I say evenly. "It is a melody that's forgotten how to end."

He scoffs. "The humans are watching. The longer you take, the more they'll try to interfere."

"They would do well to fear this," I reply. "It was never meant for mortal hands."

"Ea'mara's wards have lasted too long," he presses. "Her memory clings here like frost."

"She was a child when it was cast," I remind him.

"But she guards it now."

"Yes," I admit softly. "Though she never completed the training needed to defend it."

A silence stretches, then: "She has not done it alone."

I nod once. "I know."

I can feel them... the young ones. Especially the girl, Nia, brushing my mind like a moth against glass. Curious, clumsy, fragile. I could push her away, burn her from my awareness. But I do not. She is too bright, too unformed. Too alive.

Oberon is silent for a moment, then says, "They are interfering. Getting too close. I have sent Puck to tend to that."

I turn fully to him, one brow raised. "You sent Puck?"

His scowl is sharp. "He knows what I want."

I almost laugh. "Puck serves only whim. Chaos amuses him more than obedience, and gods help us if chaos is what amuses him today." Perhaps Oberon has forgotten to fear that. I have not.

"He will see to them."

"He will make them legends," I answer. "You do not swat flies with lightning unless you are ready to burn down the forest."

His shadows lengthen. Something dark coils at the edge of his aura. "Then I will do it myself," he whispers, voice like a knife. "If Puck fails, if these children insist on standing between me and my goal... I will end them. Personally."

My throat tightens. "They are only children."

"They are obstacles," he says, cold and final.

And then I see it clearly: the hunger in his eyes, the presence moving behind them. Ancient. Watching through him.

He turns and vanishes into the gathering dark, but his words remain:

"Obstacles are meant to be removed."

Cold settles into me... not from the wind, but from knowing the king I once knew is already half gone.

I press my palms to the earth again. The seal pulses beneath me... steady, enduring.

So I continue. Not from certainty, but resolve. If this seal is to be undone, it will be by my hands, my eyes open, even as the shadows close in. Even if the voice urging me forward is no longer Oberon's at all.

Chapter 24:
Disbelief and Magic

I am losing it, officially.

Not, like, whoops-I-forgot-my-password again losing it. Not even jumping-off-the-bed-into-my-pillow losing it. No, this is a total meltdown. Fatal error. System restart required. Every muscle in my body is on high alert, and my brain just. Will. Not. Stop. Overanalyzing everything.

My hands are trembling. They're shaking in my lap, fists so tightly closed they're practically afraid of themselves. They should be... because I am. Every time I blink I can feel it again: that absurd warmth in my chest, that surge of adrenaline through my arms, that spike of energy shooting from my hands like a literal anime finishing move. I keep my bad leg tucked under the chair, a wad of napkins is pressed against my knee.

I can still see it... that flash of light, the troll hitting the wall, the smell of burning metal. But worst of all?

I knew. It was me.

That's what's spinning me. Because that means this isn't a coincidence. I didn't trip a security laser, I didn't accidentally knock over a generator. I did that.

But that's impossible.

Magic isn't real. People don't just wake up one day and blast trolls into drywall. This isn't a game, or a show, or even one of those cringe internet videos where people pretend to be in haunted houses with bad special effects. This is Berlin. Literal, actual Berlin, and I don't care how cinematic it was... I shouldn't have been able to shoot lasers from my freaking hands.

I dig my nails into my palms until they sting. Real pain. That's good. That's normal. But my chest is still too tight, my breathing still too shallow, like my body's on autopilot from the moment before my brain caught up.

I grab my hot chocolate like it's a life preserver. Warm mug. Sweet smell. Cinnamon, sugar, and sanity. I take a sip. Too hot. Perfect. It tastes like all the good, boring moments of my life, and I clutch it like a lifeline.

Then, because I hate myself, I glance at my hands again. I stare at them like I'm waiting for a spark, a flicker, anything. But there's nothing. Just plain fingers around a paper cup. My heart does a dumb plummet anyway.

Because I know better now.

The Sherlock Holmes quote pops into my mind from somewhere:

When you have eliminated the impossible, whatever remains, however improbable...

...must be the truth.

And that truth?

Terrifies me.

Across from me, Nia is, of all things, calm. Sipping her tea like this isn't the thing that just happened. Like I didn't just punch it out of some magical girl in the freaking middle of a museum.

"Okay, so... um..." My voice wavers. "That really happened, right?"

Nia meets my eyes, calm as stone. "It happened."

The words hit harder than they should. My mug trembles.

Something inside of me snaps tight. The cup trembles slightly in my grasp. "But... how?" My voice cracks. "How did I shoot a laser from my hands?!"

She glances at her tea like maybe the answers are swirling in there. "I don't know... but I saw it. Felt it."

I blink. "What?"

"Your energy," she says softly. "It was bright. Strong. Beautiful."

I almost choke on my hot chocolate. "Beautiful?! I almost incinerated the whole museum!"

Nia laughs then... gentle, almost bashful, but honest.

And god, that laugh, it breaks something in me. The bell at the end of the day when it's been stuck in a classroom for hours. My chest doesn't unclench all the way, but for the first time since the museum, I breathe a breath that doesn't reek of panic.

"Well," she says, "you didn't incinerate the whole thing. And you saved us."

Her expression hardens again. "That troll..."

The word drops between us like a brick.

I hug my arms around myself, suddenly cold.

"That thing... it wasn't just..." I can't say it.

"It was real," Nia says again.

I don't know why, but that's worse than silence.

"You... uh... went all glowy," I say. "Oracle-mode. Lit up from the inside, then blank."

Her brows knit. "I don't remember that."

The bottom drops in my stomach. She sets her cup down. "I have to focus to use my sight. I don't just... go out like that."

Her calm only makes the silence heavier.

We sit there, both of us lost in the chaos of our minds.

I open my mouth, close it, then mutter: "How is any of this real?"

Nia's response is quiet, but definitive. "Something shifted. The air. The space around us. It warped. Like magic."

I wince. "...Magic?"

"Not tricks. Not illusions. Something else. Real. Ancient."

The word lands in my chest like a rock.

"And it wasn't just the troll," she adds.

My head jerks up. "What do you mean?"

"The boy," she says. "Blue hair."

"So what now? Salt circles? Holy water?"

Nia stares. "What? No!"

I drop my forehead on the table. "Good. Because I cannot handle a demon-possession arc right now."

Nia laughs. A real laugh this time. And just like that, the panic evaporates a little more.

We sip in silence for a while.

I look down at my hands again, turning them over slowly.

"I didn't mean to," I whisper.

Nia reaches across the table, her hand warm and solid against mine. "You were scared," she says. "You were protecting me."

Her words slice through everything else. Her hand is warm... and OMG, why am I thinking about that right now?!"

Nia's voice pulls me back before I go too far. "You saved us. That was brave."

I blink at her, throat thick. "So... what does that make me?"

Her lips twitch. "Someone with powers. Apparently."

"My eyes widen. 'Wait. I'm a magical girl.'

Nia blinks.

'Serious. Attack name, sparkles, the whole deal.'

She tries to hold it in. Then bursts out laughing."

I grin, still halfway to panic mode. "So... good thing or bad thing?"

She squeezes my hand. "It's good."

And for some reason, I believe her.

BZZZT.

The phone vibration startles me like someone shot at us. Nia's buzzes too. We grab them like we're about to cut the wrong wire in a spy movie.

> Unknown Number:
> I can explain what's happening to you.
> Come to this address.
> It's not safe out there.

Nia meets my eyes. She doesn't even flinch.

"We find out the truth," she says.

Her hand tightens around mine. Solid. Warm.

"Together."

And yeah. I'm still freaking out.

I have no idea if I can do this. But she believes I can. And that's... enough.

Chapter 25:
Operation Escape

Balam ✦ Early Evening (April 26) ✦ Berlin

We burst into the plaza and run. Sprint. We careen through it, panicked. Breathe in burning lungs, breathe out cracked glass, every stride like our legs might split. We don't stop.

"Halt! Sofort stehen bleiben!"

I don't need to know what they're saying to know what they want.

Our boots slap against cobblestone, each echo deafening, too loud, too visible. The plaza stretches in front of us... vast, open, merciless. Statues. Benches. Shrubs. No cover.

Until...

The threads flare.

Green lines, thin as ghosts, snake across the plaza floor. So pale, they might not even be real at first. They're insubstantial, the light glowing just enough to catch my eye, sliding toward alleys, darting across the bridge, slicing through people as they move, almost as if they know where gaps will appear, and where people will be seconds later. Just like the airport. Just like the museum.

No time to think. I run after them.

Aiyana follows just behind me... and that's all the space she's giving herself. Her breath is ragged, her steps uneven, and I can almost feel her legs trembling every time her foot strikes the ground.

I catch her elbow as she trips, but keep moving. "Come on," I mutter, though more to myself than her. She doesn't protest. Doesn't argue. She only goes faster, though I can see her body screaming at her for it.

Brave. So damn brave.

Sirens are closer now. The wail of them bouncing off the walls of the plaza, sounds so loud, so close they burrow under my skin. We don't have much time.

Ahead of us, a stone bridge arches across the river. It's glowing orange under streetlights. Freedom.

We hit the edge of the bridge and stop.

A police car blocks the midpoint of it, its lights a blue pulse. Two officers are outside it, both yelling at us in both German and English, their voices carrying, trying to push back a swell of tourists.

"Zurückbleiben! Alle zurück!"

Fear ripples through the crowd. People push forward, against each other. Chaos multiplies in seconds.

The green threads flutter, blink... jittering into the crowds in front of us. I grit my teeth. "Stay with me," I say to Aiyana, tightening my grip on her hand. "Don't let go."

We charge into the crowd. Screaming children. Tourists with their phones up like we're street performers. An old woman collides with us, and I half-push, half-lead Aiyana through the wave of bodies.

She trips again. I wrap my arm around her waist, hauling her back to her feet.

One of the officers locks eyes on us, suspicion flashing like knives... but someone shouts behind him, and he's gone, yanked away by a louder threat.

The bridge shakes from too many pairs of feet. Sirens are screaming behind us now, and closing in fast, but we're almost across. Almost free. Just a little further...

We make it to the main street, and I feel my stomach drop.

Blue lights are everywhere. The sirens ricochet off windows, off car doors, windows too. Police radios buzz and crackle with words I mostly understand:

"Zwei Jugendliche... dunkle Haare... braune Haut... westwärts."

I am guessing, but I think they're talking about us.

The threads flare once more... arching out like tree roots, searching for a path faster than I can even think. One surges right, glowing brighter than the rest, tugging at me so hard it almost seems physical.

I drag Aiyana after me, force her into the alley I come to first. The river looms dark against the other side of it.

Streetlights twinkle on the water. My lungs feel like they're caving in, every breath slicing glass.

"We can't... keep going... like this," Aiyana pants. Her voice is cracking.

"We have to," I tell her, though my lungs agree with her more than my words.

Coffee shops slide by to our left, painted a warm gold, tourists inside sipping wine and chatting away as if nothing is happening. They don't see us, don't know what we're running from.

"Zwei Jugendliche..." Closer this time. Everywhere now.

We veer left. Then right. The city around us twists, becoming a warren of alleys, stone walls, narrow cobblestone streets with old lanterns throwing long, distorted shadows.

Every nerve in my body screams move! Stopping is not safety... it's a cage. It's a death sentence. But Aiyana's breath hitches with each step. Her grip on my hand is getting looser. She's getting close to breaking completely, and I don't know what's going to break first... her or them.

The threads ahead of us stutter, splinter, flickering out of view every other second. Too many at a time. I can't tell which one to take.

"We need to disappear," I tell her.

"There," Aiyana says, nodding. Her voice is so soft, she's almost whispering it. A network of alleys yawns in front of us.

The threads lunge in that direction, all at once. Good enough.

We dive into it.

✦ ✦ ✦ ✦ ✦ ✦ ✦

The sound of our pursuers is gone, replaced with the harsh rasp of our own breathing. My heart is slamming in my chest so loud I can barely think past it. The green threads have dimmed, almost gone, fading away to the corners of my vision. Stress gone. Magic out. Fair enough.

We finally slow, forcing ourselves to the corner between two buildings.

The stone wall is cold behind me. I glance over at Aiyana.

She's sliding down, now sitting, her arms hanging loose at her sides, her entire body trembling. Her forehead is pressed to the wall, eyes closed tightly, her breathing so fast, so shallow.

She's not just exhausted. She's breaking.

I squat next to her, placing a hand on her shoulder. "Aiyana..."

She jerks away at the touch. Her eyes snap open... wide, glassy, haunted.

"I... I heard them," she says, her voice a whisper. "The dead. They weren't monsters, Balam. They weren't evil."

I stop. Freeze.

This is the part they don't tell you about... the part after the fight, after someone looks at you with regret in their eyes and you realize you didn't just fight monsters.

"What do you mean?" I ask, though I already know I don't like the answer.

"They were scared," she says, voice trembling. "Terrified. And I... I made them stop. I controlled them." Her hands are fists at her sides, knuckles white. "They didn't have a choice."

Guilt punches me in the gut.

"I didn't know," I whisper, even though I already do. "I'm sorry. I didn't think..."

"They were begging me," she interrupts. Her eyes are far away, unfocused like she's still there with them. "They were trapped, and I used that."

"You saved us," I say, because it's all I can. "You didn't have a choice."

She doesn't meet my eyes. Her voice cracks as she says, "I can't stop hearing them."

It's a long moment. Silence so heavy, so suffocating.

I take her hand in mine, squeezing. "You saved us," I whisper, even softer now. But I don't think she hears me.

A shout breaks the moment in two.

Blue light flares across the alley walls.

"They found us," I say.

Aiyana stiffens, her jaw clenching. No time to rest now.

We are running again.

The world blurs around us... cobbled streets, tables of café chairs clattering behind us as we shove past, curses yelled in German. Police radios buzz and crackle, always far too close.

The threads light up again, jerking unsteadily, glowing too bright, all at once. I can't think. Just follow.

"Left!" I yell, our course changing so suddenly we nearly crash into a waiter holding a tray of drinks. He yells something at us in German, but we're long gone.

Aiyana is slowing. I can feel her hand slipping again, her feet dragging just a little.

We duck into another alley, but I know the second we turn into it that this is a bad decision.

Flashlights blaze in both of its entrances. Cops are yelling, footsteps thudding closer. We're trapped.

The threads whip wildly... flashing up the walls, tangling in the air above us, all totally useless. Panic squeezes my chest in a fist.

This is it. The corner we can't turn from. All of my instincts are screaming fight, but I've got nothing left. No energy. No weapons. Nothing but Aiyana next to me, looking like she's only barely holding herself together.

"We shouldn't have run," she whispers. Her voice sounds so... broken. And the worst part? I understand. We ran to survive, but now we're criminals. Truth doesn't matter when no one's listening.

One of the officers moves closer, yelling, "Hände hoch!"

We are frozen. Trapped.

Movement, above us.

"Hey! Over here!"

Two shapes are perched on the roof of our building. A blond boy. A giant of a man next to him. Both waving like crazy.

"Come on! We'll get you out!"

I look at Aiyana. She looks at me.

We don't know them.

But we have no choice.

Chapter 26:
Confessions & Calm

Tristan ✦ Early Evening (April 26) ✦ Berlin

The night air is finally breathable again, cool and almost gentle after the last few hours.

We are not running. That is the weirdest thing. No boots pounding, no sirens scraping at my ears, just leaves rubbing the sidewalk and our breaths. For the first time since everything began, my body hates being still. My legs feel like springs, coiled to launch the second someone yells stop. My heart has not gotten the memo that we're okay. Relatively okay, at least.

I lean on the back of a beaten park bench and try to uncoil, but the tension sits too deep. Tama is pressed against the chestnut trunk, arms folded. To anyone else he might look calm. I have known him long enough to read the small tells... jaw clenched, fingers curling, like he is still seeing a fight.

The sirens have faded. That does not make me trust anything.

I glance at my phone. No missed calls from Mum or Dad. Strange. They usually text at the first hint of trouble. I ought to call, say I am fine. I do not. If I hear Mum's voice I will have to say the words out loud and then it will be true.

I keep thinking about the auras. The shimmers that showed up in the fight, bright as flares. Tama had been a molten red, all force and weight. The couple we pulled out... she glowed gold, steady; he pulsed green, quick and sharp. Now they sit like ordinary people on a fountain's edge, and that is worse somehow. It only happens when the world tilts. That is more unnerving than if it were constant.

They have said little since the alley. The boy keeps rubbing at his face like he can scrub the night away. The girl sits like a wound will open if she breathes wrong. Neither looks surprised by the madness. That might be the oddest thing of all.

Tama says, "You reckon they're okay?"

"I do not know," I answer.

"We should check on them. Can't just leave them." He sounds practical.

"Right." I stand. "You're right."

We move toward the fountain.

✦ ✦ ✦ ✦ ✦ ✦ ✦

The boy sees us the instant we are three steps away. He slams himself in front of Aiyana without a word, all posture and warning.

"What do you want?" he snaps. Not quite hostile. Ready.

I lift both hands. "Easy. We are just checking you are all right."

He does not relax. His eyes flick between us like someone running a threat assessment.

"We are fine," he says flat.

Right. Fine.

I keep my tone casual. "You were running from the cops. Not because you jaywalked, I imagine."

He stares at me long enough it feels like a test, then lets out a slow breath. "Fine. You helped. Thanks, I guess." Not warm, but honest.

I nod toward the fountain. "Mind if we sit?"

He looks at Aiyana, then back. "Fine. But no funny business."

I let a smirk edge out. "No promises."

Tama snorts. We take the empty space on the fountain's lip. Night settles around us again.

"I am Tristan. That is Tama."

The boy sniffs. "Rough night, huh?"

"Something like that." He nods at me. "I am Balam. She is Aiyana."

At the sound of her name, Aiyana finally looks up. She studies us as if deciding what we are worth. Her voice is delicate and brittle at once.

"You helped us."

"Yeah." I keep it simple.

She frowns. "Why?"

I shrug. "It felt like the right thing to do."

Balam watches me a long time. "You do not even know us."

"Does not matter."

Something moves behind his eyes... surprise, maybe hurt. He laughs, soft and skeptical. "Well, you picked the wrong people to help."

"Maybe." I give a small smile. "Or maybe not."

Silence stretches. My thoughts run on the auras and whether I should text my parents before they call. I break it with a grin I do not feel entirely.

"You two had a bad night. I will bet we win on weird."

Balam raises an eyebrow. "You want to bet?"

Tama grins. "Mate, you would lose."

"Started with a gnome fight," I say. "Real gnomes, teeth and claws. Like fighting monkeys with knives."

Balam blinks, then deadpans, "Cute."

"Cute?" Tama asks.

"Try zombies," Balam says flat.

"Zombies?" I sit up.

"Yeah. Museum exhibits came back to life. Skeletons, dead soldiers, the lot."

Aiyana whispers, "We have been running since." Her fingers twist the fountain stone.

I rub my face. "Alright. You win."

Balam smirks. "Told you."

My phone buzzes. Unknown number.

I can explain what is happening to you. Come to this address. It is not safe out there.

My heart jumps. Tama already has his phone up. "You got that too?"

I nod.

Aiyana blinks at her own screen. "I... I got it too."

Balam curses softly. "Same."

Silence circles us. We are not strangers anymore, not after tonight. Whatever this is, it has roped us all in.

Balam breaks it, his tone flat, almost amused. "If sticking together keeps us alive, fine. But I'm not holding hands."

Chapter 27:
Questions & Betrayal

The address takes us down a side street... a quiet one, at that. The kind of street where time seems to have stopped. Old buildings with stone facades pocked by age, windows faintly glowing with light from the city. There's an odd feeling about the place. Unsettling, but not dangerous. Comforting, in a way.

My chest tightens before I can pull back.

At first it's just a sense... skin tingling for no reason. But the closer we get, the heavier it feels, coiling in my ribs.

Then I see the door.

And I remember.

My hand freezes in the air, fingers hovering just short of a knock. My mind is throwing up excuses, some alternate explanation, but there isn't one. I've only been here once, more than a month ago. Professor Mara usually meets me at the university but for some reason this was her home. I would never forget it.

I remember because I told her things I've never told anyone. Things she helped me make sense of. Things she used to make me feel normal. When everything else was trying to make me feel strange.

Her home.

The professor has a house?

Before I can stop her, Airi is moving forward, hand raised to knock, but the door creaks open on its own, slow and heavy, like it's been waiting for us.

The lights are on. A fire is burning in the hearth, throwing shadows long across the walls. Someone's here. Someone was just here.

Airi stops. "Hello?" Her voice is quiet, unsure, not quite loud enough to fill the silence closing in around us.

No answer.

Instinctively, I step through the doorway, heart racing. The second I'm in the room, memory sweeps back in: the smell of parchment and old wood, shelves stacked floor to ceiling with ancient texts and scrolls, artifacts displayed like treasures. Nothing is different.

The wide picture window catches my eye... the city glowing softly under twilight, so normal it feels insulting. How can it look that peaceful when everything in me is falling apart?

"This place is... intense," Airi whispers, tracing the leather-bound spine of a thick book on the table.

"It suits the professor's personality," I find myself saying before I can catch myself.

She blinks at me. "Wait... you know this place?"

I sigh, massaging my temple. No use denying it now. "This is Professor Mara's home. I've been working with her for weeks. I intern for her."

Airi's expression twists. "What?!"

"This doesn't make any sense," I say, more to myself than her. "Why would she send us here? Why would she..."

A sudden draft of air hits the back of my neck.

✦ ✦ ✦ ✦ ✦ ✦ ✦

The door creaks.

Airi and I both spin.

We aren't alone.

Four people step into the room.

The first is a tall blonde boy, around my age, eyes sharp and appraising as he scans the room... until they focus on us. He looks at us like we're puzzle pieces he didn't expect.

Behind him, two teens with tan skin and dark hair. The boy has his hair in a small ponytail, shoulders tense, already mapping the exits. The girl beside him has a long braid and hollowed eyes. She looks like she hasn't slept in days.

And last... a giant.

Not literally, but close enough. Wide shoulders, tousled hair, and a grin far too easy for the room.

Then...

"Fry Girl?!"

The voice echoes, rousing everyone... except Airi.

She jumps, blinking in shock... then scowls. "I told you not to call me that! Urusai!"

The giant just grins wider. "Oi, small world, huh?"

The room falls silent, a pregnant pause of confusion.

I glance at her. "Wait... you know him?"

The blonde boy looks just as confused.

Airi begins to explain, like she's been waiting for a captive audience. "Okay, so I was at the Dubai airport, right? Just waiting for my flight. And this guy... Tama, his name is... ambles in like a tank and made me drop my fries."

Tama crosses his arms. "You just happened to run into me, eh? I was bein' friendly! Offered to replace 'em before you high-tailed it."

The blonde sighs. "Classic. Bull in a china shop."

Tama just laughs. Airi ignores him, words coming faster now.

"You wouldn't believe the day I've had!" she says, too bright. "I got attacked by a troll..."

Dead silence.

She beams. "Wiped out its brains. With a magic laser beam."

Tama blinks. "What?"

The blonde is still digesting. "Wait... you what?"

The boy with the ponytail steps forward, voice quiet, level. "We fought zombies."

The girl beside him shivers.

Tama nods slowly. "We got ambushed by some gnomes, too."

Airi's eyes light up. "Gnomes?! Zombies?! Trolls?! What is this, mythology bingo? What's next... Godzilla?"

No one answers. Because no one has an answer.

The room settles into stunned silence. Then finally, the blonde boy speaks.

"We've met before," he says, deliberate now.

I blink. "We have?"

He nods. "The lecture. The other day."

Oh.

The university. I was in the back, just listening. He was there... but I hadn't realized he'd noticed me.

Before I can answer, the boy with the ponytail steps forward, nodding slightly. "I'm Balam," he says. "This is Aiyana."

Aiyana lifts her head just enough to glance at me, then drops her gaze again.

The blonde straightens. "Tristan Pellinore." He nods at the giant. "This is Tama."

Tama waves. "Pleasure, Fry Girl's friend."

Airi rolls her eyes. "I have a name, you know." She plants her hands on her hips. "Airi Yugami!"

I step forward. "Nia Seretse."

Tristan's eyes flick to me. "So you were at the lecture," he says, mostly to himself. "You actually paid attention. Most interns don't."

It almost sounds like a compliment. I think.

Then his brows draw together. "I'm guessing you got the same message we did?"

One by one, everyone silently raises their phones.

Mine is still lit with the same text.

Before anyone can speak again, a noise from the back of the room cuts through the tension.

A thud. A creaking floorboard.

Every head turns.

And then... she steps into view.

Professor Mara.

My heart stops.

✦ ✦ ✦ ✦ ✦ ✦ ✦

She looks... calm, like this is normal. Like she's just walking into another class. Another late-night lab. Like she isn't standing in the middle of everything that's imploding inside me.

"It appears you all received my message," she says.

I barely register it.

She sent the message? She brought us here?

No. No, that doesn't make sense.

This is the woman who mentored me. Encouraged me. Told me my visions mattered. She opened doors I didn't even know existed.

I trusted her. My legs are suddenly too weak to support me.

I told her things I've never told anyone.

And now... she's here. Calm. Like it was all part of the plan.

My stomach twists. My brain is scrambling to make sense of it, but nothing fits. Did she always know? Was she using me?

A hundred questions rise, but none of them come out.

Only one makes it past my lips.

"...What is going on?"

The words feel too small, too fragile for everything I want to scream.

Professor Mara meets my eyes without flinching.

And says the one thing that changes everything:

"It's time for you all to learn the truth."

Chapter 28:
Untaught Lessons

This has to be a joke.

It's the only thing that makes sense.

I'm perched on the edge of this too-fancy chair, arms crossed tightly, smirk fixed into place. I'm still half reeling from adrenaline, but no way am I letting anyone hear that... not out loud. Not even to myself.

This morning was normal. Trip to the museum. Cool exhibits. After lunch... weirdness. The air started to feel thick, like it was weighing on my skin. Then I touched a railing, and it bent. Plastic. No pain, no effort. I didn't even have time to panic before things went to hell.

Gnomes. Literal gnomes. With claws and teeth. Springing out of the ground like they were waiting for me.

And now? Now we're in someone's office, and this silver-haired professor is telling me about magic and fate like she's reading the news.

I snort, because I have to. "Magic," I repeat, shaking my head. "Sure. And I suppose you'll be telling me the Easter Bunny's real too?"

She doesn't blink.

"You can laugh all you want, Tama. It won't change the truth."

Her eyes lock onto mine. Calm. Steady. Like she's not going to be fazed by me for one second.

"You felt it. When you bent the railing. When you took down the gnomes. That wasn't strength. That was magic."

I hate how that lands.

Because she's right.

I mean, she is.

Something else was in me today. Not just muscle... something deeper. Faster. Stronger. Like my body had a plan and decided to act before my brain even processed what was happening. And if that's real... if I can do that on instinct alone... what if I lose control? What if someone gets hurt because of me?

I glance around the room, willing someone to burst out laughing, willing this to be revealed as ridiculous. But no one does. Because they know. They feel it too.

The professor continues her monologue... magic, and barriers, and ancient powers... but it's all background noise to me. I'm too busy watching the other students.

Airi is vibrating. Literally. Hovering up and down in her chair like she's about to launch straight off it, eyes wide and sparking with energy.

"This is so cool," she exhales. "Magic is real! We have powers! I shot a laser. Out of my hand!"

She thrusts her hands forward like she expects them to light up any second now. "I need to try it again. Maybe I can aim better. Or charge it. Or fly!"

I groan and rub my face. "Please don't try to fly."

She doesn't listen. She's all business, now. Spinning on her seat to turn to Tristan, all wide eyes and bouncing hair. "What about you? What can you do?"

Tristan is the complete opposite of Airi. Calm. Cool. Hands resting neatly in his lap. Not excited. Not rattled. Just... watching.

"I don't know..." he says.

Airi blinks. "Wait... you haven't done anything yet?"

He shakes his head. "I've seen these auras around people, and I have some magic voice or something. But no lasers or anything."

I narrow my eyes. "And you believe all this?"

Tristan meets my gaze evenly. "I've seen enough. I want to understand."

"Seriously? That's all it takes for you?"

"You bent a railing with your bare hands."

I throw up my hands. "Yeah, and I saw gnomes trying to kill people. Doesn't mean I buy into some magic fairy-tale."

He doesn't try to argue. Doesn't try to push. He just waits. Watches. Like he knows I'll come around eventually. Which grinds my gears more than it should.

And maybe that's what does it... they're already falling into this as if it makes sense. Airi's buzzing. Tristan's calm. Even Balam looks like he's already planning his next fight. Me? I still want this to be a dream.

I turn to Balam.

He's keyed up. Feet bouncing, hands clenched, whole body coiled like he's expecting to pounce if something else attacks.

Airi notices. "Okay, but what about you? What's your power?"

Balam shrugs. "I don't know if I have one."

She gasps like he just insulted her personally. "No way. You have to! We're all in this together."

"I fought today, yeah. But it felt like me. No lightning bolts. Just a green light that showed me where to go."

I nod. "See? Not all of us are launching off into comic-book style action."

Airi frowns, but the professor interrupts.

"Magic doesn't always manifest itself the same way. Some are subtle. They develop over time."

I roll my eyes. "How convenient."

Balam mutters, "If I'm in this, I'd rather know before something else attacks us."

Fair.

Then I see Nia.

She's quiet. Too quiet. Hands balled into fists in her lap, eyes glued to the floor like she wishes she could sink into it.

Then it hits me.

She's the professor's intern. She had to know.

"You knew," I say.

Her head snaps up. "What?"

"All of this. You were in on it."

"No," she says fast, almost panicked. "I thought I was just helping with research. I didn't know any of this."

I narrow my eyes. "You really expect me to believe that?"

"I didn't know," she says again, louder now. "I get visions... that's from my family. That's it."

She's rattled. Not lying. Just... overwhelmed. And somehow, that's worse. Because for a second, I wanted to trust her. I still kind of do. But trust doesn't matter if she's been holding stuff back from us. Not when people's lives are on the line.

The professor speaks again, and every eye snaps to her.

"The world you know is not the only one. There are other realms. Separated by a magical barrier. That barrier is failing."

Gods. War. Chaos.

My fists clench automatically. I'm not scared of a fight. But a war with gods? That's a whole different ball game.

"Six of you," she continues. "Six sparks of power. That's not chance. That's fate."

My jaw tightens. Fate. Great. Because that's always worked out well for people in the stories.

She turns to each of us in turn.

"Nia, you have the Sight. You will learn to control it.

Tristan, you're a leader. Your power is deeper than you realize.

Balam, you're the hunter. Your instincts will sharpen.

Aiyana, you already hear and speak to spirits. That power will grow.

Airi, you create. Not just tech. Energy. Real power."

Airi practically hops in her seat. "So like... science magic?"

The professor actually nods. "Yes."

Then she looks at me.

"You are the unbreakable one."

Something cold slides through me. Not pride. Not relief. Just... weight. If I'm unbreakable, it means I'm supposed to stand there while everyone else shatters. Be the shield. The one who doesn't get to break, even when everyone else does.

I don't know if that's a compliment or a warning.

Tristan leans forward. "How do we stop this seal from breaking?"

The professor hesitates. "I don't know if we can."

That punches me in the gut.

"If we don't find a way to reinforce the barrier... the world will change. Completely."

Nia exhales, almost a whisper. "Then we lose."

My stomach churns. I hate waiting. I hate feeling helpless. I hate...

CRACK.

The window explodes.

Cold air pours through the room as something massive barrels through the glass. Scaled. Gnarled. Its claws lash out, quick as a whip...

It grabs Aiyana.

She screams, pure panic, and just like that, she's gone.

The room freezes.

Then chaos.

Nia lunges for the window. Balam curses. Tristan's already moving.

But I'm faster.

Chairs, tables, whatever... none of it matters. I shove past everything and barrel straight out the shattered window.

Wind slams into me, city spinning beneath me.

Four stories up. No plan. Just instinct.

And for one split second, one split second, my stomach twists with a thought I've been trying to outrun since this started: What if I'm not unbreakable enough?

This is going to hurt.

Then... impact.

The street splinters beneath me. Cracks spiderweb through the pavement.

But I'm still standing. No blood. No broken bones.

I should be dead.

But I'm not.

Aiyana screams again.

And I run.

"AYIANA!"

My feet pound the pavement, the night air roaring in my lungs.

Whatever just happened to me, whatever this "unbreakable" thing is, none of it matters.

She needs help. And I'm not stopping until I find her.

Chapter 29:
Play Time

Okay. Deep breath. Inhale chaos, exhale nonsense.

Because this? This is getting annoying.

I hover outside Ea'mara's office like an unwanted voyeur, my lovely hair crackling in the air and my patience wearing thinner than a spiderweb in a thunderstorm.

There's a barrier on the building. Of course there's a barrier. Ancient Seer magic, no trespassing, *blah blah blah.* I poke it.

ZAP.

"Ow," I say flatly, yanking my finger back and wiggling it like it's about to fall off. "How dare you. I am delicate."

I poke it again.

ZAP.

"Oooo, that one tickled. You little flirt."

I lean in, pressing my face to the shimmer like a child to glass.

And there they are.

My little fireflies.

All six of them. Alive. Together. Still glowing.

Still.

I flop dramatically backward, floating midair like a bored child.

"Ugh, seriously? You're still going? After everything?"

They weren't supposed to survive this long.

They were supposed to crack, fall apart, cry a little, scream a lot, then either flee into the night or get picked off one by one.

But noooo.

They cling. They regroup.

They talk about their feelings.

Disgusting.

And worst of all?

They keep winning. Not by being clever. Not by being strong. Not even by cheating...which, frankly, I would respect. Honestly.

But no.

They keep beating me with... ugh... friendship.

And loyalty.

And personal growth.

Gag me with a lightning bolt.

I float back toward the barrier and peer in again. My eyes catch on her.

Her. The quiet one. With the calm eyes and the glow.

Aiyana.

She's the one who stopped the draugr. She didn't fight it. She didn't run.

(Okay, fine. She ran later. But still.)

She spoke to it. Glowed at it. Whispered sweet nothings to it, soft and golden and ridiculous. And it listened.

That was supposed to be a monster, sweetheart. A big scary dead thing. I put effort into that one. Like, real effort.

And you just... calmed it.

Like a spirit whisperer. Or a grief counselor.

With glitter.

Unacceptable.

"She cheated," I mutter to myself. "She cheated with feelings... okay, I guess I respect that a little."

I flip upside down, glaring at her from a fresh angle.

Still too calm. Still too sad. Too... distant.

"She can't even have the decency to pretend to have fun."

I poke the barrier again, harder.

ZAP.

I yelp, louder this time, and stick my tongue out at the glowing runes.

"Ea'maraaa," I sing in my best whiny-child voice, "you're so dramatic. Let me iiiiiin. I wanna plaaaay!"

Silence. The spell hums smugly.

I cross my arms and sulk midair. Full dramatic hover mode.

If I go tell Oberon about this... about how the fireflies are still together, how they're adapting, how they're messing up my fun... he'll show up with all his stormy judgment and ruin everything.

Oberon doesn't play.

He cleans up.

He'll make them boring.

And then I'll be stuck on the sidelines again, while the grown-ups drone on about "duty" and "the balance of realms" and "who accidentally unraveled fate this time."

Hard pass.

I roll midair and peek back toward the window.

They think they're safe in there.

How quaint.

Safety is so last season.

I snap my fingers.

A few streets away, a griffin carved from stone shifts.

Groans.

Dust peels off its wings like breath after a thousand years.

Its eyes flare blue... my signature shade.

"Morning, sunshine," I whisper, tugging its strings. "Go stretch. Make new friends. Maybe kidnap one."

Then I pause, hovering just above the roofline, and glance directly at you.

Oh. Right. You already saw that.

(grin)

Yes, yes. I know. She's already been grabbed. That's done. Don't get all twitchy.

This is the replay. The flashback. The 'oh, that's how it got there' moment.

(leaning closer, voice mock-conspiratorial)

You think you're confused? Try being a time-bending chaos sprite with excellent hair.

(wink)

Just roll with it.

Now where was I?

Ah, yes.

It leaps.

Stone shouldn't move like that. But I don't follow rules. And neither do my toys.

Why stop there?

Snap. A lion statue growls awake.

Snap. A pair of winged warriors unfurl from the city's highest roof.

Snap. Snap. SNAP. Bronze, stone, marble, iron... groaning, cracking, waking.

The whole city turning into a playground.

My playground.

I twirl midair, arms flung wide, laughing so hard my eyes water.

"You're welcome, world!" I shout to no one and everyone. "Your public art just got a whole lot more interactive!"

I linger a moment longer, just to savor the tension. The crackle. The delicious silence before the storm.

Then I vanish in a swirl of glitter and wind, leaving only a whisper behind:

"Run fast, little fireflies... especially you, glowy girl."

A pause. A giggle.

"And Oberon? Stay on your throne, darling. I'm not done playing yet."

Chapter 30:
Stone Wings

My lungs are on fire. My legs are screaming. But I don't stop. I can't.

The streets whip past in streaks, my shoes hammering the stones. Every breath feels like broken glass in my chest. Puta madre, I can't stop.

But somewhere ahead, Aiyana is screaming.

I round a corner too fast, almost eat pavement, and then... there it is.

A shape beating against the night sky, carved straight out of a nightmare. A real maldito griffin. Its wings slice the air, each beat heavy enough to shake rooftops. Feathers glint like dull metal; stone muscles ripple where stone muscles should not move. And those eyes: glowing cold blue fire, locked straight ahead.

Clutched in its claws, Aiyana. With that same green... magic I saw earlier.

She kicks, thrashes, braid snapping like a whip. She's fighting like hell. But the thing isn't just running... it's showing off. Dipping low. Banking wide. Taunting us.

And we are chasing. Tama is ahead of me, pounding down the street like some human bulldozer. He shouldn't even be alive... he jumped out of a four-story window. Landed like a wrecking ball. And just kept running.

"Tama!" I shout, my voice shredding with the effort. "Wait dude!"

He doesn't slow. Doesn't even look back. Just throws me a nod that basically says: Keep up or shut up.

This morning, I was thinking about snacks. Snacks! And now? I'm sprinting through Berlin after a monster carved out of stone, magic in the air like smoke.

My muscles are tight and burning. But something else won't let me stop.

Something new.

It started in my chest... heat, pressure. Then spilling out, racing down my legs, sparking through my arms. The world... shifts. Thin green trails of light lace across the pavement ahead of me, darting between buildings, curving around corners like a map only I can read.

I don't even think. My feet follow. It's like this damn magic is steering me.

The griffin banks hard between two buildings, skimming so close its wingtips scrape sparks from the stone. Aiyana lashes out with her elbow, cracking it right in the chest. The glow in its core flickers... then she glows back, gold, like a sun breaking through clouds.

The creature stumbles midair. A crack spiders across its chest. Its claws open.

And Aiyana falls.

✦ ✦ ✦ ✦ ✦ ✦ ✦

Her scream cuts through the air, high and sharp.

"No!" Tama bellows.

I look up. She's too far. Falling too fast. We can't catch up.

Tama's eyes lock onto mine... wild, determined.

"I've got an idea!" he yells.

"What?! Qué idea, imbécil..."

Too late.

His arms clamp around my waist, and then the ground is gone.

Air tears at my face as I rocket skyward. Wind howls in my ears. For one insane heartbeat, I swear the green trails surge upward too, guiding me upwards, faster, like it wants me to do this.

Then... Aiyana.

She's right there. Falling. Her eyes lock onto mine, wide with terror and surprise, blazing with that same golden light. She reaches.

I reach. I am not sure I am going to be able to grab hold of her.

Contact! My arms wrap around her, yanking her tight against me. She's warm, solid, real.

"Hold on!" I gasp.

Like she has a choice.

The city rushes up to meet us. Black asphalt, glowing streetlights, and then... fountain.

We hit like cannonballs. Water explodes around us in a tidal wave. Pain detonates across my back, slamming every bone in my body, stars bursting behind my eyes.

But I don't let go.

She's trembling. Soaked. Alive.

"You..." she gasps, breathless. "You caught me."

"Couldn't exactly let you go splat," I manage, coughing. My ribs feel like they're in twelve pieces. We actually did it.

Her laugh breaks halfway into a sob. "Thank you."

"Don't thank me yet," I mutter, because I can already feel the green trails shifting again, snapping tight like warning wires.

A giant splash soaks us again. Tama lands in the fountain like a meteor, water sheeting off his shoulders.

"You two alive?!"

"Debatable," I groan.

Aiyana blinks at Tama, still clutching me. "You threw him?"

"Damn right," Tama grins. "I'm full of ideas."

"Let's not make a habit of that," I wheeze, trying to sit up.

She doesn't let go right away. Her fingers are still shaking against my arm. I am in no hurry to let her go either. For one breath, just one, we're safe.

✦ ✦ ✦ ✦ ✦ ✦ ✦

CRACK.

A sound like stone grinding against stone.

Tama freezes, turning slowly. "Oh, come on!"

Around the fountain, statues shift. Bronze warriors. Marble angels. Old kings and queens. Their stone feet scrape the ground as they step down, blue fire sparking in their eyes.

A sword drags against the pavement, shrieking. Wings spread. Shields lift. More and more wake, circling the fountain like wolves.

"They're waking up," Aiyana whispers.

I scan the plaza. No exits. No way out. Just us and a whole army of history come to life.

Tama cracks his knuckles, water dripping off him. "Because clearly, things weren't bad enough already."

Aiyana stands, dripping and fierce despite her trembling. "We stay together?"

I force myself upright, every muscle screaming. I can feel the green trails pulsing at the edge of my vision now, weaving paths across the ground, trying to lead me somewhere.

But we're boxed in and I have the others to think of now. Aiyana.

The statues take another step forward.

Chapter 31:
Taking Charge

My legs are lead weights but I don't stop. Shoes pound stone. I trip over the uneven cobbles, stumbling and gasping. The city swallows us in streaks of color as if Berlin is trying to eat us alive.

Aiyana is gone!

One second she was there, laughing and pushing us to work faster. The next...she was gone. Pulled through the air as if cut through with a knife. Something tore through the window and into the street to where Aiyana had stood just seconds before. Something that shouldn't have been real. A stone griffin. Tama leapt after it without thought, Balam following close behind in a flash of silent black speed.

And me? I'm running. I don't know what to do. But I can't stop. I can't stand still because it would feel worse. A voice inside my head shouts at me to stay put. My heart is a wild drumbeat and my hands...slippery with sweat. This is not courage. This is terror. But I can't let them be the only ones to face this.

"Where are they?" I choke. It's not a question, more a prayer to no one in particular.

"We'll find them," Nia replies. Voice is steady, even as she matches my pace.

Beside me, Airi is bouncing on her toes, frantic energy and wild eyes. But she won't stop. "What even was that thing? Like, some pissed-off gargoyle from hell?!"

No one answers. We're all out of breath.

Nia stops. Head shifts, her gaze narrowing as if she can hear something we can't.

"What is it?" I ask, trying not to sound too panicked.

She says nothing. Her eyes shift...literally shift. A dull gold light floods her irises. Faint, but impossible to miss.

"Uh," Airi says, "is... she doing that again?"

Nia points east. "There. Fast. It's like...a current. Magic. Blue, all tangled up. It's moving that way."

Magic currents. Great. Totally normal.

"Good enough for me," I reply, forcing my legs to keep moving. "Let's go."

Airi groans. "Why is it magic? Why not, I don't know, like some car? Tire tracks?"

"Because that would be easy," I retort with a smirk.

✦ ✦ ✦ ✦ ✦ ✦ ✦

We barrel through the streets, my heart trying to claw its way out of my chest but I don't stop. I don't even know them. But I can't leave someone to die. Not anyone. Not for me. Not ever.

The plaza opens up ahead.

And then... it happens again.

The world shifts. Not slows. Not exactly. But...focuses. Every sound drains into a dull roar, every movement sharpens into high contrast. I can feel the fight before I even see it. Like my instincts are reading the air.

The battlefield unfolds in my head in one breath.

Tama...center of the chaos, using his mass to barrel through attacks and strike. Balam...swift, darting around enemies, movement quick and reactive. Aiyana...on her feet, but cornered, glowing faintly, panic bleeding through every move. Statues everywhere. Heavy and oppressive, their movement somewhat predictable if you can follow the rhythm.

I don't glow. But I can read the fight. I can feel where they'll move before they do.

And they're losing.

Nia and Airi skid to a stop beside me.

"They're surrounded," I state. "If we don't draw some attention off of them, they're done for."

Airi gapes. "And what exactly do you want us to do? Throw rocks at them?!"

"Laser hands?"

"That was one time!"

"Try again."

She mutters under her breath, "If I die, I'm haunting you with glitter."

"Nia," I say, turning to her. Trying to remember what the professor said about each of us, "biggest threat?"

She sweeps her eyes over the plaza. "The ones with wings. If they get airborne again..." She doesn't need to finish that sentence. That would be bad.

I nod. "Airi, shoot them first."

"With what?" she yells back. "Do I yell 'pew pew' and hope?!"

"Honestly? Might help."

She glares. "You're not funny."

"Too bad we don't have any paper," Nia deadpans.

Airi blinks. "Wait... paper? Oh. Ha. Rock. Paper. Got it."

I don't think. I just act. Sprinting straight for the plaza, heart pounding.

✦ ✦ ✦ ✦ ✦ ✦ ✦

"HEY! YOU OVERPRICED MUSEUM EXHIBITS!" I scream, throwing my arms wide. The words are there before I have a chance to think about them. A command? Maybe. A plan? Nope.

Every stone head turns. Hollow blue eyes focus on me, unnerving and inhuman.

"Yeah that's right!" I bellow, backing toward an open area. "Come on then! Bet you can't hit me!" What else can I do? I am just trying to help...cause a distraction.

Airi screams behind me, "Oh my God, this is your plan?!"

"It's giving them time," I grit out. If my instincts are correct, I can keep them on me long enough for the others to catch their breath, regroup, hit back.

I don't glow. I'm not strong enough to punch through stone. But I can help.

Chapter 32:
Unleashed Power

Okay. Focus. Breathe.

I've done this before. Right? Sure. Totally.

I stand in the middle of a battlefield, statues closing in and I throw my hands up like an idiot trying to high-five the apocalypse.

"Kōgeki suru!"

Nothing.

"Fire blast!"

Still nothing.

"Photon strike! Laser cannon! Plasma... oh come on!"

Nothing. Not even a sparkle. Just me, standing there, looking like I'm auditioning for the world's worst magical girl anime while everyone else is actually fighting for their lives.

Tama and Balam are in full chaos mode, smashing through stones like it's a bad video game level. Tristan's there too, sword swinging, moving like he's in some historical drama he doesn't even know he's starring in. (Where did that sword even come from? Did he just pull it out of his Britishness?) Aiyana's shouting commands, voice cracking, trying to will the statues to stop.

And me?

I'm basically background NPC #3. With jazz hands.

Nia's beside me, calm as ever, glowing faintly like some elegant boss character from an RPG. She's actually doing something. Everyone is.

Except me.

I aim at a flying statue, one that looks like a bird got possessed by a kitchen appliance.

"Starbreaker! Solar flare! I don't even want what that one does but I NEED IT TO DO SOMETHING!"

Still. Freaking. Nothing.

"Yabai, yabai, yabai..." I hiss under my breath, stamping my foot like that's going to magically unlock my powers.

My pulse is racing, my breath short. There's heat coiled in my chest, like a battery ready to blow... but it won't move. Like I'm yelling at a Wi-Fi router to work harder. It's there, I know it's there, but... nothing!

The doubt creeps in fast.

Tristan said if I don't get it together... we all die.

I clench my fists. My body vibrates with frustration, panic, and that stupid gnawing voice whispering I don't belong here. That I'm just pretending again. That I'm all talk, no power, the genius who can build a robot but can't save her friends.

I think back. The museum. The troll. I did it then. I blasted that thing like it was a cartoon villain. It happened. I know it did.

So why can't I do it now?!

The others are drowning in stone. Aiyana's shouts are hoarse. Tama's getting hit harder. Balam's limping. Even Tristan's starting to slow.

And me?

Useless.

My hands drop. Cold. Still. Empty.

Then...

A hand at my waist. Steady. Warm.

"You can do this."

Nia's voice. Sure and soft. Her glow is faint, like dusk caught in amber. But her eyes... they're full sun.

"I saw your power," she says. "It's beautiful. It's strong. It's you."

Her words hit somewhere deep and aching, punching straight through all my panic. I want to believe her. Just for a second... I almost do.

But I look down at my hands. Still shaking. Still powerless.

I don't deserve her faith.

A *screech*... sharp, echoing, close.

A huge moonlit shadow falls across us.

I look up. My blood freezes.

That griffin!

The same one that grabbed Aiyana. Its massive wings slice through the air, its eagle head low and locked onto us. Across its stone chest... a fresh crack, jagged and glowing faintly blue-gold, like something inside it is still burning. I don't know what caused it. I don't want to know.

And now it's diving. Straight at us.

No... at Nia!

She shoves me back without hesitation. "Airi, RUN!"

"Baka!"

Run? I can't even breathe. My body locks, every nerve screaming. My brain flashes a thousand images at once... Aiyana being ripped away, that troll lunging at me, every anime hero who doesn't freeze like this and actually saves the day.

But me? I'm stuck. Useless. Again.

No.

It's going to take her. Just like it took Aiyana. Because I can't light up. Because I am just standing here, yelling dumb anime attacks, pretending to be a hero while my friends bleed for real.

No. No. NO!

Something inside me snaps. Not gently. Not like flipping a switch.

Like a dam rupturing. Like a hard drive frying and sparking out of control.

✦ ✦ ✦ ✦ ✦ ✦ ✦

The ground shakes. Dust spirals upward. Stones lift into the air, caught in a cyclone around me.

Power surges out of my skin like an explosion... furious and bright and unstoppable. My skin glows. Not pretty. Not soft. Blinding, like staring into a broken neon sign on overdrive.

This is what it felt like in the museum. This is what I wanted, what I needed.

I scream, "NOOOOOOO!" and my body finally listens.

A blast erupts from my hands, slamming into the griffin like a comet. It howls, cracks spiderwebbing across its chest. Wings falter. Stone groans.

And I keep going.

BOOM. BOOM. BOOM.

Bolts of light... pink and blue, glowing like rage wrapped in fireworks. They explode from my palms. Each hit is a heartbeat of fury and frustration.

I don't aim. I just unleash. The plaza ignites.

Statues crumble. Stone shrieks. Metal melts.

I don't feel human anymore. I feel... unleashed.

Tama? Safe.

Balam? Covered.

Anything that even thinks about getting near them, near Nia... dies.

The fountain explodes under the pressure. A statue lunges at Tristan... I vaporize it. Another charges Aiyana... gone.

I don't stop.

I won't stop.

Until finally...

Silence.

Smoke hangs in the air like the aftermath of a kaiju fight. The statues are rubble, glowing faintly like cooling circuits.

The power inside me flickers. Then fades.

My legs buckle. My hands fall. My whole body hurts like I've been plugged into a power grid and left on too long.

But we're alive.

I turn.

Nia is there. Staring at me like I just rewrote gravity. Her glow is still there, steady and warm. But her expression... I don't know if she's proud or terrified.

I don't ask as she rushes toward me, I don't ask as she rushes toward me. I just fall into her arms. Safe. Finally safe.

Chapter 33:
We're Not Dead (Yet)

I breathe in, slow, let it out. The crackle around us quiets to a hum in my chest. The plaza is wrecked... broken stone, scorched earth, statues toppled like a cruel game of chess. Magic still clings to the air, a faint after vibration.

We're alive. For now.

Aiyana perches on the edge of the shattered fountain, hunched, jaw tight, eyes far away. Balam sits beside her, quiet, hands loose. He doesn't push or joke. He just stays. Steady in a way I haven't seen from him before. An anchor.

Tristan leans against that oversized sword like it's the only thing keeping him up, an odd, grim grin tugging at his mouth.

Tama's slouched against a cracked wall, rubbing at his ribs. Still tossing one-liners like this is normal. I can't tell if that's comforting or terrifying.

Airi demolishes a candy bar, neon soda in her other hand, legs bouncing with leftover adrenaline.

Professor Mara isn't here. I don't know if she left, or if something happened to her. Either way... we're on our own.

"I can't believe it," Airi squeaks. "I went all glowy and..." she flings her hands... "bakuhatsu."

Tama snorts. "You went Super Saiyan. Hair and all."

"Don't call me Fry Girl," she huffs, then quieter, almost proud: "I was a Super Saiyan."

I crouch to her level and rest a hand on her shoulder. "You saved us."

"It was... kinda awesome," she mutters.

"It was," Balam says, rolling a sore shoulder. Then to Tama, "Did you really yeet yourself out a window?"

"Worked, didn't it?" Tama winks at Aiyana.

Her cheeks flush. She ducks, braid falling forward. "I... I didn't mean to... it just happened," she says, voice small. Her hands knot white in her lap. "I didn't mean to make it let go. I was scared. I shouted... and it listened."

Tristan straightens, his tone careful. "You commanded it?"

"I don't know." Her arms wrap around herself. "It felt like it heard me. Like it understood. It was alive. Angry about being controlled."

I close my eyes, reaching with that other sense... the one I can't turn off anymore. Magic still hums in the air, but under it, there's blue. Dense, curling, billowing like smoke through the cracks.

Tristan's jaw tightens. "Someone's controlling them? Sent them after us?"

Airi's soda can rattles in her hands. "W-who would do that? And why?"

My chest knots. "The blue again," I whisper. "The kid with blue hair... he isn't human."

Balam's head jerks up. "I saw a little girl. Atlanta. Blue hair."

"Also in the museum," Aiyana adds. "A woman."

Tama swallows. "Dubai. A guy."

Tristan's knuckles go white on the hilt. "Two in Berlin. They've been watching us."

Balam's voice is grim. "Whoever it is... they're not done."

✦ ✦ ✦ ✦ ✦ ✦ ✦

A groan rolls through the plaza. Rubble showers down.

"I... I did this," Airi whispers, staring at her hands.

"Yeah," Tama whistles low. "And it was pretty badass."

Her shoulders curl tighter. "What if I hurt someone next time?"

I squeeze her hand, and the leather pouch shifts against my ribs. Protection, Grandma said. Maybe it's silly, but I believe it. "We'll figure this out." I assure her.

The pull hits me like lightning. My skin lights gold, vision buckling. Blue leaks from the rubble, pulsing... eyes inside it, watching. My stomach drops. "There's more," I whisper. Louder: "There's more!"

The ground shudders. Stone cracks.

Tristan's voice goes even. "Ready."

"Oh, come on," Airi groans.

Tama rolls his shoulders. "I just got comfortable."

Tristan raises the sword, steel in his voice. "Complaining isn't in the playbook."

The statues start to move. My heart sinks. Here we go again.

Chapter 34:
Quiet Hands

Professor Mara ✦ Evening (April 26) ✦ Berlin

I was never meant for the front of the story.

I do not swing blades or trade boasts with kings. I do not hurl lightning. My work is quieter, meant to hold what can be held, to buy the seconds brave people need to do impossible things.

Tonight the storm arrives early.

The city hums under me: tram cables, copper gutters, the iron ribs of bridges, the sound of museums still ringing with alarms. I stand on the roof of my office, wind tugging at my coat, and set to my task.

My hands begin their work.

First the high ward: a dome you cannot see, flung wide and thin, no match for a king's hand if he truly reached... but enough to blur a gaze hunting from far away.

I feel the weight of Oberon's attention skim the ward. The surface shivers. Holds.

Not for long, but hopefully long enough.

I lay another ward between the children and the human eye. A soft fog for cameras; a bloom of meaningless pixels on every lens that tries to lock on to their faces. A spell of confusion and misdirection to drive the people away from the battle below.

I could go down there. These children must become what the world will ask of them... not because I push them, but because I don't hinder their chance.

And Puck? Already in the battle. Too close. Too clever to bar with my kind of magic. The children will have to turn and face that chaos with their own hands.

Oberon again. Closer.

I set my palm to the roof and drive all my magic into the ward. I hope it can buy them some time. Heat beads under my skin; the bones in my hand ache.

"Come on," I murmur, eyes closed. "Please be OK." It is so little. It is everything I have to give.

The king is angry. The ward creaks like ice.

"Good," I say, though my voice shakes. "Be angry with me."

My ward trembles again... thinner now, stretched too far. I cannot keep him out.

"I'm sorry," I tell the air, "I wish I were more. Tonight I am only a hedge."

Only. I almost laugh. "Hold," I whisper to the city, to my thread, to my trembling hands.

And for a little while... long enough, the world obeys.

Chapter 35:
Make It So

I weave between the towering statues, tripping over fragments of stone and shattered debris. The battle... a tempest of crumbling architecture, the biting clang of metal on metal, the inhuman sound of stone grinding, shifting unnaturally. Dust fills my lungs and every step is uneven. I keep trying to fight. I keep reaching for something to hold, something to help... but everything I touch is too heavy, too cumbersome.

A broken spear? Useless. A fallen sword, discarded by one of the statues? Oversized. No matter how hard I try to wield these weapons, they're too unwieldy, too heavy.

The statues don't have this problem. They move with an effortless ferocity, swinging massive stone limbs and razor-edged weapons with no sign of strain.

The voices curl around me... commands and shouts and the clamor of battle. They swirl together in a hectic, almost playful harmony of noise, echoing unnaturally in my mind. I reach for it, for the connection I know I have, for the ability I should have to hear them whispering just beneath the noise, but it's too much. The voices tangle and overlap, slipping through my fingers before I can catch on to one.

I can't make sense of it.

My voice is too weak.

I watch the others. All of them are fighting. All of them are doing something.

Nia's eyes are golden and her voice cuts through the chaos like a guiding light, warning them, directing them. Left! Behind you! Duck! Move! Her eyes are sharp and focused, seeing everything before it happens, pulling them back from the brink time and time again.

Tristan is still, calm, herding the others and keeping their movements coordinated. His oversized sword... so much larger than the one I have been using... arcs through the air with powerful, fluid motions, cutting through the enchanted stone like butter.

Tama and Balam are just wreckage, smashing and battering and tearing through anything they can reach, their strength overpowering the statues into rubble and dust. They fight without fear. Without hesitation.

Then Tama sees me. Just for a second. In the middle of battle, with dust in the air and enemies on every side, he looks for me. He grins, flashing that carefree, easygoing smile of his, like we're not in the middle of the apocalypse. Like he's saying, See? We've got this. You're okay.

My heart stutters in my chest. Heat blooms across my cheeks.

"Aiyana... duck!" Nia shouts.

I spin, just as one of the statues' tails swings toward me. I dive to the ground, barely avoiding the blow. The impact still sends me sprawling, my hands and knees slamming into the rough stone. Pain shoots up my palms and I gasp for breath, my lungs tightening into a harsh sob.

I freeze. My breath rattles in my chest. My fingers curl into fists in the dirt.

I can't fight. I can't lead. I can't protect them. I'm weak. I'm useless. I'm...

Something towers over me. Cold. Heavy. Suffocating. I raise my eyes, my stomach coiling.

A stone dragon. Towering. Wings spread wide and its body is carved from obsidian, from black stone, slick and glistening. Its eyes are glowing, an unnatural, hungry shade of light. Its mouth is open, its teeth jagged and sharp.

It snarls, and the sound rumbles in my bones.

"Airi... dragon!" Nia again, panicked and urgent.

I am still too slow to move. The dragon advances.

Its claws are splayed, ready to tear. Its teeth are bared, eager. Its eyes are on me... on me, its prey.

I should scream. I should run. I should...

A flash of light blazes in my vision. The dragon erupts.

A shockwave of energy blasts through the air. Stone shatters outward, cascading like hail. Dust fills the plaza, choking the air, stinging my eyes. The force leaves my ears ringing.

My heart races. Blinking rapidly, I tremble. When the dust clears, Airi is before me.

Her hair crackles with static, strands lifting in an electric haze. Her eyes are glowing, her pupils almost disappearing in the brightness of them. Her hands... still raised... thrum with the after-radiance of the blast, wisps of energy dancing at her fingertips.

She spins quickly, locking eyes with me. "Get up, Aiyana! You're not safe here!"

I can't reply. My throat is tight. My lungs won't work. Airi just saved my life.

Heat floods my chest, shame and frustration knotting into something sharp and unbearable.

I'm sick of this. I'm sick of always being the one who needs to be saved. I'm sick of always being helpless. I'm sick of always being weak.

Tears burn behind my eyes and I blink them away, forcing myself to shaky feet.

I'm still on the ground. My hands are clenched. My nails are digging into my palms, hard enough to draw blood. I shake... from fear? Exhaustion? A mix of all the things I can't explain? All the anger I can't shake?

Hot tears spill down my cheeks, angry and burning, cutting through the dust and grime.

I'm crying. In the middle of a battle.

I gasp on a breath, on the humiliation burning in my chest. I should move. I should do something. But all I can do is kneel here on the ground, trembling, weak.

I think of my grandfather... his hands rough with callouses from years of labor, his voice steady and unyielding. He taught me how to fashion silence into steel, how to listen when everything was shouting. He believed in me, called me his little guardian. I wonder if he would be ashamed to see me now... broken, crying, useless. Or if he would hold me and say it's okay to fall before you stand.

I think of that man. The way he touched my wrist, his fingers firm, but trembling. His eyes... the fear in them. The way I froze. The way I hated how small I felt. I thought I had exorcised that memory. But maybe instead it exorcised something inside me. Something that's been waiting to come back.

No more.

I gasp on a breath, on the humiliation burning in my chest. I should move. I should do something. But all I can do is kneel here on the ground, trembling, weak.

No more.

The words crash in my mind like a war drum.

I am not going to be helpless again.

Something lights inside my chest, a spark, a flame, something wild and ancient... something that's been buried for far too long.

Something breaks free in me, unfurling like a wildfire, tearing through my veins, boiling to the surface.

I gasp... then breathe out steady. My skin tingles. The world sharpens. A golden light blooms across my vision.

I barely register the way my skin shimmers... how it pulses with gold, how the light pulses from within, rippling across my skin like liquid sunlight. My arms, my hands, my whole body hums with power. The air around me is charged, thrumming with an invisible current.

I can hear them. All of them. Not just the others... not just Nia's orders, or Tristan's shouts, or Tama and Balam's battle cries.

The statues. The voices whisper in my ears, winding through my mind like twisting streams of sound. Orders. Commands. A chaotic symphony of voices... cold, mechanical, unyielding. The magic binding them thrums in my skull, a wall of rigid, unbreakable control.

But underneath it. Beneath it all.

Something else is hiding.

Something deeper. Something ancient. Something...

Vision swims. The golden light in my eyes sharpens. The hum in the air crescendos, building into a pulse that shakes my ribs, trembles in my fingertips.

And then... I scream. "STOOOOOOOOOOOP!"

The word doesn't just erupt from my throat. It detonates. A power explodes from my mouth, from my entire body. It's not just my voice. It's hundreds. Thousands.

A cyclone of voices crashes into the plaza, rolling through the air like a tidal wave, heaving with the weight of something ancient and inescapable. The power crushes outward, obliterating against the statues, against the very battlefield itself.

The ground shakes and the air constricts. Like the whole world is holding its breath.

The statues jolt mid-motion. A fighter mid-swing freezes. A stone dragon mid-lunge stalls. A hammer, suspended in free fall, hovers in place as if time itself has seized it. The grinding sound of stone on stone doesn't fade. It halts.

Not a pause. Not a stutter.

It just... stops.

The plaza is silent. My breath catches. The pressure in the air presses against my skin like the whole world has thickened.

And then... The statues' eyes flicker. Their eerie, glowing blue light sputters... flickers... shifts. Blue fades to gold.

One by one, the statues tremble, as if something inside of them is unraveling. Their movements stutter, become sluggish and unnatural... like marionettes with tangled strings. Their bodies shudder.

Then, slowly, they step back. Not collapsing. Not crumbling.

Obeying.

Their feet drag against the stone, heavy and stiff. Weapons are lowered. Wings are folded. Heads bow.

They return to their places. A warrior statue lands with a twitch onto its pedestal, settling like a bird returning to its nest. A stone knight eases onto a bench, his sword resting across his lap, his head dipping in a silent surrender. A dragon, who had been inches from tearing someone apart, folds its wings and claws, its burning eyes fading to black.

The magic inside them fizzles out like a candle flame.

They fall silent. They go still.

The battle is over.

✦ ✦ ✦ ✦ ✦ ✦ ✦

Weakness sweeps over me like a wave. My knees buckle, the world tilts sideways, and I don't have the strength to stop my fall. The golden glow in my vision flickers, dims. My body is too heavy, my lungs too small.

No more. The words crash in my mind like a war drum. I am not that girl anymore. I will not be helpless again.

Before my feet hit the ground, arms are there to catch me.

Warm. Firm. Balam.

His grip is strong, keeping me steady as I slump against him. His chest rises and falls rapidly beneath my weight, his heart pounding almost as hard as mine. His arms squeeze, bracing me as I try to right myself.

He's looking at me. His dark eyes are wide, his expression torn between shock and concern.

He saw. All of them saw.

"S-She just..." Airi breathes, her voice shaking.

Tama hisses sharply, rubbing a hand through his dust-covered hair. "That just happened."

Tristan is staring at me too, but his face is unreadable. His sword is still raised, his posture tense, like he's expecting the whole world to shift under his feet at any second. "...How?"

Nia, who always seems to have the answers, doesn't. Her golden eyes fade back to brown as she shakes her head slowly.

I barely hear them. My head swims. My chest aches, each breath burning as if I've been hollowed out. My vision blacks out at the edges, swallowing the plaza, the statues, the awestruck faces of my friends.

I feel like I'm falling again, even though Balam's arms are still wrapped around me.

Then... A sound. A laugh. It begins like a child's giggle... airy, light, playful. But it stretches. Warps. Becomes something else. Something cold.

It's everywhere and nowhere, sliding between cracks in the air. Slipping under my skin.

The laughter echoes. It curls around me, winding through the darkness closing in, sinking its claws into my mind.

Cold. Sharp. Mocking.

Chapter 36:
Game Over?

There's a sort of silence I love. It's not quiet. It's not calm. This silence is the pause between breaths right before something breaks. The silence that hums in your bones and murmurs in your ear: oh no, something is so wrong.

And there they are. Down there. Six weary little warriors with their shoulders slumped like a row of dominoes someone forgot to topple. Dust motes hanging in the air. Magic sucked dry. Confidence frayed.

They're spent. This is the end, they think. This is it, they sigh. Oh, sweetheart. We're only now entering Act 3.

I've been waiting all day for this. Pulling levers. Moving props. Setting moods. You don't accidentally schedule a final showdown at midnight. That's production design, darling.

It's my time to shine now. But come on... YOU think I'm storming the stage like this at random? Please. The pre-show looks? Wardrobe warm-up. Hoodies. Tourist outfit. Dismissable extras. THIS? THIS is the costume.

Porcelain skin. Skin-tight black bodysuit with enough spandex to deflect shame missiles. Neon-blue seams pulsing like fiber-optic wickedness.

Hair: silver satin. Eyes: polished chrome in the depths of your nightmares that you secretly love.

Oh, and yes... the shape of me? Oh, I am going FULL dark hero goddess costume fantasy. Think Barbie goes pop star once too many" meets "keep this book out of the school library."

My chest... fuller, my rear... more shapely. My legs... long, and the drama unfolded intensely around me.

And because this is a nighttime performance... paint to match. Winged liner thick enough to pierce a plot line. Glitter shadow in shades of bad choices. Lashes that sweep like theater curtains. Lips: poison red.

Honestly? I wish this book had art. Or even a movie. Animated, I bet. But a movie. Throw a dart... 2D or 3D? Either way, I kill it.

Snap. The air shimmers. The fountain spasms. The world is kind enough to just get out of my way.

One second I am nothing. Next second I am all.

Waiting. Like a star at the center of the stage. Legs crossed. Back curved. Smile already cocked like a weapon.

I stand. Slowly. Exquisitely. Like gravity has plans with me later.

"Well, well..." I breathe it out, letting the delicious tension settle around us like a thick fog. "Would you look at that. You're still standing." I raise one dark eyebrow.

"Color me impressed. And believe me... I don't compliment just any gaggle of half-dead adolescents."

No response from the peanut gallery. Good. Let the suspense rise.

"I wasn't sure you'd make it past the statue round," I continue, descending from my tiny throne. "But look at you now... bruised and battered and just broken enough for what's to come."

I start walking. Slowly. Indulgently. Lifting my glowing seams in a way that throws little shadows across the shattered stone. I'm practically daubing the scene with every step.

"How about a little stroll down memory lane, hmm?" I cock one gloved hand, ticking off fingers like I'm the narrator for the movie trailer version of this.

"Draugr at the museum? Moi. Gnomes at the festival? Yours truly. That cute little troll that almost squashed amidst all the machinery?" I purr, and they flinch. "Moi, also. And then there were the statues." I flash a smile that should not be as wide as it is. "Well, let's just say I was extra naughty with those."

I pause center stage. A sunbeam cuts across me like a spotlight. And yes, I pose. "I've been watching you all week."

I pause again. Because if you were me you'd pause here. "Every hushed conversation. Every sideways glance. Every chance encounter... I watched it all. Watched every clumsy, tension filled team building exercise you bumbled through in an earnest attempt at "character development."

Now I lower my voice. Let it wrap around them like velvety elastic. Tight. Pulling. "You thought this was a book about saving the world? Heroes and legend-beyond-belief? Power-ups and ancient prophecy?"

I scoff. "Nope. This is a stress test. And guess what, kiddos?" I grin, wide and wicked. "You're cracking."

✦ ✦ ✦ ✦ ✦ ✦ ✦

We begin with the obvious. I make my move on Aiyana. She's kneeling. Chin up. Eyes all big and round. So doe-y, so doll-like. Helpless princess, meets poetry major, type of thing.

"You." I say, drawling on the syllable. "The silent, pretty one. Stoic. Poised. Impervious."

I trace my eyes down my body, then up again... precise and predatory. "You don't even get red in the face?" I ask, mock insulted. "Don't shoot panicked looks all over the place? Don't even toss me a cute little 'wow, you look hot'?" I wave down at myself. "This wasn't easy, sugar."

But still nothing. She's so blank. Expressionless, if her eyes could even be said to be open, she'd be all dark with nothing inside. And, oh, how that rankles. "You were a lot more fun before... when you were shrieking."

Just then, there's a... something. A flicker. Quick. Definitely not fear. Not outrage. Something a little closer to humiliation.

"I liked you better when you were yelling." I say, stepping closer to her, grinning wide and wide. "Oh, by the way, that was my moment. The griffin? The timing? The smashing of the window? All of it? Poetic, right? Perfectly so. When everything is getting safe, yoink!... damsel to the window."

Aiyana releases a little huff of air through her nose. As if she's restraining herself from saying something.

I walk around her, now, voice dropping low and saccharine. "You didn't put up a fight. No no, not at all. Didn't resist. Didn't scream. Just sort of let it happen. As if you knew that your role was not to resist, but to be kidnapped so the real heroes could swoop in and save you."

Her jaw twitches. Right there. That one lands.

"And now look at you. Pale as milk. Shaking like a leaf. Barely able to stand after blowing vague cosmic orders at things we all couldn't even see." I cock my head. "That's your gig, isn't it? The glowing. The screaming. Hearing things. And then crumbling in someone else's arms?"

Nothing. But now her hands are fists at her sides. Lips pinched into a straight line.

"Oh, c'mon, don't get mad." I coo. "You're perfect in your role. Every crew needs a little dainty princess. Helpless kitten with a cute jawline."

She inhales. Sharp. Deep. But not fast. Not panicked. I see it. The split-second rush of heat and self-doubt behind her eyes. The way her balance shifts... subtly. Like I hit a nerve and her body knows before her mind can react.

I move in close, whispering level. "They say the quiet ones are the most dangerous. But I? I think they're just the ones who snap the prettiest."

I back away, deliberately, pleased with myself. Not a twitch. But she's got flames in her. Trust me, I can feel them. I can feel their heat in the air between us. That is what I came here for.

✦ ✦ ✦ ✦ ✦ ✦ ✦

"Balam," I purr, cooing like I shouldn't know his name. He's wound tight already. Stands there right behind Aiyana, as if his whole purpose in this narrative is to protect her. His face is a mask of stone... except for the heat in his eyes. That's not stone. That's flint. Awaiting a spark.

"Oh, there you are," I murmur, circling. "Still orbiting your little sun. Spinning around her like a loyal little moon with abs and a weapon."

I stop in front of him, lean in just a touch. Just close enough to be uncomfortable.

"You know, I always forget how chatty you are," I say. "All that fast-talking and over-explaining. So eager to throw in your opinion when no one's asking." I tilt my head. "It's cute. A little exhausting. But cute."

He scowls, and the blush is working its way under his ears.

"Wait..." I raise a finger, mock-surprised. "Do you have a speaking part in this scene?"

He opens his mouth... I immediately shush him, one finger raised, right between us. "Nope. Still not your line." He makes a noise halfway between a growl and a breathy curse word. And there it is... the confusion. The tension. The red creeping up his neck. Oh, this is delicious.

"You're fast, Balam," I say. "You're sharp. Good instincts. You're always in motion. Always in control."

I step in close, so only he can hear. "But around her?"

I glance... barely... in Aiyana's direction. "You're never still... because you don't know how to be. You don't know what to do with those feelings, so you hide behind the fight. The job. The mission." I lower my voice. "She didn't ask you to be her savior, you know. That was your fantasy."

He stiffens. "But it's okay," I add, suddenly sweet and loud enough for all of them to hear. "You're not really here to be understood. You're here to look good with your shirt half-torn while everyone else handles the important stuff."

He bristles. Shakes his head. Tries to form words. Can't.

And I grin. "See, I was going to do a whole speech about you. Really." I shrug, stepping back. "But honestly? You're not even the main event. You're just... the intermission."

I twirl a finger, dismissive. "Exit stage left, hot stuff."

And I move on... leaving him blushing, furious, humiliated, and so mad at himself for reacting to me at all.

✦ ✦ ✦ ✦ ✦ ✦ ✦

Tama steps into his stance like he's got the whole plaza framed in his arms. Fists balled. Jaw tight. "Why are you doing this?" he challenges. "Why mess with us? This isn't a game... people could've died! You think this is some kind of story?"

Oh, honey. I turn to him, smile bright. "Tama, Tama, Tama..."

I saunter closer, hips swinging like punctuation marks. "Of course it's a story. Just not the one you thought you were in."

He glares, but I can already see the gears grinding behind his big, brave eyes.

"You still don't believe in all this, do you?" I ask. "The gods, the magic, the ancient destiny stuff... still hoping it's all a bad dream or some prank show you didn't sign a release form for."

His jaw clenches. "E hika mā!"

"You don't want it to be real," I say, circling him now, letting my seams glow brighter, painting his doubt. "Because if it's real, that means you're stuck. That this matters. That you're in it. And you're not ready for that."

He glares at me, defiant. I grin.

"And let's talk about your role in this little epic," I continue. "The muscle. The hype man. The sidekick. Little John to Tristan's emotionally constipated Robin Hood."

I flick my eyes toward the golden boy and back again. "You keep telling yourself you're fine with it. That it's fun. That you're just happy to be here."

Then I lean closer, voice dropping to a stage whisper. "But we both know you hate it."

Tama opens his mouth... And I cut him off, bright and breezy. "And let's not forget your favorite coping mechanism: flirt with anything that smiles."

Glancing down at myself. "And now? You've been staring at me since I showed up like I'm a comic book goddess"

His face flames. "Oh, don't look so embarrassed," I purr. "You've got taste."

I lean in, eyes wide and mock-sincere. "You do think I'm a goddess, don't you?"

He stammers. I smirk. "I mean... sometimes." I wink. "Shapeshifter perks."

Then I turn my head ever so slightly and break into a stage-whisper. "Now, I know some of you out there like this one," I say, gesturing at Tama without looking. "He's charming. Got that messy 'forgot my homework but still passed the test' energy. He means well."

I sigh. "But come on. Really? He flirts like a golden retriever chasing sparkles and panics when it works."

A beat. I smirk. "Is he actually important? Or just here to lift heavy things and fill out the group photos?"

I glance back at Tama. "Just a little commentary for the audience. Don't worry about it."

"But here's the thing, darling." My voice softens into something almost kind. Which, of course, makes it worse. "For all your strength... you still don't know who you are in this story."

I step closer. Slower. Voice curling. "You don't know if you're the hero, the comic relief, or just the big guy who gets one epic slow-motion scene before stepping aside so the glowing ones can take the lead."

That one lands. Right in his chest.

"You want to matter. But you don't believe you do. So you hide it. Behind the jokes. The flirting. The muscles.

You play the sidekick... because at least the sidekick has a spot on the poster."

I pause. Let that settle. Then smile. "But hey," I add brightly. "You've got options."

He blinks, confused. "You could always quit this whole hero thing. Go back to your real life. Do something safe."

I tap my chin. "Like acting."

He freezes.

Ohhh, that look... like I just read a diary entry he didn't know was visible.

"You've thought about it," I say, circling him again. "Pretending to be a hero on TV instead of actually being one. Smile for the camera, say some lines, maybe get kissy-kissy with a cute little makeup artist during lunch breaks."

His mouth opens, then slams shut. The blush is volcanic.

"Oh. Ohhhh." I beam. "That's the dream, isn't it? You're not here to save the world. You're just... workshopping a character."

He takes half a step back. I don't let him breathe.

"Don't worry, love. You're cute enough to pull it off." I wink. "And if you need a reference for your next audition..."

I gesture at the plaza. "Just tell them you survived one whole boss fight before quitting to chase Hollywood life."

I blow him a kiss and turn away. "Break a leg, sweetheart. Maybe two."

✦ ✦ ✦ ✦ ✦ ✦ ✦

"Tristan. Nia." I click my tongue. "Mommy and Daddy of the group."

I turn to Tristan first, tilting my head. "Still roleplaying as a leader, huh?"

I stroll up, real close, lift his chin with one finger. "Chin up, golden boy. Posture is everything."

His eyes flick downward. I raise a brow. "My eyes are up here." I toss a handkerchief at his chest. "Clean up your drool."

He catches it. Barely.

"Let's be honest," I sigh, dramatically. "You're not a leader, Tristan. You're a placeholder. You're just doing what Mommy and Daddy expect of their perfect little legacy. Say the lines, wear the suit, wave to the crowd..."

I lean in, whisper-soft: "But deep down, you know, don't you? You're not guiding anyone. You're playing dress-up... just like every cursed knight in your bloodline."

His face stills.

"Oh, did they never tell you about the Beast?" I grin. "The endless chase. The family gift. The legacy of failure wrapped up in gold trim and noble lies."

I step back and mock-bow. "Sir Pellinore would be so proud. Or maybe just exhausted."

I spin and land on Nia, smile already sharpened. "And you, glowy girl."

I circle her like a spark about to catch fire. "Always proper. Always precise. Always doing what everyone expects. Life color-coded and future-proofed."

She lifts her chin... defiant. Brave. Predictable. "College. Career. Honors. Titles," I purr. "The good daughter. The bright scholar. The polite little prophet."

I lean close, lowering my voice. "All while the Professor puppeteered your every move. Funny, how she never told you the whole truth, isn't it?"

There's a flicker in her expression... doubt, just for a moment.

"Planted you like a flag in Berlin and called it guidance." I pause, then whisper: "And my Queen noticed, you know. She felt your thoughts brushing hers. Poking where they don't belong. I wouldn't keep doing that, little light. She doesn't like being touched."

Nia swallows. Barely.

"She's watching too, you know. She thinks you're funny when you panic."

I glance... just briefly... toward Airi. "And let's not pretend you're as composed as you act."

Nia's face flushes.

"A little spark of something there?" I tease, voice sugar-sweet. "Or are you still pretending you don't know what you want?" I grin. "Blind to your own feelings... and missing what's right in front of you."

I tap her forehead with a single glowing finger. "You see everyone's future but your own. Isn't that tragic?"

Stepping back, shake my head. "You're so much alike, it's tragic. So afraid of being wrong, you've forgotten how to be real." I wave them both off with a flick of my hand. "If you survive this, do me a favor... go find something that'll actually make you interesting."

✦ ✦ ✦ ✦ ✦ ✦ ✦

"W-wait!" Airi squeaks. Her voice cracks like a dropped plate. "N-Nia's not boring! None of us are! W-we're... we're heroes!"

I freeze in my steps. Turn slowly to face her. And smile like she just offered me dessert.

"Oh, Cotton Candy," I say sweetly. "There you go again. Always jumping in to defend people who forget you're even in the room."

She flinches. Blinks fast. "Th-that's not true!" she stammers. Her cheeks flush deep pink. "They... they like me! I... I help, I fight, I'm not... I'm not just some... "

I raise one hand gently... shushing her with a single finger... then turn away from her entirely.

"Oh, dear reader," I say. Voice brightening with mischief.

I begin to pace, slowly, deliberately. "Here she is. The fan favorite. The sparkly one. The chaos gremlin. The cute disaster in oversized sleeves."

Airi freezes. "Wh-who are you talking to?!" she squeaks. "There's... there's no one there!"

"She shoots lasers," I continue cheerfully. "She talks too much. She stumbles, fumbles, explodes, then smiles like nothing happened."

I glance sideways, stage-whispering now. "Admit it. You love her."

Airi's face is pure confusion. And offense. "I... I don't understand! Are you... are you just ignoring me?!"

I stop mid-pose. Tilt my head dramatically. "Oh, I'm talking about you, Cotton Candy. You're just... not really the main character of the moment."

Her mouth falls open. "I'm...? I'm not... what?!"

"You're a glittery little firecracker in a cast full of moody drama bombs." I circle her now, letting my glowing lines cast ripples across her stunned face. "Comic relief. The energy drink in human form. A cartoon action character dropped into a real-world tragedy."

"I'm not a joke!" she blurts. "I... I'm not just a-a-a sidekick or something! I try... I'm... I do everything I can!"

I lean in, eyes glittering. "And I've loved watching you try."

"We all have." gesturing behind me.

Her breath hitches. She's blinking faster now, like she can't decide if she's angry, heartbroken, or just deeply confused.

I lean closer, voice soft and razor-sharp. "But come on... do you really think they take you seriously?"

I glance at the others... all watching in stunned silence. "Or you're the one they keep close... not because they trust you... but because they're afraid of what'll happen if they don't."

She shakes her head hard. "No... no, I'm... I'm trying! I'm part of this... I belong here!"

I step back, letting her flounder in the silence she can't fill.

"You are," I whisper. "You're bright, unpredictable, and so much fun to watch."

I flash a grin. "You've always been my favorite little player."

She stands frozen, visibly shaking. "Wh... what happens now?" she manages to ask, voice cracking halfway through.

I sigh and stretch, dusting off my shoulders like the scene's over. "Well," I say breezily, "that was the cutscene."

"W-wait... wh-what?!" she stammers. "W-what cutscene?!"

Smiling wide. "You know. That quiet moment before the big fight. The save point. The room with the health packs and the suspiciously generous loot drop."

She stares at me, breath caught in her throat.

"This is the part where the music fades," I whisper. "Where you check your inventory... and wonder if you're ready."

Her voice is barely audible. "Is... is this the final boss?"

I let out the most delighted gasp. "Ohhh. Yes. YES. I love that." I twirl once, basking in the moment. "Final level. Final fight. Final fun."

I lock eyes with her one last time. "You've been such a treat, Cotton Candy. Really."

Snap. The air warps. Light bends. My form flickers...
once, twice... And then I'm gone.

But my laugh? That lingers. Bright. Mocking.
Weightless. Unforgettable. Like static in the air right
before everything falls apart.

And it doesn't stop. Not for a long time. You know, for
the drama... too much?

Chapter 37:
Not-Dead Celebration

The plaza is too quiet. Not peaceful-quiet... the bad kind, like when the laughter cuts off after someone says something that hits too close. Dust hangs in the air, glowing in the stuttering lamplight, throwing monstrous shadows across the busted statues that were trying to squash us like bugs twenty minutes ago.

Everything aches. My ribs, my shoulders, even my teeth from clenching them. But worse than that is Puck's voice still echoing in my skull, oily and smug. I hate how it sticks.

I stretch until something pops in my back and force out a groan, louder than necessary. "So, that sucked."

"Catastrophically," Tristan mutters, still white-knuckling the sword like the statues might hop back together.

Good. At least he answers.

Airi is sprawled across a broken bench like she owns the ruins, cracking open a soda she "rescued" from a shattered stand. "Could've been worse. We could've died."

"Not-dead," I say, dropping onto a slab of stone like it's a beanbag chair. Chips jab into my back, but I lean into it. "Not-dead is my new favorite status."

Nia shoots Airi a look. Aiyana just breathes, slow and shaky, like every inhale is a struggle.

And me? I keep talking. Because if I stop, I'll remember Puck peeling back my secrets in front of everyone. My dream. Acting. The one thing I wanted for myself, and dangled it like a punchline. She laughed, and it still burns. So no... I'm not giving her the silence too.

Airi waves her soda like she's making a toast. "We walked away from a magical death match. Which is... kind of impressive?"

Nia folds her arms. "That's your take-away?"

Airi flushes. "Anyway! Puck is super weird. Like... world-champion weird."

I groan and wave a hand. "Seriously... what even are they? Him? Her? Whatever? My brain's too fried for pronouns."

Aiyana starts ticking off fingers. "We've seen Puck as a little girl, a teenage boy, a businessman"... she shoots Tristan a look... "a professor, a tourist, a scary woman in heels, and now a supermodel. That's at least seven forms."

"Pick a look already," I mutter.

I grin suddenly. "Chaos Gremlin."

"Too playful," Nia says, deadpan.

"Existential Nuisance?" Aiyana suggests.

I snap my fingers and point at her like she's cracked the code. "Perfect. Foreboding, accurate, rolls right off the tongue."

We almost laugh. Almost. But then Airi kicks at rubble and mutters, "Do you think she was right?"

"Puck," Airi says, voice small. "About me. Being too much. Not enough. Always the one who screws it up."

For once, she's not the loudest or flashiest in the group. She's just a kid asking if we secretly hate her.

"No," Nia says instantly, solid as bedrock.

Airi shrugs like she hadn't expected an answer. But she goes quiet, and the silence that follows has edges.

Balam clears his throat. "There's no way we're fighting again tonight... right?"

Groans of agreement ripple through us.

"Yeah," I hear Tristan mutter. "Let's not kid ourselves. This isn't a break. Just a pause."

I throw my arms wide. "And that means I'm officially declaring this Not-Dead Celebration before the next horror show begins. We need snacks."

Airi raises her soda. "To later!"

Nia is still focused on Aiyana, steadying her. Aiyana's face is pale, her hands trembling.

"I... I don't know how I stopped them," Aiyana whispers.

"You trusted your instincts," Nia says softly, keeping her grounded. "And they didn't lead you astray."

Aiyana shakes her head. "It didn't feel like instinct. It was... emotional. I don't know if I could do it again."

"You don't have to figure it out now," Nia assures her. "You kept us alive. That's enough."

Airi rummages in her bag and dumps out an impossible mountain of candy. "Oh! Snacks achieved!"

Aiyana arches an eyebrow.

"They were abandoned," Airi says defensively, pressing a chocolate bar and soda into Aiyana's hands. "Post-mystical-statue-fight recovery kit."

Aiyana gives her a faint smile. "Thanks."

I whistle low. "That's a serious stash. Running a black-market candy ring on the side?"

Airi hugs the bag closer. "Hey, a girl's gotta be prepared."

She's still clutching it when Nia plucks a gummy, then Balam grabs a bar, then I swipe a handful of gummies myself.

Airi gasps, cheeks puffing. "Don't clean me out!"

I unwrap a chocolate with mock gravity. "Relax. You'll live."

"You're the worst," she huffs, but there's no real heat.

"Deliciously the worst." I stuff a bite in my mouth, exaggeratedly.

Even Aiyana chuckles. That sound... fragile but real, loosens something tight in my chest.

"Alright, but seriously," I say, "Aiyana, you need something better than scavenged candy?"

She shakes her head. "This helps. Really."

"Okay." I grin, masking the worry under my ribs. "Offer stands though. Tama Snack Delivery Service, open twenty-four hours."

Balam shifts on her other side, too neutral, eyes flicking between us. Just for a second his shoulders go tight. What is he sensing?

✦ ✦ ✦ ✦ ✦ ✦ ✦

I clap my hands, chasing the moment. "Anyway! Survival equals team status. That means we need a name."

Airi lights up instantly. "Yes! The Magic Six!"

"Sounds like a card trick," Balam deadpans. "The Legendary Guardians?"

"Ew, no," Nia mutters.

"The Statue Smashers," I say proudly.

"Absolutely not," Nia and Tristan say together.

Aiyana chuckles, faint but real. "Please, no statue names."

"Fine. Mystic Misfits?" throwing out another.

Balam tilts his head. "That's a bad punk band name."

Airi gasps. "Wait, we could be a band!"

I strum an invisible guitar. "Already the air-guitar legend, thank you very much."

Nia crosses her arms. "Which means you have no musical talent."

"Not even a little," I say with pride.

"I played piano for a few years," Tristan says with a laugh.

"Cello," Nia adds.

"Ha! Classy ones confirmed. Every band needs one. And we've got two." I grin.

Airi jabs a thumb at herself. "And I'm the lead singer."

I snort. "Nah, you're the mascot."

Her gasp could wake the statues. "Take it back!"

Balam smirks. "He's not wrong."

Aiyana, faint but smiling: "You did steal all your candy from the battlefield."

"It was a rescue mission!" Airi throws her hands up. "The snacks were homeless!"

"Definitely mascot behavior," I say, ducking her half-hearted swing.

The laughter that follows isn't loud, but it's warm. The kind that pushes the darkness back a little.

I lean into it, even as the ache in my chest stays. We're exhausted. Scared. Still bleeding in places we haven't checked yet. But the fact that we can still laugh... still feel like something close to normal kids... means we haven't lost ourselves.

And maybe... just maybe, we really are a team.

Chapter 38:
Take Me To Your Leader

Tristan ✦ Late Evening (April 26) ✦ Plaza Ruins

There is one thing we do need to discuss.

I take a breath, steadying myself before I go there. "We need a leader."

The conversation stops dead.

A second ago, we were laughing, throwing out absurd ideas about team names and uniforms. But now, the air shifts. The others turn to look at me, and I realize... too late... that I just handed them an opening I didn't intend to.

"We already have one," Tama says without missing a beat, shrugging. "You."

I blink. "...What?"

Airi tilts her head. "Wait. Did I miss something? When did this happen?"

Nia crosses her arms. "You're the one who's been keeping us together, Tristan."

I shake my head, a spike of panic flickering through me. "No. I was thinking you should lead."

Nia doesn't even hesitate. She shakes her head firmly. "A Seer is a guide, not a leader. Besides, we already chose."

Something in my stomach twists. "Choose?" My voice comes out more strained than I'd like. "When did we choose?"

Tama smirks. "Oh, it was an unspoken vote. We figured you'd catch on eventually."

I stare at them, the weight of their expectations hitting me like a punch. They actually believe this. They think I'm their leader?

No. No, that's wrong. That can't be right. "I don't know if... "

"You kept us moving," Balam says, voice even. Not pushing, just stating.

"You made sure we didn't lose focus," Aiyana adds, watching me carefully.

"You think things through," Nia says. "Even when the rest of us act first."

"You make decisions when no one else will," Tama points out.

I open my mouth to argue, but I don't have a response to that. Because... they aren't wrong. But that doesn't mean I'm the right person for it.

"That's just... I was just trying to keep us from getting killed," I protest. "That's not the same as leading."

Balam tilts his head slightly. "What do you think leading is?"

I hesitate, clenching my jaw. I don't have an answer.

Airi leans in, tapping her chin. "Okay, but if this isn't official, I really think we should've done a proper vote. Or, like, a trial by combat. Maybe a scavenger hunt?"

Tama snorts. "If it's a scavenger hunt, you'd win by cheating."

"I would not cheat," Airi says, scandalized. Then she pauses. "...Okay, I'd probably cheat. But I'd be really charming about it."

"You just agreed with the rest of us, so technically, you did vote," Nia says, amused.

Airi huffs. "I hate how you guys keep tricking me into agreeing with things."

I barely hear them. My mind is still spinning. This is wrong. I was just trying to help. Trying to do what made sense in the moment. That's not leadership. That's survival.

But... when I look at them, I see no hesitation. They've already made this decision.

At some point, without me even realizing it, I stopped being just another person trying to get through this alive. I became the person they were looking to.

I run a hand through my hair, exhaling slowly. The weight of it... of all of it... settles onto my shoulders. "...I still don't think I'm the right choice," I admit. "But I guess that doesn't matter, does it?"

Nia shakes her head. "No, it doesn't."

I glance around at them one last time, searching for some sign that this is a mistake. That someone else will step in. No one does.

I straighten my posture. The words feel heavy, but I say them anyway. "Alright," I murmur. Then, stronger... more certain, even if I don't quite believe it yet... "Then let's start acting like a real team."

✦ ✦ ✦ ✦ ✦ ✦ ✦

The earth shakes. A slow shifting, deliberate and inexorable like a great beast rolling out of sleep from below. Dust flies from the shattered bodies of the statues, through the thick, choking air. The sharp, disturbed scent of earth and rock rises as if the ground itself knows to expect the terrible thing. A presence builds in the air... big, wrong. Crushing at my chest, stealing my breath.

But I do not see it yet.

Then Nia goes rigid. Her eyes flash gold. Aiyana's do, too.

I can't breathe.

"I sense a great concentration of energy," Nia says. Her voice is far away, detached, as if she's not there at all. Her eyes harden, focused and distant, as if she's looking past this world and through to something we cannot see.

But Aiyana isn't seeing it. She is hearing it. Feeling it. Her expression is twisted, her fingers fluttering, as if something unseen is stroking past... reaching. Her shoulders rise at a sharp inhale but she does not exhale for a long moment.

"I sense an old thing," she whispers, her voice strained, ragged. "Angry."

The ground trembles again, more urgently, warning.

"I do not sense anyone directing it," Aiyana says, but her eyebrows furrow in thought. "Not directly. But..." She falters. "There is more than one mind... in contact with, but not..."

Nia's golden eyes dart, sweeping the unseen energy in the air. She frowns. "I do not see Puck's touch on it," she says. "No force shaping it. No puppeteer directing it."

The stone under our feet fractures in a shuddering crack.

Airi's hand tightens on my sleeve. "I... I think this is worse than a bunch of statues."

Tama sighs, shrugging at his shoulders, trying to sound casual. But his fingers clench at his sides, already at the ready to strike.

Balam is eerily still, watching Aiyana. "Aiyana," he says cautiously. There is something in his tone... cutting, urgent... but she does not acknowledge him.

Nia's lips move now, silent words as she works to understand the shape of the energy she is seeing.

But Aiyana isn't seeing it. She is hearing it.

Her fingers curl around Nia's arm, as if she is trying to hold herself in the moment, as if whatever she is hearing is trying to drag her down.

A breath, finally, a whisper of fear.

"Hydra."

Chapter 39:
Who am I?

It explodes.

For one second, it's still a mostly intact fountain; broken and missing most of its statues but otherwise standing proudly. Then the next, it isn't. Stone and water and plumbing explode into the air. Rain down like the very sky is crumbling on our heads. I raise an arm and duck under as the rubble hits the ground around me.

Then I see it.

It rises from the fountain's destruction, larger than I could ever have imagined anything being... at least six stories tall, no exaggeration. Muscle twitches beneath slick, scaled skin. Three titanic heads rise up on thick, powerful necks; each with an eye that glows like a searchlight: red, and blue, and green.

They don't hesitate. They don't roar or posture or wait.

They breathe out.

The gas hits like a wave of rot and ash. My stomach flips, part of me wants to cry, part to run. I settle on gagging and coughing as the sickly green-gray fog rolls over us. It stings my eyes, burns my throat, sinks into my skin like it wants to stay. I stumble back, vision swimming. The others are yelling... Tristan curses, Tama shouts something I can't make out.

My power flares, golden and hot. I feel it in my chest first, then my fingertips, then my eyes as they start to glow. I reach out with it... searching for a thread, a spark, a twist of thought that might tell me what this thing wants.

But there's nothing. No spell. No control. Just rage. The creature isn't bound. It isn't being used. It's loose. And it's angry.

Worse; it's hungry.

Each of the three heads moves independently of the others, snapping and twisting in different directions. One locks on to Balam. Another swings to the left, its full focus on Airi. The third lunges forward toward Tristan. They don't fight like one creature... they fight like three minds sharing a single monstrous body.

Fast. Focused. Terrifyingly aware.

And they all want the same thing. Us.

"It's not controlled," I cough, voice raw and rough from the gas. "It wants this. It wants to hunt."

And we're the prey.

"OI!" Tama's Kiwi bark slices through the chaos... sharp, raw, urgent. "Any ideas, Fearless Leader?!"

Tristan doesn't miss a beat.

"Stay together! Don't let it separate us!" he barks, voice cutting clean through the rising panic in my chest. Even with everything falling apart, he sounds like he belongs here... like this is what he was made for.

He points sharply, already dividing us.

"Tama and I; head-on attack;

Balam, Aiyana; keep it distracted;

Airi; blast it."

Simple orders. But nothing about this is simple.

I can barely see through the shifting fog of that toxic gas... green-gray and clinging to everything like oily mist. It burns going in, thick like smoke but heavier. My eyes are watering, my throat on fire. We're all coughing, ducking, scrambling to stay clear of the worst of it. And it's everywhere. It seeps in the cracks between movements, swirls beneath our feet. Even the wind can't carry it away fast enough.

The hydra lunges. Three heads, three directions... one snapping forward toward Tristan, another swinging low at Airi, the third arching like a whip toward Balam and me.

I shove Balam sideways and dive in the opposite direction, rolling hard. The tail smashes behind me with a thunderous crack that shakes the pavement. My ribs ache but I force myself to my feet, blinking through the blur of gas and grit.

Tama... somehow still grinning despite the fact we're one breath away from death... yells over his shoulder, "Just don't level half of Berlin while you're at it!"

Airi growls, puffing her cheeks like a balloon about to burst. "ONE TIME! I lose control one time and suddenly I'm a city-leveling threat!"

Balam snorts beside me, crouched down and watching the heads slither through the air. "To be fair... you did take out like twenty statues and half a building."

Airi throws up her hands. "Okay, the building was collateral damage. Let it go!"

The banter helps. Just a little. But it doesn't last.

The hydra lunges again... its movements terrifyingly fast for something so massive. One head moves as bait, while another snaps from the side. Tristan barely blocks in time with a length of pipe he must've grabbed from the rubble. Metal clangs, bending under the impact.

He ignores the back-and-forth, his focus laser-sharp. His gaze lands on Nia.

"Nia... you're our eyes. Keep us moving."

Nia's jaw tightens. Her eyes glow softly... her power flaring as she sees what we don't. She nods. "It's watching how we move. We can't be predictable. Shift positions often... don't let it anticipate us. And don't stay in one place too long... the gas is getting worse!"

She's right. I can feel it. Even with my golden energy crackling just under my skin, it's not enough to keep the burning out of my lungs. I'm starting to feel dizzy. Slower.

Tama coughs hard behind me, waving a hand like he can swat the air clean. "Ugh, yeah. Definitely don't wanna be breathing that in for long."

Balam's crouches down beside a crumbled statue, rubbing his eyes and squinting through the fog. "My lungs already hate me. Let's make this quick."

But nothing about this fight says quick.

Every time we move, it adjusts. Every time we dodge, it tracks. It's not just strong... it's smart. And it's not going to let us go.

Three minds. One monstrous will.

We have to be better than that.

We have to be one.

We move. Not perfectly. Not cleanly. Not like warriors in some battle-hardened movie scene. But we move.

Tama and Tristan charge first... Tristan leading the way, face tight with focus, and Tama right behind him, moving like a human freight train. They don't have weapons that should work against something this size, but they go anyway. Because we don't have time for perfect. We have now.

"Nia... what now?!" I yell, barely dodging a tail swipe that craters the ground where I'd just been.

Her voice cuts through the choking fog, fierce and clear. "Tama, Tristan... GO!" she shouts from somewhere behind me. "Balam, Aiyana... KEEP THE HEADS BUSY!"

I don't hesitate. I push forward into the haze, golden light flickering off my skin. One of the hydra's heads swings low, jaws snapping inches from Balam's back. He pivots sharply and jams a metal staff... no, a fence post... into the thing's nose.

The head reels back, just a little.

Balam grins, wild and thrilled. "I've always wanted to fight a dragon!"

My laugh comes out as a squeak; dragons are supposed to be stories. "It's a hydra," I laugh, coughing as I drag him away from the snapping teeth of another head.

"Eh, close enough!" he yells back.

The hydra bellows, all three throats roar in mismatched fury. The sound vibrates in my bones. I can feel it in my teeth.

Then Tama's voice, cracking through the madness: "Dude, you just bopped a hydra on the snoot!"

Somehow, we all laugh... short, breathless, but real.

The banter doesn't fix anything, but it keeps the fear from winning. At least for a second.

I swing out wide, trying to draw the green-eyed head's attention away from Airi, who's building up a glowing charge between her palms. "Airi... NOW would be a great time to level something on purpose!"

"I'm trying," she growls. "But this fog is killing my concentration!"

Another plume of gas swirls through, and I cough hard, dropping to one knee. My lungs are on fire. My eyes sting. I can barely see two feet in front of me.

I can feel Balam's hand on my arm a second later, dragging me back. "Don't stop. We stop, we die."

I nod. I know he's right. But gods... this thing.

This isn't like the statues. Or the draugr. This is something else. Bigger. Older. Wrong. This is a monster.

I don't know how the others are feeling... but I'm not just scared. I am terrified.

Not just because of what's in front of us. But because somehow, this is still the same day.

One day ago, I was a regular girl on a group trip. Now I'm glowing, gasping for breath, dodging the claws of a creature out of storybooks... and trying to pretend like I'm not coming apart at the seams.

How are we still standing? How are we not broken?

I brace myself and reach inward, past the ache in my lungs and the sting in my eyes, past the noise and the panic, into that warm center where my power lives. The golden light builds behind my ribs, rising like a tide, waiting.

This thing... this monster... won't stop unless I make it.

I reach out, not to its body but to its mind. Or minds. The moment I connect, I understand the difference.

It's nothing like the draugr. They were scared, confused, their thoughts clouded and begging for direction. And it's not like the statues, empty vessels being moved like pieces on a board.

This is raw, living will.

Three minds crash into mine the moment I touch them. They aren't whispering... they're roaring. Ancient, furious, and aware. There's no space for me, no crack to slide into, no weakness to exploit.

Every time I try to assert control, I'm thrown under again, like drowning in a storm of sound and hunger. Their thoughts are heavy, brutal. Their rage is sharpened by intelligence.

Still, I don't let go.

The light inside me flares brighter, burning through the fog. I draw on every shred of strength I have left and send the command like a blade slicing through the storm.

"STOOOOOOOOP!" Power lashes out, golden and blinding. For a heartbeat, I feel it land.

The red-eyed head shudders violently. Its pupils blow wide, muscles locking up mid-strike as if something inside it short-circuits.

I almost collapse with relief... until the other two heads turn. They aren't frozen. They aren't stopped.

They're angry. And their fury shifts instantly to Tristan.

He's already in motion, charging forward, sword raised. He doesn't see the shift, doesn't notice that the opening has collapsed.

My voice rips out of me. "Tristan...!"

He sidesteps the green-eyed head just in time... but the blue-eyed one lunges and sinks its teeth into his shoulder. His scream splits the air, high and raw.

Blood sprays across the broken ground. His sword hits the concrete with a metallic clatter as he stumbles back.

The hydra rears up, triumphant.

I tried. I fought for control. But it wasn't enough. These aren't broken monsters waiting for direction. They are predators. Ancient. Powerful. I can still feel their voices twisting around the edges of my thoughts, pressing in, mocking me for daring to challenge them.

The others rush forward, vanishing into the gas, shouting his name, charging toward the danger without hesitation.

But I don't move. Not right away.

My legs won't listen. My chest feels like it's caving in. My power is still there, burning like wildfire under my skin, but my will to use it flickers.

Tristan's scream echoes in my head.

And now he's bleeding because of me.

I drop to my knees, breath burning in my throat, the world spinning with gas and noise and fear. Tristan is bleeding. The hydra is still moving.

And I can't stop any of it. All I feel is that old, sickening heaviness curling in my stomach.

Helpless.

I know this feeling too well. It's the same one that's haunted me for years... creeping in through cracks I never asked for, twisting into the corners of my life.

It started the night someone stole something I didn't know could be stolen.

And after that, everything changed. The world wasn't safe anymore. My body didn't feel like mine. My voice didn't feel like it mattered. People said all the right things. Therapy. Support. Time. But no one could put me back together. Not really.

I smiled through it. Sat still through it. Numbed myself through it. I've pretended that I'm okay more times than I can count.

But I'm not. Not always.

And now here I am again, powerless in the face of something bigger and meaner and ancient and cruel. Something that doesn't care who I am. That wants to crush and devour and erase.

And deep down, some part of me is still that girl. Frozen. Quiet. Waiting for someone to save her. But no one's coming this time.

It's me. I'm here. I'm alive. And I refuse to let that old pain define me. I refuse to be the girl who disappears when things get dark. Because I wasn't alone then... not really.

My grandfather was there. He never asked me to be stronger than I was. He never told me to move on. He listened. He held space for my silence. And when I was ready, he reminded me of who I still was beneath the hurt.

"That pain is real," he told me. "But it's not all of you. You are sacred. You are whole. Even when you feel broken."

And when I couldn't find a way forward, he gave me one... through our values.

> Woohitika. Bravery.
> Wówačhaŋtognake. Compassion.
> Wóksape. Wisdom.

They weren't just ideas. They were roots. They were medicine. And they carried me through the worst parts of healing.

They carry me now.

My hands shake as I push myself off the ground, golden light trembling around my fingertips. The fear is still there. But it's not stronger than me.

If I can't stop the hydra, I'll move it.

If I can't win, I'll fight.

If I can't silence its voices, I'll scream louder.

"I'M OVER HERE!" I shout, throwing every bit of power into the command.

The red-eyed head jerks violently to the side, its neck spasming as it tries to reorient.

I sprint away from the others, lungs burning, vision blurry. "NO, HERE!" I yell again, waving my arms as I duck beneath a twisted pipe and veer hard to the right.

It roars, furious, confused... torn between instinct and the sudden shift in its prey.

It wants to go back to Tristan. I can feel it. But I keep yelling, keep pulling. I don't give it the chance.

I can't stop it entirely. But I can hold its attention.

Just long enough for...

Out of the corner of my eye, I catch movement.

Pale, hunched, blood smeared across his arm... Tristan grits his teeth and explodes to his feet. One hand grips the hilt of his sword, knuckles white but steady.

"T-Tristan, wait...!" Nia calls out, voice cutting through the fog, panicked. Tama's already outstretched, reaching for him, to steady him, to drag him back. "Bro, stop! You're hurt!"

But he's not hearing them. His eyes are on the opening I've torn, where the red-eyed head twitches, stunned and disoriented, drawn off by my voice. The others are still retreating, on pause, their guards coming up just a moment too slow, unbalanced by the shock.

Tristan acts. Swiftly. Quicker than any of us anticipated. His blade flashes through the viscous air, locks onto the weak spot at the base of the neck. And then...

Slice. The hydra's blue-eyed head rolls away, and the body convulses with animalistic violence. Its eyes roll once, then go black.

The head doesn't fall. It melts. A wet, gurgling sound fills the plaza as the severed chunk of flesh dissolves into a sludge the color of the gas... gray-green and glistening.

Silence. No one moves. The hydra stops thrashing. The plaza is silent. Even the fog seems to pause in place. All of us are caught, staring.

Then... "HA!!!!" Tama shouts, a maniacal laugh, fist flying triumphantly into the air. "Take that, spaghetti-lizard!" Airi is jumping up and down like a hyperactive bunny. "He did it! He did it! I knew we could…"

SCHLURK. A gross, wet sound like someone tearing into a mud pie pulls all of us out of our trances.

We spin around. The severed neck is bubbling. Gas is spewing out in thick jets. Flesh is writhing around the wound, pulsating and grotesquely ballooning.

And then… it splits. And two new heads erupt out of the stump… one a serene blue, the other an angry yellow. Both glaring. More angry.

Tristan reels back, breathing heavily, with a look of utter disbelief on his face.

Tama is just wide-eyed. "That's… that's not good."

Tristan's voice is flat. Empty. "You've… got to be kidding me."

The hydra lets out a roar… not from one mouth, but four. A sound so loud it makes my teeth rattle, the ground quake.

Then… It's coming at us. All four heads. At once.

Chapter 40:
Strategy, Anyone?

It lasts for three seconds. Three epic seconds.

There are now four. The new heads buzz in perfect, terrible unison... four mouths with acid-dripping fangs and no chill whatsoever.

Airi tilts her head to the side, already calculating in the moment like a living, breathing doomsday spreadsheet. "That's a 33.3% increase in mouths. Assuming proportional venom production, we're now at 33.3% increased toxic breath. Or 40% if they're agitated."

"Pretty sure they're agitated." Balam deadpans.

I stare at her blankly. "Why would you say that?"

"I thought it would motivate!"

"Airi, never tell me the odds!"

She beams at me. "Oh. Han Solo. Classic. He also ran, by the way."

"Exactly! So maybe... " The hydra bellows, and all four heads snap toward us in one grotesque motion.

"... RUN!" My heart thuds so loudly in my chest, I can't hear the roaring heads.

Tristan leads the way. Balam disappears into the trees like some kind of professional vanishing act. I'm right behind Airi, who is now laughing... laughing... as she runs.

She's shouting, and it's a terrible Jeff Goldblum impression. "Must go faster! Must go faster!"

"Not the time for Jurassic Park!" I gasp.

"We are running from a dinosaur... how is it not Jurassic Park time?"

I step away from the gas, glancing over at Tristan... still down from the earlier attack. He's pale, and hunched hard against a hunk of stone, that giant statue-sword of his half-buried in the dirt next to him. His shoulder is bleeding pretty badly.

I wedge myself in between him and the fight, fists tight, heart still racing. I've got no weapon, just me. But if any of those heads try to come this way, I'm gonna make sure they regret it.

I don't even notice Aiyana until she's already there, dropping to her knees next to Tristan like the earth itself pulled her straight in. Her hands hover over his wound, not quite touching. Just shaking.

"I... I should have stopped it," she whispers, voice breaking. "I wasn't strong enough."

Tristan grits his teeth, but shakes his head. "Aiyana, you distracted it. You gave me a chance."

"But you still got hurt," she says. Her voice is so quiet, I almost don't catch it. "I... "

"Aiyana," Tristan says, softer this time. "We're all getting hurt."

She goes still. For a second, her golden light stutters, a hairline crack where the strain shows. He takes a breath. "You've done more than you know. That first opening? I missed. I was careless. The second... I took the shot. It was just the wrong one."

She blinks. I don't think she's quite counting it as a win.

"Yeah," I add, stepping forward. "If it weren't for you and Balam keeping those heads off us, we'd all be lizard jerky by now."

Her eyes flick over to me, surprised. Not used to being seen in that way, I think. Not for what she brings to the fight.

Then she nods... once. And stands. Shoulders square. Eyes sharp. Without a word, she turns and runs straight back into the fray.

I watch her go. The girl's got steel in her spine.

✦ ✦ ✦ ✦ ✦ ✦ ✦

Tristan is still on the ground, pale and clutching his shoulder like he's trying to convince his arm to not fall off, when suddenly...

Airi gasps. Full dramatic gasp, hands to mouth, like she just realized she forgot to feed her robot dog back in Tokyo.

"WAIT... WAIT! I KNOW THIS!"

Everyone's looking at her. (Well, most of us. Balam's still actively ducking monster limbs like it's his job.) She's waving a hand. "This is TOTALLY classic hydra behavior! Cut off a head? Boom... two more! I can't believe it didn't click sooner!"

Balam, ducking low, groans, "You're figuring this out now?!"

"I was distracted, okay?! Tristan went all Jedi and I geeked out from coolness!"

Tristan, face-down in the dust, mutters, "It was kind of epic. For like three seconds."

"But the solution!" she continues, practically bouncing. "In the myths, and the movies, and that one video game... you stop the heads from growing back by burning the stumps!"

There's a moment of silence.

I cough through the ever-thickening poison fog. "So... who brought a flamethrower to the monster fight?"

Slowly, everyone turns to Airi. Balam points. "Laser girl."

Not a bad nickname actually.

She freezes. "Okay, yes, technically, I can shoot energy blasts, but have you SEEN my aim?! I've blown up five benches, a couple of food carts, half of a building, and a tree that was literally just vibing!"

"That tree didn't deserve what it got," Aiyana says calmly.

"I SAID I WAS SORRY," Airi wails.

"You said, 'whoops,' and then high-fived yourself," I point out.

"I was being brave in the face of my own failure!"

Before she can spiral further, Nia's voice comes in... steady and clear, but warm.

"Airi... it's too risky. Not with the heads moving like this. You've already done so much. Let's not take this chance unless we have to."

Airi blinks, just for a second, thrown off by the kindness in her tone. "Right. Yeah. No, that makes sense. Totally. Kakkoii"

Tristan, somehow hauling himself upright, eyes the monstrosity looming over us. "Then we adapt. We don't go for the heads anymore."

He nods to the now multiplying horror. "We aim for the body. The heads are too risky."

I grunt. "So basically... don't make it worse."

Tristan waves me off. "We hit fast, and we move. Don't stay in one place too long. The gas is spreading, and it's only getting worse."

I narrow my eyes. "Dude. You're in no shape to fight."

"I will survive," he says with a pained smile. "It's only a flesh wound."

Airi gasps again... happier this time. "Monty Python!"

Tristan gives her a wobbly thumbs up. "Finally. Someone gets me."

"You can barely stand, Tristan," Nia says gently, the worry now audible in her voice.

"I can lean dramatically if needed." Tristan grins.

Balam wipes sweat from his forehead. "So... hit and run? Keep it moving?"

Tristan nods. "Exactly. Nia, you've got the best eyes on this thing. Call it out. Track the heads. Tell us when to move and where to strike. If we keep it off-balance, we can wear it down."

Airi nods, more serious now. "Okay. No heads. No necks. Just body shots and rapid movement. Got it."

I crack my knuckles, feeling a grin sneak across my face. "Now that's a plan I can work with."

We spread out... moving constantly, no time to stop, no time to breathe. Just movement.

Nia calls out from the center of the battlefield, sharp and focused like a general playing 4D chess.

"Tama, left side... go now!"

I duck as a claw crashes down behind me, sending cobblestones flying. I grab a broken chunk of a lion statue... mane and all... and smash it into the Hydra's knee joint like I'm trying to break up a giant reptilian bar fight.

The hydra staggers, hissing and shrieking like it just stubbed all twelve of its collective toes.

Nia doesn't miss a beat. "Balam, two heads tracking you! Eyes on you... now!"

Balam dives, tucking into a roll just as twin jaws snap down like a Venus flytrap from hell. He springs onto a crumbled column, kicks off, flips over the hydra's writhing spine... and lands with ballerina precision right behind it.

Then he whacks one of the heads in the face with his staff. The hydra sneezes. SNEEZES. The stench hits like rotten eggs on steroids.

"That is still WEIRDLY effective!" I yell. Balam grins mid-spin. "I'm full of surprises."

"Red one always lunges first... watch it!" Nia calls, tracking every movement like she has cheat codes.

The red head snarls and darts... right where Tristan was standing. He's already sliding under its line of sight and lunging forward, sword raised. He drives the massive blade into the exposed underbelly, then rolls away as the creature rears up and roars, tail thrashing behind it.

It misses. All of us. Too slow. We're too fast.

Airi zips past me, blasting a chunk of stone to distract one of the heads. It bites the rubble instead of her.

"I'M HELPING," she shouts triumphantly.

"Try not to laser me!" I call back.

"NO PROMISES!"

Then, Aiyana's voice cuts across the chaos... calm and clear, like a bell through fog. "Turn left. Strike low. You've been tricked before." One of the hydra heads hesitates. Like it's trying to process the words, or argue with her somehow. It twitches... confused... and blinks the wrong way.

Tristan takes the opening. Sword up. One clean, burning slice across the monster's side. Aiyana steps back into the smoke, unflinching.

"She's messing with its head," Airi whispers. "Like... verbally gaslighting a hydra. That's SO COOL."

Nia calls again. "Tama... flank right, now!" I don't even question. I just move.

The hydra whips around... but it's off-balance now, confused, swaying like a drunk snake monster at a concert it didn't want to attend.

We're turning the tide. Not with raw power... but with rhythm. Timing. Teamwork.

And maybe a little bit of reckless luck.

This might actually work.

I hurl another chunk of broken stone at the hydra's flank, timing it just as Balam vaults off a pillar and lands a blow with his staff. The monster reels sideways, dazed... and I grab more rubble without thinking. My muscles move before my brain does.

Nia calls out... clear, quick, perfect: "Left head turning... Tama, now!"

I let the next piece fly. Crack... right into the hydra's shoulder. It roars, stumbling again.

Balam flips over its tail like gravity doesn't apply to him and shouts, "Nice one!"

Aiyana's voice rings out, low and cutting: "You can't see them coming. They're behind you. You're failing again."

One of the heads twitches violently, snapping at air like it's fighting a ghost.

Tristan rushes in through the gap, sword raised, and slices clean into the monster's ribs before it can even react. Then he's gone again... retreating, repositioning. Hit, move, hit, move. The guy's bleeding and barely upright, but somehow still managing to look like a storybook hero.

Airi's at the edge of the plaza, hands glowing, unleashing a nonstop volley of blasts into the hydra's body. Boom. Boom. Boom. A steady rhythm of pure chaos.

"I THINK I'VE FINALLY GOT THE HANG OF THIS!" she yells.

"Please don't jinx it!" I shout back.

The hydra shrieks... frustrated, staggering, backing up. It's retreating. It's actually backing off. We're winning.

And suddenly, I'm laughing. Not because it's funny... because it's ridiculous. Me. In a crumbling plaza in the middle of Germany, chucking chunks of ancient statues at a mythical monster while my maybe-magic teammates fight like they belong in a movie trailer.

And I do too. For the first time, I'm not just reacting... I'm part of this. I'm moving in sync with the others. Watching the signs. Trusting the timing. The adrenaline is still there, sure... but so is the certainty.

This is real. All of it. The hydra. The gods. The barrier. The magic.

It's not just some weird fever dream I've been trying to deny since the professor told us all this back in the office.

That was hours ago. Feels like days. Back then, I was scared. Okay... I still am. But I'm not alone. I've got a team. A real one. And somehow, I'm part of it.

I grab another chunk of debris, roll my shoulders, and grin.

"Let's finish this."

Chapter 41:
The Long Unbinding

Three nights.

The seal has held me through moonrise and moonset.. Runes rasp my bones with every breath; the old magic hums where my palms have pressed for hours, then days.

We planned this centuries ago... Merlin and I... on parchments worn thin by argument. We argued over every rune, every spell, every fail safe in the weave because the seal was not a door, it was a vault. It was built to hold the thing that gnawed at the edges of everything, the darkness that could not be killed, only contained.

Now I... finally, reverse our own craft.

I taste copper and ash as I draw the last counter glyph. Threads tighten, then loosen one, then another, like unhooking stars. The seal trembles.

"Easy," I whisper, to the ward, to myself, to the memory of the man who stood here with me and said the price of mercy is vigilance.

The final knot unspools.

The world breaks like glass.

A shockwave blooms from the anchor stone... soundless, merciless. It punches the breath out of me and hurls me backward across the flagstones. My shoulder hits hard; lights burst behind my eyes. Runes gutter and die. For a heartbeat there is only ringing.

Then I feel it.

This is presence. Cold like deep water and close like a whisper on skin. It seeps from the hairline crack in the barrier, tasting the air, tasting me. Curious. Patient. So quick...

I lurch to my knees, stunned by how fast it is here, how eager. As if it had been waiting, face pressed to the glass, counting down my breaths.

"No," I say, and the word skids in my raw throat.

It presses harder, testing the shape of my name, the edges of my will. Instinct says flee. Duty says stand. I plant my palms against the trembling stone and hold the hole to the size of a needle's eye. I am not strong enough to push it back; I am strong enough not to yield.

For a terrible moment it feels like being remembered by a predator.

You opened the door, it seems to say without words. You did this!

I feel it the way the dark makes a mirror of my doubts. Balance, I remind myself. Renewal. The world has starved without the magic we locked away. But as the first trickle of power slips past my guard, bright and wild and not clean, another thought blooms, acid and sharp:

What if the darkness is all that returns?

The night falls silent. I am on my heels, panting, dust in my mouth, shoulders aching, blood warm on my palm. The barrier is thinner. Avalon hums from the other side with returning current. And underneath the sweetness, grit.

I rise, unsteady, and the new magic licks at my heels like a tide. Somewhere far off, I feel Oberon's satisfaction open like a cold flower.

I hug my doubt to my chest like a warning bell and go to find him.

Chapter 42:
Beyond Exhaustion

Pushing it back. Órale...just a little more," I mutter.

One of the heads shrieks as Airi's light smashes into its chest. Scales crunch. The beast staggers. Four heads lash and whip about, a dim green trail flickers where the hydra's feet drag; flickering left; new, strange, but I trust it. Trust her. It's off-balance now... defensive.

Tama's grinning as he tosses another rock like it's a volleyball. Nia chants next to him, her light curling around the creature's arms, tightening. Aiyana's holding its gaze with steady, golden light. Even Airi's gone mad and electric... like the storm she always was.

For a second, I feel it too... that buzz. That almost-belief.

We might actually be winning this.

But then I look at Tristan.

He's still fighting. He's moving. He's still swinging that stupid sword. But it's too slow. Too heavy. And he's been hurt... more than he's letting on. I saw the shoulder wound earlier, but now it's clear. His swings are sluggish. His steps are off. Every time he hoists that sword back up it's like he's bench pressing a car with one arm.

He's in pain. Bad pain. But of course, he doesn't say anything.

The hydra lashes out. He parries...barely. The momentum tosses him to the side and he drops the blade with a groan.

"Mierda," mutters under my breath. No one else notices. Or they're too focused to care.

But I notice. And I notice something else too. We're not winning. We're surviving. Retreating. Hurting it.

But we're losing ground. Every time we hit it, it chews back. Takes pieces of us with it. Every minute drags on the fight, stretches it out. And that thing... it's not wearing down the way we are.

It's adapting. Changing. We don't have time. That's the angle no one else is seeing.

This thing doesn't have to beat us quickly. Green lines spiderweb across the plaza, tracing where its weight shifts, where it's going next. It just has to last longer than us.

And if we keep fighting like this... it will.

I file that under "nightmare math."

Tama's still at it... of course he is.

Throwing rocks like he's a kid at gym class tossing foam balls back and forth. The kind of strength that'd make ol' Hercules blush. He laughs in between throws, flashing that ol' signature grin like this is just another wild weekend, not a deathmatch against a regenerating beast from the underworld.

But I'm watching closer than that. I am seeing more than that.

His jokes are slower now. His grin doesn't quite make it to his eyes. There's a hitch in the way he grabs the next hunk of rock, like his arms are just starting to notice the weight he's been pretending not to feel since day one.

He's winded. No one wants to admit it... not even him... but he is. Subtle. Like the pause between waves before a hurricane crashes ashore.

But the weird part? His throws are getting stronger. More precise. Like the exhaustion is honing something inside of him instead of wearing it down. That's not normal.

"Left side, Tama!" Nia calls out over the din, crisp and clear. Tama doesn't even blink...he pivots, grabs a monstrous chunk of rock as if it's nothing, and hurls it.

CRACK! The hydra lets out a roar as the rock smashes into it square in the side. All five heads whip about, jaws clacking, staggered by the force of the impact.

Tama grins, already reaching for the next. "Oh yeah, that's right! I rock your world, don't I?"

I groan, eye-rolling as I roll out of the way. "Tama, cálmate!" But he's already mid-toss again, and this one smashes into the beast's knee with bone-shaking impact. The hydra staggers. One claw sinks into the cement, screeching as it digs in to keep from falling.

We're doing damage. We're pushing it back. But to what end?

We're not going to win by pushing it. The edge of the plaza, the crumbling building, the street beyond... it doesn't matter. There's no finish line here. No magical point where this thing just quits.

This isn't tug-of-war. It's a countdown. And we're burning precious seconds we don't have.

Compared to the rest of us... even Tristan... Nia fights differently. No sword. No blasts. She doesn't swing or throw. She just watches, listens, and knows. If Tama is brute, I think as I twist away from a swiping claw, then Nia is precision. She's not just calling out what's happening... she's predicting it.

A glowing arrow tugs me toward the hydra's rear ankle... a gap only I can see, and maybe Nia.

"Balam, two heads tracking you... move now!" I drop and roll left, dirt spraying as two mouths snap down where I was just a heartbeat before.

"Airi, three-second delay... fire!" Airi hesitates...only for a few seconds... but when she fires, it's perfect timing. It connects right as the hydra lurches at her. Perfect. It reels backward, out of balance again.

Nia doesn't react. She's reading. The hydra's movements, the ground, us. Like a conductor leading an orchestra only she can hear. We wouldn't have lasted this long without her.

And she knows what I know. This isn't working.

Tristan's slowing. Tama's still throwing stones like a one-man wrecking crew, but even he's beginning to show wear. His grin is tighter now, his arms a little slower between each toss. Even Airi, for all her power, is starting to miss by inches.

The hydra's hurting... but it's still coming. Still learning. We keep pushing, and it just keeps resetting.

We're tiring. It isn't.

And me? I'm running. Dodging. Striking when I can, keeping low, staying quick. It's what I do.

I slip between a tail swipe and charge across one of its legs with the staff I found earlier. Not hard enough to matter, but just enough to keep it off balance and distracted. I duck, roll, sprint five steps and leap...springing off of a chunk of broken pillar, flipping over one of the heads.

I land silent. Eso sí.

My footfalls don't even kick up much dust. The hydra doesn't even notice me until I'm already gone.

This is what I'm best at. The professor's voice flares in my head, crystal clear as if she's standing right beside me.

"You are the hunter. Fast, silent, untouchable." I didn't get it at first. I thought she was just giving me a pep talk, making me feel good about what I was good at. But now... now I know.

Not just speed. Instinct. I've always been fast. Always seen plays before they happened... on the track, on the field, dodging through crowded streets like I knew where people were going before they moved.

I never thought it would be what saved me. But it is. I see the hydra's claws flex. I'm already moving before it strikes.

I catch the shift in its weight... subtle, the way only one of its heads is moving instead of two... and adjust my angle, slicing just wide enough to stay out of reach, just close enough to cut deep behind the knee. I don't need force. I need precision.

I'm not guessing anymore. I know. The fight's too big, too loud... but I find the rhythm underneath it. A pattern. A pulse. I move through it like I've done this a thousand times. Like my body knows something my mind's still catching up to. Every movement leaves a fading emerald trail, like the path's drawing itself in front of me as I go.

Something that was always there, but I never noticed. Never tapped into.

Until now.

✦ ✦ ✦ ✦ ✦ ✦ ✦

Aiyana should've collapsed hours ago. She's been tired since before this fight even started. The weight of everything that's happened today... the fear, the gas, the monsters, the gods. I've seen it in her eyes when she thought no one was looking. That quiet kind of fear that doesn't yell or panic. The kind that sits low and silent and heavy.

And yet... she's still here. Still fighting. That soft golden glow around her isn't bright or showy. It flickers. Wavers. But it's still there. Still burning.

She's moving like she's running on fumes, but her voice is steady, her hands don't shake. She doesn't attack the way Tama does, or dive forward like Airi. She's looking for gaps. Looking for ways to protect us. To distract the hydra. To help... even when she can barely stand.

I've fought beside her all day. I've watched her take hits. I have seen the emotional toll of the things she's seen and heard... the things she's sensed. She always gets back up. Always finds a way to stand, even if it's just for the rest of us.

But this... this is different. Not because she looks strong. But because she isn't. She's tired. Injured. Pushed past her limits. And she keeps going anyway.

The first time I met her, back in the airport, I felt it. Something quiet and strong in her. A kind of gravity. I didn't know what it meant back then. But I do now. She's the one I've been searching for without realizing it.

Through the draugr. The statues. The escape through the city. She's been there with me every step of the way and I've told myself I'm here to protect her... but the truth is, I've been holding on to her.

Her glow pulses softly through the haze, and her voice rings above the hydra's snarling... "If two fathers and two sons go fishing, but they only catch three fish, how is that possible?"

One of the hydra's heads stops, confused. She's moved from gaslighting to just straight up riddling it. Oddly it seems to be working just as well.

"Because there are only three people. Grandfather, father, and son."

It snarls again, eyes unfocused. It doesn't understand. But I do. She's using what she has. Her voice. Her mind. Her presence. Even through the smoke, even with red-rimmed eyes and tangled hair and dirt on her cheeks... she's the most incredible thing I've ever seen.

Not because she's perfect. But because she isn't... and she's still here.

Still fighting. Still trying to keep us safe.

I don't even see the tail coming. CRACK.

"¡Híjole!" I can only moan as I hit the ground.

The impact rams into me like a train. My ribs wail. I'm out of air before I can even cry out. I land hard, rubble erupting around me, sharp pain ripping through my shoulder as the world skids sideways.

"BALAM!" Tama's voice barely registers over the blood in my ears. I'm on my back, half-buried, the sky spinning above me. I'm gasping for breath. But I force my head up.

And she's still there. Still glowing. Still holding the line.

And all I can think, through the haze and the pain and the dust in my mouth, is...

She's the bravest person I've ever known.

✦ ✦ ✦ ✦ ✦ ✦ ✦

Airi is chaos. Unchecked, unbridled, unrelenting chaos.

Every time one of her blasts hits, the hydra recoils with a shriek...not just distraction. Real damage. But it's not clean. The ground's scorched, chunks of rubble fly in every direction, and everything near the blast gets wrecked... hydra or not.

Her aim's not good. Honestly, it's never been. But she's trying. Hard to blame her. She's had these powers for less than a day and been forced to figure them out while running for her life. The fact that she's still on her feet, still hurling energy with this kind of force is nothing short of insane. Especially considering she's been running on soda, stolen candy, and pure panic since sunset.

Tama yelps as another blast zips past him, incinerating what's left of a column. "OI, Airi! AIM!"

"I'M TRYING!" she snaps, voice cracking with effort. I believe her.

Her hands are shaking. Her shoulders are hunched. Sweat streaks her face, mixing with dirt and smoke. Her mouth is dry and open as she pants between attacks, her energy fading faster than she can manage it. She doesn't really know what she's doing. But she keeps going.

I duck under the sweep of a claw and slash across the hydra's ankle with the blade I picked up earlier. It's not hard enough to matter. Real damage. But I need to stay moving... if I stop now, I won't get up again. I circle wide, looking for an opening, one eye on the hydra and one on her.

Because I know what it's like to feel overwhelmed. To feel the weight of something too big, too fast, too much... and fight anyway.

That's what she's doing. Even as her power spins out of control. Even as she misses.

And then... One blast goes wide. Too wide. BOOM. One of the hydra's heads explodes. A sickening pop of flesh and flame. A stray shot right down its throat.

"Oh, COME ON!" Tristan groans, dragging his sword and his pride across the field.

Airi stares, horrified, hands clapped over her mouth. "I... I didn't mean to! I was aiming for the body!"

Tama throws up his hands like the universe personally offended him. "WHY?! WHY WOULD YOU DO THAT?!"

And then... of course... two new heads burst forth from the bloody stump.

Five. We're at five.

Aiyana sounds broken. "We were doing so well..."

The hydra doesn't give us a moment to catch our breath. It lunges faster now. Smarter. Deadlier.

I throw myself into a slide under its legs, barely dodging a claw and land hard next to the rubble.

Everything is falling apart.

And when I look at Airi... arms trembling, face streaked with soot and ash, eyes wide with panic... I see how close she is to falling. She's swaying on her feet. Blinking like she's trying to stay conscious. Her hands are still up, but barely. There's no fire left in her blasts. Just effort. Desperation.

She's scared. So scared. But she's still here. I've never seen anyone try so hard with so little left.

I watch her suck in another breath. Stand her ground. Bring her trembling hands up again.

And I realize...

She's not chaos. She's courage. Raw and untrained and barely holding it together.

But courage, all the same. And right now, that's all we need.

✦ ✦ ✦ ✦ ✦ ✦ ✦

The fifth head reverses our odds. Just like that. It's as if we never had the upper hand in the first place. It speeds up. Gets more intelligent. Its attacks are organized. Coming in waves, then pushing us back... back and back... until there's no more options, no more tactics. Just a single, instinctive choice.

Retreat.

I push to the front, slash at the legs and generally make as much of a distraction as I can. But I'm not holding my position anymore. Not even close. I'm just stalling. Buying time. Time for the rest of them to catch a break. Time for them to run.

Aiyana moves to my left, arm extended and golden light flickering, dimming. I know she's trying to hold on to it. Stuttering around it. Whispering riddles to the hydra. Tossing it off-balance when she can... but she's fading. It's taking more and more out of her to do less and less.

Then one of the heads swipes out. Quick. Low. She flinches, too close, too late. It catches her side, glancing... but it's enough to stagger her. I grab her arm, wrench her behind the broken remains of a fountain and sink to my knees behind her.

"Go," I whisper. "Help the others get out." Her eyes widen, like she wants to argue... like she wants to stay. But she sees it, too. I can tell by the way she's hanging onto the moment. This isn't our fight anymore. Not like this. She nods once and slips away, her light spilling out after her.

Tristan's already got Nia pulled to the edge of the plaza. They don't say a word. Tristan, at least. He doesn't have to. He's got her hand. He feels the moment go the same way I did. Our fleeting advantage slipping away.

It's over.

We're not winning. We're barely holding on.

Nia goes still. Not the sharp, tactical calm she has had all night... just blank, as if someone turned her head inward. Her eyes flare gold, then go wider, distant. She doesn't speak for minutes.

Her lips move on their own. "Titania," she whispers, and then, "Oberon." "Mara" follows like a question. The words are clearer to her than to anyone else in the plaza.

Nia snaps back, fingers clawing at the air as if she's been pulled from a deep pool. Her face goes white. She blinks hard, looks at Tristan, then at me, and the apology spills out before she can steady it. "Sorry. I... I saw them. For a second. I thought... he *touched* me."

Her voice is small, shaken. The look on her face says she got a glimpse of something worse than anything we've fought tonight.

And then... the ground pulses. Not a quake. Not an explosion.

A shockwave? The whole plaza bursts green, my vision swimming.

It washes over the plaza in a wave of force, past all of us. Everything stops... for a moment. The hydra, the movement, the smoke. Everything halts in a single breath.

Then the air shifts. Toxic gas lifting, spiraling away like dust in a wind tunnel. I take in a breath and... it's clean.

The weariness in my bones flips like a switch. Limbs steady. Lungs clear. For a heartbeat the world is clean.

Aiyana's golden glow burns brighter, steadier than before. Aiyana looks... stunned, like she can't quite believe how solid she feels.

Airi's hands are glowing... blinding. White-hot with energy crackling between her fingertips.

Tristan stands taller. The way he's moving... his shoulder doesn't seem to be bothering him at all.

And Tama... Tama's grin is back. Full and reckless and unstoppable. He rolls his neck like he just walked out of a nap.

We feel good. Stronger. Lighter. Ready.

For a heartbeat, it feels like everything's about to swing back in our favor.

But then... The hydra lifts its heads. All five pairs of eyes flash, glowing brighter than before.

Its scales ripple... then shift. Darken. Harden. The shimmer across its body twists from dull armor to something alive, gleaming. The ground under its coils cracks.

Because whatever just empowered us... It empowered it, too.

"Claro... no podía ser tan fácil."

Chapter 43:
Your True Colors

Airi ✦ After Midnight (April 27) ✦ Plaza Ruins

"Kuso," I mutter, and hear the awe and horror in my own voice.

Something just zapped me with 1.21 gigawatts of raw, unfiltered whoa.

Everything's changed. The shockwave lingers in my bones, buzzes in my fingertips like static just about to snap. I don't hurt anymore. My lungs don't burn. My arms don't feel like lead. I flex my fingers and... snap, crackle... KA-BOOM!

My hands flare brighter, somehow, more intense. But they're not just pink and blue now. Red, yellow, green, teal... all swirling together in a bright crazy light show. My own personal rave, tiny sparklers crackling in my palms.

I blink. Then grin. I don't just feel good. I feel unreal. Like I could bench-press a truck or ace a history test without even looking at the notes.

Okay, maybe not the last part. But the truck? Hell yeah.

The hydra thrashes back, heads screeching and lashing out like it can sense the change in the air.

I don't wait. I dive. My body answers, barreling forward at full speed before I even think to call it, and the world goes a blur. I toss my first orb up mid-stride... this one bright yellow instead of my usual pink or blue. It smashes into the hydra and the yellow head recoils, eyes snapping, scales splintering, breath cut off.

Did I just get a critical hit? That yellow head hated that!

"Ohhh yeah," I groan, already charging my next one. This time I throw two... one from each hand. WHUMP-WHUMP!

"Shōnen power-up, baby!" I laugh.

My orbs leap from my hands, this time a blazing bright red and a neon green. Two of the heads shriek, twisting like I dumped salt on an open wound.

I feel the others moving with me...

Balam's darting in and out of the shadows (I've tagged a few street lights) slashing quickly and ducking out, all sleek and feline. Aiyana quickly darts just out of reach, her eyes glowing, and her weird riddles, clearing a path just as Tama barrels in front of her with fists like bombs.

I hear Nia call sharply, voice piercing through the madness, crisp and clear: "Head, the green one, is weakening! Keep it off balance! Tristan... left flank!"

Tristan, sword aloft, shouts back: "Push it back! Tama, with me!"

They don't need to ask me twice. I hold up both hands, charging another orb... bigger this time, heavier with light and fury... and fling it forward like a volleyball spike.

It connects. BOOM. Another body shot, jaws snapping in pain like they're not even a part of this animal anymore.

I grin like a maniac. This isn't chaos. This is control. This is electricity.

I start flinging orbs like an arcade game on overdrive. Blue hurts blue... the head shrieks like it's about to combust. Green enrages green, and it actually recoils, scales sizzling. Holy crap, it's not random... it's color coded pain! Matching colors deal critical damage. Like Pokémon, but deadly! Did I just get EV training?

And for the first time in my life, I don't feel like the weirdo holding back, scared she's gonna mess everything up.

I feel like lightning with a body. And I'm only just starting. Lightning still fries its handler, Airi... focus.

Combat becomes rhythm. Distractions make openings. Openings let Tristan and Tama strike. Nia shouts, ever-present, voice sharp and sure in my head like we're chess pieces in some strange, deadly game.

And me? I'm just here blasting everything I've got.

My orbs hit harder now... tearing scales clean off, leaving scorch marks, smoking craters in the hydra's armored hide. Every time I let one loose, the monster jerks and bellows in agony. I don't even wince anymore. I want it to scream.

My head's clearer than it's been all night... whatever that shockwave was, it knocked the cobwebs out of my brain. And wow, it turns out that aiming is way easier when your mind isn't scrambled eggs.

BZZZAK! A beam of multi-colored energy erupts from my palms, cleaving through the gas-filled air like lightning out of a cannon...

AND SLAMS STRAIGHT INTO THE HYDRA'S RIBS.

The thing howls, its entire massive body convulsing from the impact and for a split second I swear I see actual fear in its eyes.

YES. I did that. ME. I actually hit the stupid thing where I was supposed to.

I do a little dance...

"Yatta!" I yell... spinning, sparks still crackling off my fingers. "I think I'm getting better at this."

For a heartbeat, maybe two... we're winning. We're actually doing this.

Then Tama snorts mid-swing. "Oh sure, now you figure it out."

Balam vaults off a toppled column like he's got some wires rigged under his hoodie. One of the hydra's heads swipes at him, but he twists in mid-air, spins, and brings his staff smashing down onto the snout.

CRUNCH! The hydra sneezes. I swear it actually sneezes.

Balam grins. "Still works!" Tama barks a laugh. "Are we seriously booping a hydra to death?"

"Hey, if it ain't broke..." I start, but Nia's already stepping in: "Tama, left!"

Tama growls, scoops up a boulder the size of a motorcycle, and tosses it like he's throwing a beach ball.

CRUNCH. The hydra stumbles. For the first time since this nightmare began, it actually looks slow. Like it's wearing down.

We're not winning yet... But we might be close.

And I'm not backing down.

Tama's eyes narrow. Picks something up from the ground. A glint of bronze in the rubble, half-buried under broken stone and ash, shining like it was made for the light of my last blast. He kneels down and wrenches it free... a twisted, curved piece of some ancient statue. It's big, sharp, and heavy enough to do real damage.

He flips it in his hands, weighing the heft. "Solid."

I nod. "Go for the ribs. Hit it hard."

He hurls it... fast, perfect spin, right for the hydra's side. But right as it reaches the target, the beast shifts. One of its heads drops to lunge forward... and the bronze disc slices straight through it.

SHNK.

The head thumps to the ground with a sickening smack. Time stops. I don't cheer. I don't breathe. I know what's coming before it happens.

SQUELCH. The wound bubbles. The flesh splits and writhes... And two new heads burst from the stump.

Now it has six. Tama stares in horror. "I... I didn't mean to. I wasn't aiming for the head. I swear, I wasn't."

Hot bile rises; the plaza suddenly feels three sizes too small.

"I know," I say, voice hushed. "I saw it. It... it moved."

Nia pivots, eyes huge. "Get ready! It's about to..."

The hydra screams. All six heads whip toward us like they know exactly what we did... and they want to make us pay for it.

Tristan's sword is up, but there's no joy left in his face... just grim finality. "We need to fall back. Now."

"I'm sorry," Tama repeats, louder this time, shuffling back. "I'm sorry! I thought it would help."

"We all did," I whisper. My fingers still spark weakly, but I'm not sure if it's courage or fear.

Balam is already moving. "Cover each other! Nia, get us a route!"

The hydra lunges.

"RETREAT!" Tristan shouts. And this time, no one argues.

"Eat rainbow, kaiju!" I screech, tossing a double-shot.

✦ ✦ ✦ ✦ ✦ ✦ ✦

We're running. Not the fun kind. Not the laughing-through-the-mayhem kind. This is the break-your-lungs, legs-jerking kind of running... where all you're doing is trying not to die.

I'm at the back, throwing blast after blast, trying to keep the hydra from closing the distance. Energy hums from my hands, ribbons lighting up the air. The blasts crack into its thick body, its legs... anything to slow it down.

It doesn't stop. Six heads. Six mouths. Six jets of toxic gas and snapping jaws and venomous teeth. Six coordinated attacks headed in all six directions.

Nia's voice is staccato now, barely a breath between commands:

"Tama, back!"

"Tristan, right!"

"Balam... MOVE!"

We're retreating, one step at a time, while the hydra just keeps coming. It's relentless. Towering. Too many heads. Too much strength. We're getting beaten.

And the worst part?

Each head isn't just attacking aimlessly. They're looking at us. Those glowing eyes are scanning, locking in... tracking.

Red.

Green.

Blue.

Yellow.

Magenta.

Cyan.

I skid behind a chunk of toppled pillar, panting, hands glowing again as I hurl another blast. It connects right in a head's jaw... it barely flinches.

My stomach plummets. We can't win like this. Not like this.

I duck as a head sweeps across the air above me, jaws snapping, gas whirling. Another blast shoots from my palms to cover Tristan as he stumbles back.

Then... I look up.

Red. Green. Blue. Yellow. Magenta. Cyan.

My brain sizzles like someone plugged me into a wall socket. The heads. The colors.

It's light.

"Wait..." Matching colors. Hits harder, RGB, CMY... what if instead of matching one-to-one, I combined all the colors into one supercharged blast? One perfect, obliterating beam of pure white?

Not just light. Balance. Interference. If I can line them up, sync the wavelengths...

I can collapse the entire spectrum into one perfect, obliterating beam of pure white.

Additive color theory. RGB. CMY. My brain pieces it all together all at once... art class, physics class, coding tutorials, all crashing together in the middle of a battlefield.

I freeze. Then I laugh... once, sharp and wild. "I'm such a nerd," I whisper. They always told me I saw the world in different colors. But I have an idea. I just need time.

✦ ✦ ✦ ✦ ✦ ✦ ✦

I try to shout my idea... try... but no one seems to hear. The hydra is everywhere. Six heads, six directions. Gas, claws, mayhem. I'm just one voice in a hurricane of noise.

And I realize... what was I thinking? Some random art-class trivia? This isn't a plan... this is just my brain throwing a game idea at a knife-fight.

Brain: great time for an existential spiral! Thanks, executive dysfunction.

I start to lower my hands...

The others are real heroes. Fighters. Leaders. I'm an awkward fifteen-year-old with laser hands and a brain full of useless trivia. The one people pat on the head and call "gifted," like that makes up for not being invited to anything else.

So I lower my hands. I start to give up.

And then...

"GIVE AIRI AN OPENING!" Nia. Fierce. Commanding.

"LET'S GIVE HER SOME TIME!" Aiyana. Steady. Unshaken.

I freeze. They heard me.

They heard me. They understood.

And they believe in me.

Something clenches in my chest... like a sob that never made it past my lips. And suddenly, I feel it. All of it.

Because back home? I'm alone most of the time. My parents provide... they function... but they're always too busy, too tired, too distracted.

My friends? We talk games and fandoms and art and books, but when the screen turns off, the silence creeps in.

I'm the youngest. Too smart. Too weird. Too much.

Teachers admire me. But they don't know me.

The other kids smile, but I can see it... the hesitation.

I'm a curiosity. An afterthought.

Pity hurts worse than teasing.

The whispers echo:

"She skipped two grades."

"She's kinda intense."

"Just let her do her thing, she's like, smart or whatever."

No one really knows me. No one really wants to.

But right now? They do. Aiyana. Nia. All of them... they're fighting to give me a chance. Because they think I'm worth it.

I take a step back, hands shaking, light already crackling between my fingers. Sparks dance at my fingertips. I grin, remembering that night I couldn't sleep and fell down the rabbit hole of physics tutorials and additive color theory. Who knew that might actually come in handy?

I hold my hands to one side and breathe in, tears hot in my eyes.

"HAKAI-KŌ!" A point of light ignites... furious and bright.

"SHŪHASŪ!" The colors swirl, pulled from the air, from the hydra, from me.

"HAKAI-KŌ!" The world goes still. Gray. Empty. Silent.

All color drains from the plaza... except six glowing eyes:

Red. Green. Blue. Yellow. Magenta. Cyan.

And the orb in my hands. The light screams, growing too fast, too wild, too much me. The colors spiral tighter, brighter, blending faster and faster... red, green, blue, yellow, magenta, cyan.

My hands tremble from the overload. If this takes out the power grid, we're gonna fry us all. No pressure.

Feels like hitting X to beat a boss with one hit-point left.

And I don't stop. Because this?

This is everything I never said. Every time I smiled when I wanted to scream. Every empty birthday. Every fake friend. Every time someone called me gifted and thought that meant I didn't need anyone.

All the times I was too loud. Too proud. Too me.

And the worst part... the voice that believed I didn't belong.

And worse... the part of me that believed it.

"SHŪHASŪ!" The orb swells, beach-ball-sized and barely containable.

My body shakes. My fingers burn. My bones feel like they're cracking from the inside out.

And I let it. Because this is my voice. My anger. My light. Mine.

I fling my hands forward and scream:

"BĪĪĪĪĪĪĪMUUUUUU!" The beam erupts. Not just light. Not just energy. A cyclone of color and fury and heartbreak. A scream wrapped in a rainbow inferno.

The hydra twists too late.

The beam connects.

It's not just bright... it's everything.

But it doesn't go down.

It just digs in. Claws the ground.

The beam shudders... starts to gutter. My knees hit the stone. My pulse staggers. I feel it slipping, slipping, slipping... It's too much.

I can't...

"Don't stop."

Tristan's voice. Low. Rough. Not a command... just recognition. Like he knows what it's like to be right at the edge and want to fall anyway. "You're almost there."

The beam steadies, a heartbeat more.

"Hey, Fry Girl!" Tama. Still breathing like he's winded and cocky at the same time. "You better not let that overgrown lamp-eel win! You're the big gun, remember? Pull the trigger!"

I almost laugh. Almost.

"Airi." Aiyana's voice now. Quiet. Grounding. Not panicked. Not desperate. Just steady. "We're here. We've always been."

Simple words. Somehow more grounding than anything else.

The light swells again. But my arms are shaking. It's too much. The hydra isn't giving up.

"You've got this," Balam calls. He's close now. I can feel it more than see it. "Even if it doesn't work... we're with you. You're not alone."

And then... arms. Around me.

Nia.

She doesn't say much. Doesn't have to. She wraps herself around me like armor. A hand on my stomach, her forehead resting against the back of my head. And her voice... barely a whisper:

"You don't have to carry it all by yourself."

She glows. Not for show... just because it's who she is. And I let her hold me up. Just for a moment.

And it's enough.

The color shifts.

The orb detonates.

And this time... there's no pushback.

Only light.

A spiraling helix of light... raw, radiant, absolute... colors cracking like thunder around a burning white core... tears through the hydra like it's made of paper and bad decisions.

Its heads thrash, eyes reflecting every color I've ever seen and more.

Scales peel. Jaws crack. The ground shudders.

And then... Silence.

Please stay dust. Monsters love sequels.

Ash. Nothing. I fall to my knees, chest heaving, arms numb.

✦ ✦ ✦ ✦ ✦ ✦ ✦

We won. But something inside me still aches... like a fuse burned too hot. I wonder if it'll ever stop buzzing.

The others are standing again, blinking like they've just stepped out of a dream.

The plaza is still.

And for the first time in my life, I feel I did something right. Not just because I was smart. But because they trusted me.

They chose me.

I sag to the ground. The world tilts sideways... my vision swimming with static and color trails. My chest heaves. My arms feel like jelly. My hands twitch, little sparks still flickering at my fingertips, like they haven't realized the fight is over.

I gave it everything. Everything I am. Everything I had. And now I'm barely holding on.

Then... footsteps. Rushing. Hands are on me... gentle, steady.

"Hey. Airi. We've got you." It's Nia. Her voice is soft. Grounding. She kneels beside me, already digging through my bag. Somehow she knows exactly what to look for... she pulls out one of the stolen sodas I hid under the zipper flap and a handful of candy I forgot I liberated.

"Sugar. You need sugar," she murmurs, tearing open a wrapper and pressing the candy into my hand. "Here. Drink."

My fingers fumble, but she helps me hold the can. Helps me tilt it. The soda is warm and way too fizzy, but I don't care.

I inhale the soda, burp like Kirby, mutter, "mana potion achieved". The sweetness hits my tongue and I sigh, eyes stinging.

She's still here. They all are.

Tristan crouches beside me next, gently squeezing my shoulder. "That was insane", he says, a little breathless. "You vaporized it."

Tama flops down on the ground with a groan, hands behind his head. "We're officially adding 'Airi nuke mode' to the team strategy."

Balam grabs a chocolate bar. "Next time, warn us so we can be behind a wall first, yeah?"

Aiyana just smiles and quietly grabs a piece of candy, then settles beside Nia, legs folded. Her eyes meet mine... kind, steady.

We sit there. All six of us. Exhausted, bruised, still buzzing with leftover adrenaline... and eating stolen candy in the ruins of a broken plaza like we're kids on a break between classes.

It's quiet. Safe. And for a few minutes, I don't feel weird or left out or like I'm too much.

I feel with them.

I'm not the awkward little sister. Not the sidekick or the mascot. I'm just one of the team.

I lean my head against Nia's shoulder, eyelids fluttering.

And then...

Clap. Clap. Clap.

We all turn.

Puck sits atop the cracked remains of the old fountain, legs crossed like a queen on a throne of rubble.

"Good game, Cotton Candy", she purrs, voice soaked in mischief. The slow clap continues... mocking, measured.

Clap. Clap.

Her lips curl, eyes glinting like twin daggers. "That was an impressive finishing move. Very dramatic. Very bright."

She leans forward, lacing her fingers under her chin. "But..."

She lets the word stretch, teasing it like a cat with a mouse.

"...the first seal is already broken. And the fun?" Her grin widens, wicked and thrilled.

"Oh... it's only just beginning."

And then... She's gone. Vanished like smoke. But her laughter? It lingers. Sharp. Cold. Echoing off the stone.

Chapter 44:
We're Still Here

Nia ✦ EarlyMorning (April 27) ✦ Plaza Ruins

We sit in the middle of the ruined plaza, surrounded by broken stone, scorched earth, and silence. It should feel like a victory. The hydra is gone. The city is still standing. We're still standing.

But all I can hear is Puck's voice, echoing in my head like a bell that won't stop ringing. "The first seal is broken." No jokes. No riddles. Just those words, dropped like a blade.

I don't know what I'm supposed to feel. Relief? Fear? The adrenaline is gone and what's left is a hollow ache in my chest that doesn't seem to go away.

I stare across the plaza. Ripples move outward from the east... not sound or light, but something deeper. Like waves in a pond.

That has to be it. The seal. And now I see the aftershocks. I see the way the world has shifted. Magic is everywhere now.

It hums beneath my skin, buzzes in the corners of my vision. I see it bleeding through the cracks in the stone, winding around the broken statues, soaking into the air like mist. And I see it most clearly in them... the others.

Their auras haven't faded. If anything, they shine brighter now, clearer. More themselves. Each one distinct.

Tristan's is a steady silver-blue, calm and commanding. Aiyana glows warm gold, grounded and still. Tama's pulses red-orange, bold and alive, like sunlight on water. Airi's flickers in sharp bursts of rainbow, chaotic and brilliant. Balam's dances like smoke and starlight ... quiet, dangerous, controlled.

And mine... mine stretches between them. Threads of golden light, unseen by anyone else, but I know they're there. Connecting us. Binding us.

We're different. We always were. But now I see how we fit. Not just a team. A pattern. A circle. A spark.

"We won," Tristan says softly beside me.

I glance at him. There's blood on his temple and shoulder, dirt on his hands. His voice is steady but his eyes are searching. Like he needs me to say it too.

I want to believe it. I think I do.

"The professor said we couldn't stop the seal from breaking," I say. "She knew it was going to happen."

"Then maybe this was the best outcome," Aiyana says. Her voice is calm but there's something heavy under it ... something I think only I can feel. "We made it through."

"Barely," Balam mutters, leaning back against a chunk of shattered wall. "But yeah. We did."

"No," Tama says, his mouth tugging into a tired grin. "We crushed it. Come on, don't sell us short."

That actually makes Airi laugh ... short and sharp, like she's surprised to hear the sound coming out of her own mouth.

We're bruised, burned, exhausted. But we're alive. And even if it wasn't a clean win, even if the seal broke and nothing will ever be the same again... we're still here.

That has to count for something.

I let out a breath and lie back on the warm, cracked stone. The sky above us is dark but open. No gods. No monsters. Just stars.

The world feels different now. More alive. More dangerous.

Everything has changed. And somehow... I know this is only the beginning.

✦ ✦ ✦ ✦ ✦ ✦ ✦

Tama groans and flops onto his back beside me. "Okay, real talk ... did anyone wake up this morning and think they were gonna beat a hydra today? Like, be honest."

Airi raises a hand without even sitting up. "I absolutely thought I was going to die. At least twice."

"Three times," Balam mutters. "That green head almost got you. I was this close to dragging your sparkly corpse out of the rubble."

Airi grins. "Please. If I go down, I'm taking at least half of Berlin with me. Minimum."

"I still can't believe you fired a laser through it," Tristan says, shaking his head. "That was... genuinely terrifying."

"And awesome," Tama adds. "Terrifying and awesome."

"Thank you," Airi says, beaming like she just won a medal. "I accept your fear and admiration equally."

"Can we talk about when Balam jumped off that broken fountain?" I say, propping myself up on my elbows. "Because I'm pretty sure gravity just gave up trying with him."

He shrugs, trying to look casual but there's a little smirk on his face. "Gotta stay unpredictable."

"You landed on its head," Tristan says, still looking half-offended. "I was trying to distract it. Not give it a concussion."

"I was assisting."

"You were showing off," Aiyana says, smiling faintly. "But it worked."

Tama sits up suddenly, pointing. "Okay but nothing beats Tristan fencing that thing like it was a school tournament."

"Hey, muscle memory is muscle memory," Tristan replies. "It's not my fault the hydra didn't bring proper footwork."

We all laugh.

"Oh! And what about when Tama punched a whole boulder in half?" Airi says, eyes wide. "That was anime-level stuff."

He stretches his arms behind his head. "Yeah, I'll sign your shirt later."

"You cracked the pavement when you landed," I add.

"I do have great form."

"Not after you tripped five minutes later," Balam says with a grin. "You landed in that fountain like a sack of potatoes."

"Strategic hydration," Tama replies, deadpan.

We laugh harder this time. It feels good. Stupid and warm and good.

"Honestly," I say, looking around at them, "we were a mess."

"A beautiful mess," Aiyana says.

"The best kind," Tristan agrees.

And for a moment, sitting here in the middle of ruins and starlight, I forget about seals and monsters and what comes next.

We're just us. Banged up, still standing. Still together.

✦ ✦ ✦ ✦ ✦ ✦ ✦

A flicker of movement at the edge of my vision cuts our laughter short. I straighten, suddenly alert. Footsteps pound across shattered stone, frantic, uneven. The urgency snaps me fully awake again.

Then a voice. "Nia!" It's Professor Mara. Her voice breaks. And then she's running.

I barely have time to process before her arms are around me. Tight. Fierce. Not like a polite teacher's hug ... like something desperate. Like she's been holding her breath this whole time and only now remembers how to breathe.

Her breath hitches. Her fingers grip the back of my jacket like I might disappear if she lets go.

"Oh, thank the spirits... you're safe... you're safe..." Her voice shakes, breaking on the last word. "I was so worried... I thought..." She swallows hard. "I thought I'd lost you."

I freeze, stiffening in surprise. Professor Mara is always composed. Controlled. The steady presence who made me feel like anything was manageable. Seeing her shaking, vulnerable... it hits me like a punch in the chest, knocking down barriers I didn't even realize I'd put up.

But now... Now she's shaking. And something in me cracks. I hug her back. Hard. Because after everything today, after what we've seen and fought and barely survived... I think we both needed this.

She pulls away just enough to grip my shoulders, scanning me from head to toe. Her face is pale. Eyes wide. "Are you hurt? Are you...?"

"I'm okay," I say softly. "But the others... "

Her eyes widen... and then she's moving.

Her hands glow faintly with light as she rushes to Tristan, then Aiyana, then Airi. She kneels, touches each of us with careful urgency, checking for wounds, wiping away dirt and blood with trembling hands.

Relief washes over her face as she sees us all alive. Bruised, tired, scraped up and sore ... but whole.

"You did well," she whispers. "All of you."

Airi lets out a breathy, tired laugh, still staring at her hands like she doesn't recognize them. "I... used too much... I'm... empty." Her voice wobbles. "I can't feel it anymore."

Professor Mara kneels beside her, her touch soft and steady as she places a hand on Airi's shoulder. "You saved them," she says gently. "I can still feel the echo." The surge of energy ... it came from you."

"Huh. I guess I did." Airi smiles, a little stunned. Watching her soften at Professor Mara's reassurance, a quiet warmth settles in my chest. She's part of this strange, chaotic family we've become.

The plaza becomes quiet again.

Not the kind of silence that feels heavy or haunted … but the kind that comes after. After the battle. After the storm.

For the first time all night, we feel safe.

✦ ✦ ✦ ✦ ✦ ✦ ✦

The sirens are everywhere now. Distant at first, then closer … until they echo off the broken stone, a scream that won't stop. Flashing blue light spills across the plaza, catching on the broken pillars, the blood, the soot. On us.

Police pour in, shouting into radios, flashlights sweeping the rubble. A man stumbles forward, babbling about cameras. A woman snaps at her phone about earthquakes. Someone sobs quietly. Another person throws up into the bushes. No one knows what happened, just that something impossible tore the plaza apart.

A woman in a sleek gray suit storms past, yelling into her phone. "No, I don't know what happened! I was in a meeting and now the plaza's gone! I think... maybe a gas explosion? Or a sinkhole?"

Another woman, pale and shaking, stands just outside the barricade, crying quietly. She doesn't seem to realize she's filming the rubble on her phone with one hand, muttering to herself about an earthquake.

There's shouting now ... overlapping voices in different languages. People pointing. Asking questions no one can answer.

Someone sobs nearby. Someone else throws up in the bushes.

A man in a neon vest tries to take control, waving his arms and barking in German. "Zurück!" "Back up! Everyone back... clear the area... do not touch anything!" "Räumen Sie den Bereich frei!"

It's chaos. The kind that comes after something unthinkable.

And in the middle of it all: us.

Six teenagers.

Bloodied. Burned. Exhausted.

We're sitting on broken stone like survivors pulled from the wreckage of a building collapse ... except there's no building. Just what used to be a plaza. We can feel the stares. See the confusion painted on every face.

How did they survive?

How are they not dead?

Were they here when it happened?

It's written in their eyes ... the civilians, the officers, the EMTs. No one says it out loud, but I can feel it: we don't make sense.

We don't fit the narrative. Because if this was a natural disaster ... a gas explosion, a tornado, an earthquake ... then how are we alive? And how is so much gone?

There's a fracture line running through the stone beneath us. A perfect arc where the hydra's final thrash split the earth. The buildings around the edges are scorched, destroyed, windows shattered. Some of the trees are blackened to ash.

But we're still here. That's the part no one can wrap their heads around.

✦ ✦ ✦ ✦ ✦ ✦ ✦

Then I hear someone shout ... a name, sharp and urgent. "Tristan!"

His parents break through the crowd like a wave, parting people without a second thought. His mother gets to him first. She stumbles to her knees, her heels snapping against the stone, and wraps her arms around him with the kind of force that says she hasn't breathed in hours.

His father is only a step behind, jaw tight, eyes wide as he grips Tristan's shoulders.

And then ... they see it. The blood. Dark and soaked into the shoulder of Tristan's shirt, smeared down his arm, crusted at the edge of a long gash.

His mother's breath catches. "Oh... Tristan... your... " Her hands hover helplessly, not sure where to touch. "There's so much blood... where are you hurt? Look at me... where is it?"

Tristan tries to speak, but she's already checking him ... pushing back his sleeve, brushing hair from his forehead, searching his face like she expects to find him fading in front of her.

"I'm okay," he says quickly, gently. His father wants to push ... I can see it in the tight line of his mouth, the way his hands twitch like they want to fix this, to control it.

But then his gaze shifts ... takes in the plaza, the broken stone, the crater where the hydra fell. And his shoulders drop. Whatever they thought they were walking into... it wasn't this.

For a moment, I think he might push them away. But then I see it ... the way his shoulders drop, the way he lets them in. Maybe for the first time tonight, he doesn't try to be perfect. He just lets himself be a kid.

His mother pulls Tristan into another hug, fingers trembling against his back. No speeches. No politics. Just fear and relief, wrapped together in silence.

Aiyana's chaperones aren't far behind.

They emerge from the crowd like a unit ... calm, focused, deliberate ... their traditional clothing half-obscured by heavy coats, their eyes already scanning her from a distance.

When they reach her, they don't cry. They don't panic. They assess.

One of them steps forward and gently lifts her chin, checking her eyes. Another moves silently to her side, running practiced fingers down her arms, across her ribs, her shoulder ... checking for breaks, burns, bleeding. There's a quiet hum of words in low Lakota from the third ... too soft for me to catch, but it sounds like a prayer. Or a protection.

Their movements are careful, reverent. As if touching her too fast might shatter something.

Aiyana doesn't flinch. She meets their gaze, steady and calm, and nods once ... but it's like watching someone respond from behind glass. Her face is composed, almost serene, but her eyes are far away. Like her body's here, standing in the wreckage of a Berlin plaza... But her spirit is still elsewhere. Somewhere deeper.

One of the chaperones cups the back of her head briefly, murmurs something I don't understand, and Aiyana closes her eyes.

Only for a moment. Then she opens them again, and she's solid. Present.

She doesn't speak, but something in her posture changes. Not lighter, exactly. Just... anchored. Like whatever storm she's weathered inside has passed, and now she's ready to walk forward again.

✦ ✦ ✦ ✦ ✦ ✦ ✦

Balam swivels on his heel just as a voice slices through the crowd ... quick, jagged, thick with emotion.

"¡Dios mío! Mírame, mírame, ¿estás bien?"

The kind looking woman is practically running, bouncing from side to side with her bag flailing off her hip and her coat slipping off one shoulder. Her words stumble over each other, breathless and frantic.

"Tu cara... ¿tu brazo está bien? Ay no, tu cabello... mira nomás lo sucio que estás... "

She pulls up to him and pauses, blinking owlishly as her eyes dart over him. Blood on his temple. Dirt smudged across his cheeks. One sleeve half-torn through. Her hands flutter, fingers twitching with indecision ... not knowing where to begin ... if she should scold him or hug him or check him for fractures.

In the end, she does all three at once.

She's crying and laughing and mumbling a whole hurricane of Spanish, brushing dirt off his shirt one second and cupping his face in both hands the next. Her voice cracks halfway through a sentence.

Balam just stands there, grinning. Bone-tired. Bruised and ash-smeared.

He lets her fuss over him. Lets her run anxious circles around him. And when she finally throws her arms around his neck and presses herself into him like she can hold him to the ground, he hugs her back with the sort of love that says he understands.

And maybe for the first time, he's not trying to be brave or self-assured. He's just letting someone hold him. Letting himself be seen.

✦ ✦ ✦ ✦ ✦ ✦ ✦

Tama's standing off to the side, hands on his hips, like he's trying to act totally fine even though there's a gash across his pant leg and a bruise blooming across his jaw.

Then I see him. His uncle? Tama's mentioned him a few times.

Barreling toward him, face grim, eyes wide, boots crunching over the rubble. "Tama."

Just his name ... low and sharp, like a warning and a prayer all at once.

Tama lifts his head and gives him a tired grin. "Hey, Uncle." But before he can say anything else, his uncle pulls him into a hug so hard it knocks the breath out of both of them. His thick arms clench around Tama like he's trying to hold back the whole world, and for a moment, Tama just stands there ... stunned.

Then he gives in to it. "I told you to stay out of trouble," his uncle mumbles into his hair, voice breaking.

"Technically," Tama mumbles back into his shoulder, "the trouble kind of found me."

For all his wisecracks, he doesn't deflect this time. Watching Tama quietly drop his guard, even for a moment, clench my chest with a gentle ache. It's important, to see him just be cared for. He stills and lets someone care. His uncle pulls back and seizes him by the shoulders, eyes scanning every inch of him, from the dried blood on his temple to the rip in his shirt. He mutters something under his breath in Māori ... I don't understand it, but I can tell from the cadence that it's both a reprimand and a blessing.

Tama just grins again, softer this time. "I'm okay," he says. "Really."

His uncle doesn't answer. Just seizes the back of Tama's neck and presses their foreheads together for a long, silent moment.

✦ ✦ ✦ ✦ ✦ ✦ ✦

Her parents are the last to arrive... not panicked like the others, more like they're checking on an inconvenience.

Her dad barrels in first, still talking into his Bluetooth headset, barely glancing up as he steps over a chunk of broken concrete.

Her mom comes in right after, holding her phone high and filming the wreckage like it's a tour. She glances toward her husband. "Junbi dekita?" Not a word for Airi. Not even a glance.

Then, in English, her voice drops low and dramatic for the mic: "We're here live at the scene..." With practiced ease she flips the camera. "It looks like there's been some kind of explosion, or earthquake, we're not sure yet, but the damage is extensive."

They walk right past her. Not even a glance.

My stomach lurches, anger and grief tangling together. After everything Airi's survived... how can they ignore her?

But Airi?

She doesn't flinch. She doesn't call out. She doesn't even look disappointed. She watches them for half a second... just long enough to confirm what she already knew. Then she lets the moment go. Not with bitterness. Not this time. Just release.

She turns to me instead, eyes soft, tired but still there. Without a word she slips her hand into mine. Her fingers are warm and steady. Grounding.

"Stay in touch, okay?" she says, a small smile that is not fake, not strained. Just quiet and real.

I squeeze her hand back, tight. "Always."

✦ ✦ ✦ ✦ ✦ ✦ ✦

One by one, they leave.

Tristan.

Airi.

Tama.

Balam.

Aiyana.

No one says goodbye like it's forever. But nobody says it lightly.

Aiyana lingers the longest, standing just outside the chaos. Her eyes are fixed on the horizon, still and unreadable in the strobing lights. Then she looks at Balam. Then at me.

A single nod. Quiet. Certain. A silent promise passing between us. And then she's gone.

Tama claps Tristan on the back as he turns to go. "Next time, I get the sword," he jokes.

Tristan smirks. "You'd break it in ten seconds."

"Exactly," Tama says, grinning. Their handshake turns into a firm clasp ... the sort that means we're not done yet.

We exchange numbers. Emails. Anything we can. Anything to stay connected.

Because we know. This wasn't the end. This was only the beginning.

And then they're gone. Swallowed by flashing lights and shouting crowds. And I'm left standing in the middle of it all ... smoke still curling up into the air, the scent of ash and ozone clinging to my clothes.

The adrenaline ebbs. The numbness with it.

What's left is this strange, heavy ache in my chest. Not pain. Not grief. Just... everything.

I feel like I'm standing on the precipice of something bigger than I understand.

The professor steps quietly beside me. She doesn't say a word ... just slips her coat around my shoulders and rests a hand on my back.

I let myself lean into her, just a little. Just enough.

She pulls out her phone. "Let's call your family," she says softly.

I nod. Swallow hard. "Yeah. Okay."

And as we walk away together, stepping over shattered stone and through lingering smoke, I don't look back. I don't need to. The world has changed. So have we. Whatever storm is coming, we'll weather it... together.

Chapter 45:
Shadows of Doubt

Avalon is too bright, too sharp-edged. Flowers open too fast, as though excited to see. Oberon waits by the fountain, motionless as a knife left in ice. Moonlight curves around him, instead of lighting him.

"It's done," I say. "Three days. The first seal is broken."

"Good." He does not trouble to turn.

"One word... and nothing for what came through with it?" I step nearer. The air clamps, thin and metallic. "You feel it. Do not pretend you do not."

"I feel what is ours returning." He looks at me, and the old warmth in his eyes is a mask drawn over something brighter and hollow. "I feel your reluctance choking it."

"Reluctance?" I laugh once, harsh. "I was almost crushed by what was waiting. The darkness leaked the instant the seal was broken... as if it had been waiting, watching for the first unguarded moment." I lower my voice. "It knew me. Oberon, this is what we sealed."

He takes a step, stones shivering under his heel. "And this is what you will not keep naming like a bedtime bogey. We let our own birthright be contained to quiet mortal panic. No more."

"I helped Merlin create this seal," I snap. "We did it because something hungry was rising to devour us all. We saved both worlds. Today it touched me. It was glad." I watch his face, and the hairs on my arms lift. "And now I can hear it in you."

A filament of silver flares behind his eyes... wrong, cold. For a heartbeat the man I love is there, stung, reaching. The next heartbeat something leans through him, and the reaching stops.

"Choose your words," he says softly, "or choose exile."

Power flows from him... bigger, blacker at the edges than I have ever known in this court. The fountain's surface quivers. Pennants luff in a wind that is not wind.

I draw myself up. "Then hear mine first. Pull back. Listen. If you drive this through before we understand the cost, you will rip Avalon or drown it. That is not kingship. That is madness."

A shape swings down to sit on the fountain's rim, boots on water that will not wet him. "My king...the seal fell as you predicted," Puck says lightly, watching Oberon without blinking. "You told me to harry, not to harvest. I harried. You told me to end the children...."

"...and you disobeyed." Oberon's voice hardens, the courtyard dimming around the syllables. "Had Ea'mara not raised her wards, I would have crushed them myself while you japed."

Puck's grin thins. "Mm. Yes. That would have been tidy. Also dull."

"Enough." The word cracks a fissure through the fountain's lip. Power seethes, darker now, as if something in him has decided restraint is no longer necessary. "I will not be delayed by your riddles or her sentiment. The second seal will fall. The wards will fail. Those who will not bend will break."

The seal's ache still lives in my bones; fear rides it... but so does a steadier thing. I step between them, the simplest line I can draw.

"If you are set on that path," I say, calm and clear, "I will not walk beside you."

Silence. The kind that gathers weight. "Then you will not walk here at all." He lifts his hand. The court recoils with the gesture... stone, air, light. Magic clamps my ribs, cold bands tightening. The world tilts to throw me out.

Puck is suddenly at my shoulder, one hand on my sleeve, the other sketching a lazy sigil that turns the worst of the shove. "She's leaving," he says, bright and insolent, "which is exactly what you asked for. Consider it the first thing I've ever done exactly to command."

Oberon looks past us, through us, at horizons only he can see. "Run, then," he murmurs, voice rich with that borrowed chill. "Gather your little heroes. When the seals fall, you will have a choice: kneel...or be destroyed."

Epilogue:
Before the Next Storm

Professor Mara ✦ Morning (April 27) ✦ Professor's Office

Morning light streams through the broken window. Bits of jagged glass still lodged in the frame catch the light... a ghost of the night before. Too tired. Too scared. No longer the woman they used to call Ea'mara.

Somewhere in the distance I can hear the sound of breaking stone and a girl's voice screaming light into the dark.

I sigh and the ash seems to settle on my shoulders.

On the other side of the room Nia sits hunched over with her phone to her ear and a small leather punch in the other. Speaking in Setswana her voice is strong, but strained by exhaustion. She's telling her family that she's fine, that she's safe.

She's trying to convince herself as much as them.

Some have already gone, or are getting ready to leave. Families are being found and reconnected. Teams are packing and flights are being organized. Life, as it is in the first seconds after something changes it, moves on. As much as I want to make them stay, gather them to my side and lead, I know I can't force it. Not now. Not after they've been through what they have.

I made the call that they would be safer awakened than hidden. But now... they need space. Time to rest, to process the things they've seen, done, become. To reclaim some of the pieces of the ordinary lives that were stolen from them, in an instant.

Oberon won the first round. The seal is broken ... and there's nothing I can do to stop that.

But he's still contained. Limited ... checked by myth and belief and culture.

Six seals remain. For now, they are safe.

We have things to do.

The seals. The damage. Keeping these six extraordinary children safe... all of it now falls on me. I will learn. I will search. I will find a way to repair what's been done ... to learn what still stands in the way, and how to strengthen it.

But I can't do it on my own. And neither can they.

They will need training. Guidance. Learning. They will need to come to terms with the power they've been given, how to control it.

But not today. Today they need rest. Time to not feel so different. Time to reconnect with the lives they were living, before.

I look back at Nia. The tension in her shoulders, the weariness etched in the lines of her face. She's seen too much... more than any child her age should ever be witness to. They all have.

And still, they survived.

They fought against something they should never have had to.

And they lived.

I stand and walk over to the window. Fingers tracing the splintered wood of the frame. Outside, the city is waking up. Horns. Footsteps. Voices. Laughter. Life.

As if nothing had happened. But it did. Everything has changed. The world might go on around us, none the wiser.

But we won't forget. I will contact them again. And together, we will meet what comes.

"They are safe. They are aware.

And when the time is right. They will understand what's happened ... and what's to come."

For now, that will have to be enough.

Tristan, Nia, Tama, Balam, Aiyana, and Airi
will return, their journey is only beginning.

Echoes of the Lost World:
Journey of Doubt

A year has passed since the seal was broken in Berlin. The
world is different. So are they.

Drawn together by a shared and strange vision, the six
heroes embark on a road trip across the United States...
guided by cryptic clues, hunted by mythic creatures and
the traumas they've tried to bury.

From desert ruins to urban legends, from ghost stories to
gods, the journey will test their strength, their trust and
the truths they tell themselves.

Magic is rising. The next seal is waiting.
And this time, surviving might not be enough.

**Ea'mara's Field Journal... exclusive bonus content
available at echoesbooks.com**

Acknowledgments

This book would not exist without the encouragement and support of so many people. To my family and friends... thank you for believing in me and reminding me why stories matter. To my early readers, who took the time to dive into these pages and share your thoughts, your feedback made this book stronger. And to every teacher, librarian, and author who inspired me along the way... I am deeply grateful. Finally, to the readers holding this book: thank you. You are now part of the world of Echoes.

About the Author

Seth Mohs lives in Atlanta, Georgia. When he isn't writing, he's usually reading, exploring new places, or chasing down good food. Echoes of the Lost World: The Hidden World is his debut novel and the beginning of a seven-book series.

**Stay updated on new books,
behind-the-scenes content, and extras:**

Facebook: @echoesofthelostworld

Instagram: @sethworld.media

TikTok: @sethworldmedia

YouTube: @SethworldMedia

Reddit: u/echoesbooks

Bluesky: @sethworld.bsky.social

Website: echoesbooks.com